How could she h

This wasn't like her at all.

Andrea had invited the Vidtel people in, wedding gown for traveling clothes and thrown a couple of pairs of jeans and her medical kit into her already packed bags.

The contest officials had noticed her veterinary school certificate and questioned her about her occupation. A female vet and bride-to-be dumping her career and fiancé to accept their prize was apparently great tabloid fodder.

Oh, God, she *had* dumped her fiancé. She'd literally left him at the altar!

A sharp pang of guilt swept through her. Here she was, exhilarated to have made her escape, while her family and friends probably thought she was lying dead in a ditch somewhere.

No, that wasn't true. Mother and Jeffrey were no doubt reveling in the attention they were receiving. And she'd left messages on their machines. She'd call them again when she reached the ranch....

Dear Reader,

Buffalo Gal, my first novel, was inspired by my visits to
North Dakota with my husband, Ron, a native of that state.
Many of the events in the book are based on experiences
we've had there, including the Memorial Day ceremony on
the plains, the picnic and the white elephant auction.

The fictional town of Rorvik is similar to many of the little
towns in central and eastern North Dakota, and the old
Amundson homestead was based on the cabin where my
husband's grandfather lived. Even Bert's UFO activities have
a basis in fact—Ron's adolescent experiments with hot-air
balloons and model rocketry.

From a scientific perspective, the likelihood of
electromagnetic fields (EMF) causing the problems
described in *Buffalo Gal* is remote, but research into the
effects of EMF on human and animal health is still
inconclusive. The relationship between EMF and melatonin,
however, has been documented and is still being studied.

These are just some of the facts that made writing
Buffalo Gal so much fun. The rest of the book is the
product of my imagination. I hope you'll enjoy it.

Sincerely,

Lisa McAllister

BUFFALO GAL
Lisa McAllister

HARLEQUIN®

TORONTO • NEW YORK • LONDON
AMSTERDAM • PARIS • SYDNEY • HAMBURG
STOCKHOLM • ATHENS • TOKYO • MILAN • MADRID
PRAGUE • WARSAW • BUDAPEST • AUCKLAND

ISBN 0-373-70810-6

BUFFALO GAL

Printed in U.S.A.

To my favorite author, my husband, Ronald Wanttaja,
whose home state inspired this book and whose support
and encouragement made it happen.

PROLOGUE

DR. ANDREA MOORE STARED at the clock on her bedroom wall with rising terror. Two more hours and it would all be over. She'd be married.

She tried to tell herself her nervousness was simply prewedding jitters. But she knew it was more than that.

She could envision every detail of the next few hours: The church decked out in pink and white roses, their petals vibrating to the chords of the massive pipe organ. Mother in the front row, beaming in rose chiffon. Jeffrey at the altar, gorgeous in his black tuxedo, the man with whom she'd spend the rest of her life.

Another burning wave of nausea gripped her, and she shoved a clenched fist hard against her venetian-lace-and-whalebone-encased stomach. Popping two more antacid tablets—at least she wouldn't have to worry about calcium deficiency—she stared at her reflection.

Mother's wedding gown looked as if it had been made for her. It practically had, she thought, considering the extensive alterations necessary to make it fit her size-twelve frame. Mother still prided herself on her own petite size eight and had never quite accepted the fact that at five-eight and one hundred and thirty pounds, Andrea definitely favored her father.

The thought brought her father's face to mind. She imagined him watching over her. Would there be sadness in the crinkled deep green eyes that had nearly always sparkled with good humor?

Daddy, if only you could be here. You'd know what to do—how to get me out of this.

But her adored father, in whose footsteps she'd followed to become a veterinarian, was no longer around to offer his patient, sensible and comforting advice. His death, three years earlier, had left a void in her life nothing could fill.

"How could I let things go this far?" Andrea groaned. She snatched up a hairpin and shoved it hard into her beaded lace cap. Too hard. It poked through her thick, dark curls to stab her scalp painfully, sending a bolt of anger through her.

Anger at herself.

She had only herself to blame for her predicament and she knew it. If she'd had the nerve to stand up to Jeffrey and Mother, she wouldn't be in this situation.

Now she was going to pay for her cowardice by marrying a man she didn't love.

Andrea glanced at the clock again, then back at the mirror, and grimaced. Her hair appointment had fallen by the wayside when an emergency surgery took up most of the afternoon. Had she even remembered to ask Patti, the receptionist at the clinic Jeffrey owned, to call and cancel? She couldn't remember. Between the surgery and her state of mind, the afternoon had been a blur.

Well, her hair would have to do—the limo would be here soon.

As if on cue, the doorbell rang, its two-toned notes like a funeral dirge. Andrea sighed deeply. There was no chance for her now. She was trapped.

She slipped on her white satin pumps, shuddering in anticipation of what they'd feel like by the end of the evening. Then, gathering the voluminous skirt of her wedding gown, she walked to the door.

When she opened it, no uniformed chauffeur greeted her.

Instead a surprised-looking trio, two women and a man, huddled on the porch step in the Seattle spring drizzle.

The well-dressed man held a huge bouquet of carnations and lilies. One woman clutched a mass of helium balloons that read Congratulations, and the other, standing back slightly, operated a video camera.

A wedding-day surprise from the gang at the clinic? Andrea wondered. Then the man stepped forward and thrust the bouquet into her arms.

"Andrea Moore?" he asked.

Unable to talk through a faceful of flowers, Andrea mumbled, "Mm-hmm?"

"Congratulations, Ms. Moore," the man continued. "We're the prize committee from the Vidtel Music Network. You're our grand prize winner."

"Grand prize?" Andrea spit out a fern frond, vaguely recalling the contest entry she'd pulled from an entertainment magazine one quiet afternoon at the clinic. Had she actually mailed that in?

The balloon lady piped up, "Yes. You're now the proud owner of White Thunder Ranch near Rorvik, North Dakota."

"A ranch in North Dakota?" A sprig of baby's breath caught Andrea's lashes and made her eyes water. She blinked back tears.

"Yes," the woman said. "We even have a plane ticket for a flight this evening to whisk you away to claim your ranch."

Andrea stared at them and struggled to make sense of the news. She'd prayed for escape, but *North Dakota?*

Her stomach lurched. No, she couldn't possibly. The very idea was insane.

What about Jeffrey?

What about Mother? She'd never understand.

But a voice of calm reason sounded in her ear. Her father's voice. *You have to live your own life, Andrea. This is the chance you've been waiting for. Don't pass it up.*

He'd spoken those very words to her when she was accepted to veterinary school. Mother had objected, urging her to pursue a more traditional vocation—business, accounting, something that would offer her stability and comfort. But Andrea knew what she wanted, and her father had supported her decision.

He'd want her to take this chance, too. In a way, this was like a wedding present from him. He was throwing her a lifeline. She couldn't pass it up.

"May I see some credentials?" she managed to ask, her hopes rising.

She reviewed the official-looking documentation while the balloon lady studied her gown.

"I hope we haven't caught you at an inconvenient time," the woman purred, her smile sly.

Satisfied as to their identities, Andrea smiled back, calmer than she'd been in weeks. "Not at all," she replied. "I'm even packed."

CHAPTER ONE

TUFTED BURGUNDY VELVET enclosed Andrea on all sides. Plush claret carpeting rose from the floor, almost obscuring her green lizard-skin boots. The odors of disinfectant, stale champagne and other, well, biological aromas assaulted her nostrils.

She sat embedded to her hips in the overstuffed back seat of the limousine billed as "Minot's Finest" and wondered at what she'd done.

Yesterday she'd been on the brink of marriage. She imagined Jeffrey scowling impatiently at the front of the church, her friends in the pews wondering, Mother...

Mother would never forgive her.

How could she have done it? This wasn't like her at all.

She'd invited the Vidtel people in, discarded her wedding gown for traveling clothes and thrown a couple of pairs of jeans and her medical kit into her already packed bags. They'd noticed her veterinary school certificate and questioned her about her occupation. A female vet and bride-to-be dumping her career and fiancé to accept their prize was apparently great tabloid fodder.

Oh, God, she *had* dumped her fiancé. She'd literally left him at the altar!

A sharp pang of guilt that rivaled her earlier nausea swept through her. Had she hurt him badly? Would he ever forgive her?

Here she was, exhilarated to have made her escape, while

her family and friends probably thought she was lying dead in a ditch somewhere.

No, she argued with herself, she *had* called from her apartment and again from the airport. Mother and Jeffrey would know she was alive and well.

At least they would as soon as they checked their answering machines.

She hadn't had the nerve to call the church and tell them in person. Not moments before her scheduled wedding. If she'd actually spoken to them, she'd never have gotten away. Mother would have talked her out of it, convincing her to do what was right, what everyone expected of her. Like she always had.

She'd call them both when she got to the ranch, Andrea promised herself, and tell them what had happened. It would be better that way, she rationalized. After all, her mother would have been mortified to learn the news in person, in front of all her friends. This way she could play the distraught mother-of-the-bride. The guests would be sympathetic and comforting, both to her mother and to Jeffrey. They'd revel in the attention.

Andrea had had more than her share of attention, as well. A Vidtel executive producer was accompanying her to the ranch. She'd met the producer, Connie Chambers, at Seattle-Tacoma airport for their flight to Minot via Minneapolis, and the woman had been her constant companion, her shadow, every minute since.

No, she amended, shadows didn't talk. Connie, however, had babbled constantly.

The crowded flight to Minneapolis, which Connie had grumpily referred to as "the squalling baby shuttle," arrived after midnight, local time. Their connection to Minot wasn't scheduled till the next morning, and some clerical snafu combined with the presence of a convention in town had resulted in their party having no hotel accommodations.

They'd sat up in the airport terminal all night, Connie complaining incessantly about the flight, the food, the organization of the trip and the airport decor, offering little pointers on contest-winner etiquette and basically driving Andrea insane.

The arrival early the next morning of the rest of the Vidtel entourage—photographers, production assistants and a Seattle rock band with the winsome name of Rusting Hulkk—had distracted Connie's attention enough to allow Andrea a couple of hours' fitful sleep in a chair at the terminal gate. She'd dozed another hour on the flight to Minot but was still exhausted, stiff and rapidly approaching nervous collapse.

As bad as the trip had been, though, the clothes were worse. In Minneapolis, Connie had insisted they shop for extra clothing at one of the overpriced boutiques in the airport concourse. The store's merchandise leaned, inexplicably, toward western wear, much to the delight of the Vidtel producer.

Connie selected several outfits to supplement Andrea's trousseau. Packed for her Hawaiian honeymoon, her wardrobe ran heavily toward shorts and sundresses, not really appropriate for springtime on the prairie.

Andrea wiped a damp hand over her snug, silver-studded, salmon-colored jeans and cringed. Few colors could have clashed more violently with the opulent upholstery. The cream cotton western shirt wouldn't have been bad, except for the salmon-and-green cacti and coyotes embroidered across the chest.

Then there were the boots. She wriggled her toes, encased in soft green reptile skin, and grimaced. The boots had sat in the shop a long time if the thick coat of dust covering the box was any indication. Connie convinced the store manager to throw them in as part of the package, and the woman eagerly complied, obviously having been unable to sell the bilious green things, anyway. Andrea had analyzed lab specimens of more appealing shades.

At least they were her size. She wouldn't have put it past Chambers to try to squeeze her size-eight feet into size-six boots if it meant getting them for free.

She studied the woman who occupied most of the opposite seat. Connie Chambers wore a similar but more subdued western outfit, befitting her age, which Andrea guessed as late forties. Swathed in yards of blue denim and chambray, she sprawled at an angle across the wide seat, her head tilted back and her mouth open. Each vigorous, gusty snore rustled the bleached strands of hair that had fallen into her face. The white leather fringe on her blouse shuddered with each inhalation.

The snoring was a welcome respite. The relative quiet provided Andrea an opportunity to organize her thoughts.

Only a few more hours, she realized, and she'd be free. Free of Jeffrey, free of Connie and her entourage, free to explore her ranch in peace.

"My ranch." Andrea mouthed the words with pleasure and gazed out the window at rolling fields just beginning to turn green. She'd heard North Dakota winters were harsh, bitter and lengthy. Today, though, the crisp May morning seemed to promise abundance for the plains.

A few hours of hell was worth it, she thought as she forced herself to relax against the cushions and marveled at her brand-new start.

She didn't kid herself that it would be easy. She knew almost nothing about ranching, and although she'd enjoyed large-animal medicine in veterinary school, all her experience in practice had been with pampered pets.

Once or twice she'd hinted to Jeffrey that they should mix some large-animal practice into the clinic he owned—even offered to take it all on herself so she wouldn't get rusty—but he'd been adamant about maintaining a pets-only practice.

She knew all the reasons for it, even the ones he wouldn't admit to.

Pet owners were more willing than farmers to spend money on expensive medical procedures. Facilities and equipment for small-animal practice were cheaper. Jeffrey was too fastidious and fond of his comfort to involve himself in emergency calvings and such.

Now she'd not only have the opportunity to work with large animals, she'd actually own a buffalo herd. No, not buffalo, she corrected herself, *bison*.

If twelve bison constituted a herd.

Andrea grinned at her sudden possessive feeling, looking forward to being a land baron.

The car slowed and turned off the main road onto a stretch of rough, well-rutted gravel, followed by the attending vehicles. The ride took on the characteristics of a ship in heavy seas, and Andrea's queasiness became physical as well as emotional.

Connie Chambers's nap ended with a snort. She hauled herself upright on the seat.

"Where are we?" She squinted out the window with bleary eyes. "Where'd the pavement go? Don't these yokels know about asphalt? How much longer till we get there?"

Andrea, now all too familiar with Connie's conversational style, knew that answers were neither expected nor appreciated. She smiled politely as Connie twisted in her seat to rap on the glass panel separating them from the driver. The panel dropped with a soft electric hum.

"How far to the ranch? We've been on this road for hours. Are you sure you're not lost? Do you have a map up there? Let me take a look at it."

The chauffeur returned her gaze unflinchingly in the rearview mirror, reminding Andrea of the Greek hero who'd faced Medusa.

"Looks like we're coming up on the ranch now, Ms. Chambers," he said flatly.

Connie squinted past him out the windshield. Just ahead on the left was a long driveway with an aluminum gate. A white wrought-iron sign above it proudly proclaimed White Thunder Ranch.

"About time," Connie harrumphed, and subsided back into her seat as the chauffeur once again raised the barricade.

They turned into the drive, and Andrea stared past Connie, straining for a glimpse of the ranch and anticipating her escape.

A big two-story farmhouse, a large barn and a modest trailer comprised the main ranch buildings. Smaller sheds, probably for farm machinery, lay just beyond the house. Near the barn was a large corral containing a loafing shed and hayrack.

The house, surrounded on two sides by a rambling porch, looked charmingly traditional, the kind she'd always dreamed of owning. Perhaps the worst of her ordeal was over.

The limo pulled to a stop near the house, and their escort of cars and vans circled it like covered wagons fending off an attack.

Andrea glanced down at the gaudy embroidery on her chest and wished she'd spent the past hours unraveling the unsightly stitches. Muttering a prayer of thanks that she'd convinced Connie to forgo the cream felt cowgirl hat, she ran a sweaty hand through her hair, tousled from the static electricity generated by acres of nylon velvet.

The grounds looked deserted.

One of Connie's minions appeared from nowhere to assist Andrea from the car while cameras clicked around them. Andrea took a moment's guilty pleasure in the static discharge that loudly shocked the man when he grasped her hand.

"What a dump." Smoothing wrinkles from her chambray, Connie clambered from the car and looked around. "Where the hell's the welcoming committee?"

Connie's secretary, two production staff members, a pair of cameramen and the four members of Rusting Hulkk piled from their vehicles and milled around.

"Wait here." Connie detached herself from Andrea's side and charged toward the house. The rest of the group followed in her wake, a swarm of bees around their queen.

Andrea, momentarily forgotten, hung back to take advantage of her unexpected freedom. She inhaled fresh, clean air rich with the earthy scents of green grass, animals and newly turned soil. After the stale miasma of the limo, no perfume could have smelled sweeter. She glanced toward the corral, and a hint of motion caught her eye.

She walked toward the enclosure, and inside the loafing shed, an enormous bison stood gazing at her. *A female,* Andrea thought, proud of herself for recognizing the shorter beard and smaller size that, along with the lack of the obvious organs, distinguished bison cows from bulls.

She moved closer.

She'd read once that adult female bison could stand five feet tall at the top of the hump. This one was every inch of that. The size had sounded impressive but manageable when she'd read it. Standing next to the real thing, however, Andrea felt dwarfed, despite the two-inch heels of her acid-green boots.

The bison cow regarded her with eyes the color of melted chocolate. Thick horns curled up from the sides of her head, their wicked points aimed skyward. Dense brown wool, easily several inches deep, covered her head, hump and forelegs.

The cow was scruffy, shedding her winter coat, but here and there, patches of sleek, dark hair peeked through the wool of her sides and hindquarters.

Andrea made soft chucking noises and was rewarded and surprised when the huge animal sauntered toward her, flicking an ear at a buzzing fly and eyeing her curiously.

Cautiously, taking care not to spook her, Andrea reached through the corral rails toward the cow's side. Her fingertips had just brushed the soft wool when a loud scuffling sound, followed by a series of high-pitched whirs and clicks, caused the bison to dance sideways out of reach.

Andrea turned toward the now-familiar noises and watched the photographers jockey for position. Surely there had been only two of them when they'd left Minot. Where had the others come from? Was Connie breeding them in the vans?

"Great photo op, Andrea," shouted a man she didn't recognize. He wore a badge proclaiming he was from the *Rorvik Herald.*

"Andrea, honey," a Vidtel photographer called, "see if you can coax her back over to the fence."

"Hey, maybe she can get into the corral and pet it," a third suggested.

Yet another straddled the rail on the opposite side and made shooing sounds to chase the bison toward her.

Andrea stood paralyzed, every avenue of escape cut off. She looked at the bison cow, stock-still and terrified in the center of the corral, and empathized.

"What the hell do you people think you're doing?" The roar from the direction of the barn effectively silenced the throng.

At first Andrea couldn't see the man who'd shouted, but the swarm of people around her parted without argument before him. As he approached, she understood why. He stood well over six foot and seemed at least four feet wide at the shoulders. His short black hair gleamed in the sun, and his bronze arms, bared by the rolled sleeves of his shirt, glistened with perspiration.

"Get off there, Wes," he snapped at the man on the fence. "That cow's pregnant, and if she gets frightened, she might lose the calf. Not to mention what she'll do if she gets fed up with the commotion and decides to charge. The *Valley Times* can't afford the damages, believe me."

The photographer scrambled down and quickly melted into the crowd.

The tanned giant turned his attention to Andrea, who unconsciously took a step backward and found herself pressed against the corral rail. She stared up at him.

His eyes, remarkably light colored for his dark complexion, flashed like sunlight on steel. Below them, his nostrils flared from a strong nose. His finely chiseled lips were set in a tight line.

He seemed constructed of solid muscle, taut and powerful, his wrath barely held in check. Andrea suddenly realized her racing pulse was only partially the result of fear. The recognition annoyed her.

He held her gaze a moment and took a deep breath as though fighting to keep his anger under control, then glanced at the photographers and reporters and swore softly.

When he spoke again, the crisp control in his voice reminded Andrea of a tour guide whose ignorant charges had gone astray.

"Please move away from the corral. Gypsy has had a rough pregnancy, and we can't afford to have her spooked."

As if his command wasn't enough, the man's stance hinted at the consequences of noncompliance. The crowd recognized the threat and flowed back toward the house.

He watched them go, his tension ebbing visibly, then

turned back to Andrea, imprisoned against the corral railing. His gaze traveled over her, from her disheveled hair to the embroidered desert life on her shirt to the green leather encasing her feet. He shook his head, then shaded his eyes and exaggeratedly scanned the horizon beyond her.

"What are you looking for?" Andrea asked slowly, struggling to keep the irritation out of her voice. As if she didn't know how ridiculous she looked!

"I'm just expecting some movie cowboy to come riding in, sweep you onto his horse and carry you off into the sunset." Amusement, or sarcasm, tinged his silky baritone.

Andrea's cheeks grew hot and she bit her lip to stifle a sharp reply. *Great, a comedian.* It wasn't bad enough that she had to parade around the prairie looking like an escapee from a low-budget western. Now she had Jerry Seinfeld here, pointing out that fact to her. How much luckier could she get?

She looked away abruptly, hoping he wouldn't notice the blush she felt burning her face.

He apparently *had* noticed. "Sorry for the outburst," he said grudgingly. "I'm a little protective of Gypsy. She's due sometime next month. The longer she carries the calf, the better its chances." He held out his hand. "I'm Mike Winterhawk, foreman here at White Thunder. For now, anyway."

"Andrea Moore," she replied through clenched teeth, and allowed her hand to be swallowed by his, expecting him to crush it in a typically *manly* grip.

His grasp was firm, but warm and amazingly gentle.

"I thought you might be Ms. Moore," he said slowly, after he released her hand. "Or should I say *Dr.* Moore? When Vidtel called to tell us they had a winner, they mentioned you were a vet." He paused, his brow furrowing slightly, then he added, "Welcome to the ranch."

"Thank you, and it's Andrea, please." She knew she

wasn't imagining the tension underlying his greeting. Hostility? Or just uncertainty? Whichever, here was one inhabitant of White Thunder Ranch who wasn't thrilled to make her acquaintance.

She looked from Mike Winterhawk to the milling crowd. "Who are these people? They didn't *all* come with me."

He glanced at the throng, some of whom, Andrea noticed, still watched him nervously over their shoulders. "You're big news, Doctor, er, Andrea. It's not every day some stranger takes over a few thousand acres of local real estate. Most of the small towns have sent reporters to check you out, but don't worry, they'll only hang around until the novelty wears off."

Definitely hostility, Andrea decided, stunned into silence. Before she could gather her wits to make a comment, she heard Connie Chambers's all-too-familiar bellow.

"Oh, Andrea-a-a."

Andrea fought the urge to duck behind the foreman's bulk, a move he probably wouldn't have appreciated. He raised an eyebrow at her, then turned to face the onslaught as Connie approached, an elderly man in tow. Connie stopped abruptly and gazed up at Mike from her five-feet-nothing.

Andrea had to give the man his due. Nothing short of a brick wall had halted Connie so thoroughly since she'd met the woman. To her credit, though, Connie recovered quickly. She sidestepped the foreman and swung the old gentleman in Andrea's general direction.

"So sorry to have left you—" Connie darted another glance up at Mike "—alone, Andrea dear. But some things one just has to do oneself. Would you believe headquarters didn't even let these people know when we'd arrive?" She patted a straying strand of hair off her face. "No wonder there was no one to greet us. You do have phones out here?"

This last remark, addressed to the old man, was obviously rhetorical, since Connie plunged on without waiting for a reply. "But I'm getting ahead of myself." She clutched Andrea's arm and swung her to face her prisoner. "This is Dan Amundson, former owner of White Thunder Ranch. Dan, meet Dr. Andrea Moore, new owner."

Andrea went rigid with embarrassment at the woman's tactlessness. Around her, roaring silence had fallen. Mike Winterhawk stood only inches from her, and she could almost feel the tension in his body. She didn't dare look at his face. His feelings were only too easy to imagine.

Connie beamed, oblivious to the insensitivity of her remark. Andrea forced herself to look at the woman's newest victim.

Not as frail as he'd seemed at first, Dan Amundson was tall and wiry. Age and the elements had seamed his tanned face, now weathered like a rock exposed alternately to the sun's heat and winter's frost. His light hazel eyes, sparkling as with some secret humor, reminded her of her dad.

Andrea felt surprise, then relief as a grin lit Dan's face, and he held out a large, callused hand.

"Dr. Moore. Pleased to meet you."

Andrea took the warm, rough hand in hers and felt some of her qualms dissipate at the genuine warmth in his eyes. He hadn't even registered shock at her awful clothing. "Thank you. And please, call me Andrea."

"Ya get that, boys?" Connie's voice rent the silence.

Andrea had been so caught up in her discomfort, she hadn't heard the photographers' approach. Now, under Connie's direction, she and Dan were grabbed and posed for pictures. When the photo session ended, Connie linked arms with both Dan and Andrea, edging them out from under Mike's watchful shadow.

Andrea glanced over her shoulder at the foreman as they walked away. He'd settled against the corral fence, one foot propped on the lowest rail. Their eyes met briefly, then he turned away to watch the crowd with an expression that promised grievous bodily harm to anyone who dared threaten Gypsy again.

"We'll need a couple hours for filming," Connie rambled. "We want to shoot Dan turning the keys, or whatever, over to Andrea. Then we want to go out and see the buffalo, of course. The band wants to shoot some scenes for their video, too. Finally we'll all have supper, then wrap it up and head back to Minot." She paused for breath. "Except for Andrea. I expect you'll stay a few days at least, won't you, dear?"

Andrea could only nod before Connie continued, turning to Dan. "Why don't you take Andrea in to freshen up a little. I have to meet with the cameramen before we start." She relinquished their arms and headed off toward the Vidtel crew.

"Uff da," Dan muttered.

"You can say that again," Andrea said.

"So you've heard that expression, eh?" He raised one gray brow.

Andrea nodded. "Kind of the Scandinavian version of *oy vey,* isn't it? I've heard it back home. There are a lot of Scandinavians in Seattle."

"Well, you have to admit it fits." He offered his arm. "Come on, let's go up to the house. I bet you could use a break."

Andrea accepted, and together they walked across the yard.

From the corral rail, Mike watched them go. He heard a snuffle behind him, and something moist and bristly brushed his arm. He turned to face Gypsy, who, now that the noisy photographers were gone, had decided she needed some attention after all.

Mike raised a hand, and she pressed her muzzle into it.

"Well, old girl, what do you think of the new boss?" He absently rubbed the bison's face and glanced back toward the house.

Andrea Moore wasn't what he'd expected. He'd been amazed to learn the winner of the ranch—his ranch—was a veterinarian. Apparently not all Vidtel viewers were giddy teenagers.

The discovery gave him some much-needed hope.

She probably had a practice back home. She wouldn't want to relocate to the middle of nowhere. If she wanted out fast, he might have a chance. She'd take less than the place was worth to unload it and go back where she came from. He'd get a loan, make payments to her, whatever. She'd still come out ahead, and White Thunder would finally be his.

He clutched the corral rail with his free hand, and his knuckles showed white.

Damn it, it wasn't fair!

He needed the ranch. This land had made him whole again after the injury that had nearly killed him and cost him his fiancée. Dan should have given him more time to come up with the money. He'd have found a way.

But that wasn't fair to Dan. The old man had no choice. In declining health and facing a mountain of bills, Dan chose the surest way of paying off his loans and securing his old age—selling the ranch to Vidtel. The big ranch, complete with bison, had been just the slice of Americana the video network had been looking for to promote their new season.

Gypsy butted his shoulder. Lost in thought, he'd stopped petting her. He laughed and grasped her muzzle in both hands. Her massive pink tongue darted toward his face, and he leaned away to avoid a bison spit bath.

"Sorry, girl. Didn't mean to ignore you. How about some lunch to make up for it?" He walked to the barn to pull an armful of hay loose for the bison. The rich scents of sweet alfalfa and old wood mingled with the warm animal smell, and he breathed deeply, almost at peace again.

Two short years ago, he'd never have thought the smell of a ranch would mean home to him. Now he couldn't imagine life anywhere else.

He walked back to the corral and tossed the alfalfa into Gypsy's hayrack. The bison pressed her face into it and was soon chewing eagerly. Mike looked toward the house. *No use postponing the inevitable.* He headed inside.

CHAPTER TWO

THE BUTTERFLIES IN Andrea's stomach eased slightly as they approached the solid and inviting farmhouse. Maybe this wouldn't be so bad, after all.

Dan led her up the steps to the broad porch, pausing at a front door intricately carved with interlaced flowers and geometric designs.

"Since you're getting the two-dollar tour, I'll point out all the sights as we go," he said. "My great-grandfather brought this door with him from Norway, where his father carved it." He brushed his fingertips lovingly over the deeply incised wood before looking back at Andrea.

"Great-grandpa settled in Minnesota for a time, then came here after he'd saved enough money for his own place." He gestured toward the prairie that spread out beyond the house, a rolling sea of green and gold. "There's a creek out there where he built the original homestead. My father was born there. He built this house when he married my mother."

Andrea ran her fingers over the design, anxiety returning with a vengeance.

When Vidtel told her she'd won a ranch, she thought it would be some sterile corporate-owned property. She never expected to displace a family that had been here for generations.

"It's lovely," she said weakly.

"It'll stay with the house, of course," Dan continued. "The old place would look kinda naked without it."

"Oh, no," Andrea protested. "I can't keep an heirloom like this." She was taking this man's home, for God's sake. She didn't have to claim his family treasures, as well. "I can easily buy a replacement."

Dan's gentle smile cut her to the core.

"I don't have any family except for a cousin in Fargo, so there's really no one else to take it. Anyway, I have a feeling you'll take good care of it." He opened the door and ushered her inside before she had a chance to argue further. "Come on. Lena's anxious to meet you."

The front door opened onto an immaculate living room filled with rugged, durable furnishings made comfortable by years of use. Large rugs warmed the hardwood floors. To the left, a steep staircase led to a small landing. On the right, a set of double doors stood open, and the aroma of baking bread wafted through.

Dan gestured toward the doors. "Kitchen's straight ahead. There're two bedrooms in back of the house and two upstairs. Lena uses one for a sewing room."

He led Andrea into the sunny, spacious kitchen. "Dr. Moore, I'd like you to meet Lena Olsen, our cook, housekeeper and mother hen."

Andrea held out her hand to the tall, rawboned woman who grinned broadly at her from beneath an unlikely billow of titian hair.

Lena's glance flashed to Dan briefly before returning to Andrea. Her blue eyes registered a moment's surprise as they swept her costume and finally settled on the green boots. She gawked with the sort of morbid fascination one usually reserves for car wrecks and shook Andrea's hand vigorously.

Lena Olsen stood nearly six feet tall and had the grip of a lady wrestler. Andrea thought she could see the tips of her fingers turning blue before Lena finally let go.

"Sure'll be good to hear another female voice around

this house.'' The strapping redhead tore her gaze from Andrea's feet, to cast a teasing glance at Dan. ''Sometimes I
think the men around here forget I'm a lady.''

''Don't let her fool you, Andrea.'' Mike Winterhawk
came in through the kitchen's screen door.

Despite the spaciousness of the room, he loomed even
larger than he had outside. Andrea revised her earlier impression of him. Brick could never have formed the hard,
smooth contours of his body. In here, out of the sunlight's
glare, she could trace every muscle, tendon and ligament
beneath his skin; the depth of his tan simply enhanced an
already coppery complexion. Hispanic? she wondered. No,
Winterhawk definitely sounded Native American.

Mike continued, his gray eyes meeting hers steadily,
''No matter what Lena says, she's the real boss around
here. When she says jump, we'd better have our boots on.''

Lena chortled. ''That's because I'm the only one on the
place who can cook. You're all just afraid of starving.''

Andrea looked away abruptly, realizing she'd been staring, caught up in Mike's gaze. Grateful for the distraction
of Lena's remark, she smiled at the woman while surreptitiously massaging her mangled hand.

When she risked another quick glance at Mike, he was
still watching her, his expression measuring.

What was the Vidtel crew doing? she wondered, almost
wishing they'd make an appearance, if only to divert the
foreman's watchful gaze from her.

Lena seemed to read her thoughts. ''How long till that
swarm of locusts finds its way back here, Mike?''

Mike shrugged. ''They're setting up for filming. I've got
to hand it to that Chambers woman. She knows how to
organize that crowd. She's even bossing the locals
around.''

''No surprise there,'' Dan said. ''She was bossing Andrea, here, and she's the guest of honor.''

"Harrumph!" Lena snorted. "Let her try it in my house. How long are they staying, anyway?"

Andrea spoke up, self-conscious. "They're a little vague about that. Till after supper, I gather. I'm really sorry for the inconvenience." She forced herself to look at Mike once more. "Especially for Gypsy."

"It's not your fault." Mike's grudging tone implied exactly the opposite. "But if they don't stay away from my animals, I'm going to break some heads, publicity be damned."

"Lena," Dan said. "Show Andrea to her room so she can freshen up. Mike and I'll keep an eye on things outside."

Lena nodded and turned to her.

"Your room's upstairs, Dr. Moore," she said, and led the way from the kitchen.

Relief washing over her at the chance for escape, Andrea followed the housekeeper out from under the disturbing stare of Mike Winterhawk.

They climbed the narrow steps to the second floor. The two bedrooms opened off either side of the landing. Lena paused in the doorway of the right-hand room.

"Here you go," she said. "Just make yourself comfortable. There're clean towels in the bathroom, and if you need anything else, just give a yell. I'll be in the kitchen getting the roast in the oven."

"Thank you, Lena. I won't be long. And please, call me Andrea."

"Take your time, Andrea." Lena grinned broadly. "Like Dan says, you're the guest of honor. That bunch won't make a move without you."

She stepped back into the hall, her smile slipping a little as her gaze fell once more to the green snakeskin boots, then she pulled the door closed.

Alone at last, Andrea released a long-held breath, slumped against the wall and closed her eyes.

What was she doing here?

Had she imagined the measured glances between Dan and Lena? She was sure she hadn't. Just as she hadn't imagined Mike Winterhawk's hostility.

She massaged her temples, willing herself to relax, but her thoughts continued to whirl.

How could she stay with these people? They didn't want her here. Especially Mike Winterhawk.

The idea of returning with Connie and company was almost tempting.

No!

That would mean going home to face Jeffrey and Mother. She couldn't do it. Not when she'd finally made the break.

The truth was that almost from the moment she'd accepted Jeffrey's proposal, she knew she'd made a mistake.

They'd been friends for years, their mutual interest in animals drawing them together, despite a four-year age difference—nearly an eternity for high school kids.

After college and veterinary school, their marriage had been a foregone conclusion. At least to Jeffrey and her mother, who treated him like the son she'd never had. Andrea hadn't been so sure.

She'd changed a lot over the years she'd been away at school, and her broadened perspective gave her new insight into her old boyfriend—insight that made her question whether she wanted to spend the rest of her life with him.

Except for their careers, they shared few common interests. In addition, she discovered he'd developed an unfortunate tendency to be controlling—a trait that chafed at her awakened consciousness from the moment she'd entered practice with him after graduation.

She recalled how he'd taken her to lunch one afternoon and told her how he had her life all planned out.

They'd marry and share the ideal husband-and-wife practice, a comfortable and lucrative urban clinic with regular hours and little stress. Eventually, when the children came along, she'd leave to devote her time exclusively to them and to the care of their household.

He hadn't seemed to grasp that she preferred the variety and challenge of a mixed practice to working exclusively with pets. Nor could she make him understand that she hadn't just spent eight long years and thousands of dollars on college and veterinary school simply to kill time until her children were born.

Nonetheless, she'd eventually succumbed to the concerted pressure from Jeffrey and her mother. Father would have wanted it, Mother said, adding the traditional dose of daughterly guilt to her own forceful opinion on the issue.

Andrea was trapped.

If the Vidtel crew hadn't shown up to whisk her away to the hinterlands, she and Jeffrey would be winging their way to Hawaii at this moment.

The thought still infuriated her. How could she have let things go so far? She'd plodded along like a dull-witted sheep, letting everyone else make her decisions for her. Letting everyone else run her life.

Well, no more. She couldn't go back. She'd have to make the best of things here. A few days and the worst would be over. White Thunder was hers, after all, regardless of what the current residents thought of her.

She took several steadying breaths, then opened her eyes and looked around.

An ancient-looking bed with a towering carved mahogany headboard dominated the room. Beside the bed crouched a blocky nightstand, and across from it stood a large marble-topped dresser, its mirror wavy with age.

Lace-trimmed, lavender-print curtains, which billowed at the open window, balanced the heavy furniture. A matching comforter covered the bed, and a thick rag rug in soft pastels cushioned the floor between the bed and dresser.

The overall effect was light and airy, yet cozy and inviting.

Andrea sank onto the bed and stared at her reflection in the rippled glass. Pulling a comb from her purse, she ran it through her tangled hair, cursing the rash impulse that had led her to have it permed only a week before the wedding.

When her hair looked reasonably presentable, she touched up her lipstick and powder, then studied the bed longingly.

In the past twenty-four hours, she'd had barely three hours' sleep. Not to mention the two hours she'd gotten the night before her scheduled wedding.

If only they could postpone the filming a few hours.

Of course, a few hours' rest would mean a few more hours of Connie Chambers.

No one wanted that.

She rose reluctantly and headed downstairs.

Connie met her at the foot of the steps. "Come on, Andrea dear. We don't have all day."

Andrea bit back a whimper as Connie took possession of her hand and dragged her out onto the front porch, then pulled her into the sunlight for a quick inspection.

"Makeup and hair look fine. I don't suppose we could get that housekeeper to press your jeans before the shoot. They're wrinkled from the drive." Connie paused for a moment's contemplation of the idea, then shrugged it off. "No, they'll be filming you mostly above the waist. Shouldn't make any difference."

Andrea sighed with relief. She could just picture Connie ordering Lena to the ironing board. And Lena's response.

"Now, where's Dan?" Connie scowled. "Is it too much to ask that everyone be where they're supposed to?" She pressed Andrea against the porch railing. "Stay right here. Don't move. I'll go find him." She stormed off around the side of the house.

Andrea looked out across the yard.

The camera crew was setting up nearby. An invisible barrier, enforced no doubt by Connie, separated them from the curious onlookers gathered out near the barn.

She caught a glimpse of Mike Winterhawk's head above the crowd. Her breath caught in her throat as he eased out of the throng and headed toward Gypsy's corral. He moved like a creature of the prairie, sinewy and graceful.

Connie rounded the corner of the house arm-in-arm with Dan, who was doing his best to keep up. She led him down the porch steps to where the Vidtel entourage was gathered, gesturing to Andrea to follow.

Andrea already knew the group. Now the woman introduced them to Dan. She rattled off the names of the cameramen, her production assistants and her secretary. Then she turned to the four skinny leather-and-jeans-clad youths lurking at the back of the group. Andrea held her breath awaiting the introduction.

"And lastly, I'd like to introduce the terrific new band who'll be filming their debut video here at White Thunder. Dan Amundson, meet Rust Bucket."

Dan's eyes widened, and he raised a gray-tinged eyebrow, but he shook hands all around.

A spiky-haired young man Andrea knew as Todd gave a heartfelt sigh of resignation. "Pleased to meet you, sir," he said. "And it's Rusting Hulkk. With two *k*'s."

Connie snorted, "Whatever."

Andrea hid a smile. In the few short hours since she'd met Rusting Hulkk, she and the band had become comrades-in-arms of a sort, united against a common enemy—

Connie. The woman had yet to get their name right. Andrea had begun to eagerly anticipate the Vidtel producer's mangled guesses.

Formalities out of the way, Connie shooed the band and nonessential personnel aside and conferred with the cameramen, then she turned to Andrea.

"Okay, we'll start with Dan on the porch and you going up the steps. This'll be Dan greeting you on your arrival at the ranch." She positioned everyone and stood by watchfully, ready to jump in and take control at any moment. The cameras rolled.

Two hours later, the scenes at the house were done. Andrea slapped dust from her salmon jeans and marveled that she'd thought she was tired before they started. Now she really knew what exhaustion was.

But they weren't finished. Connie ordered the vehicles brought around so they could drive out to where the herd was grazing.

Mike pulled up in the ranch's battered pickup. He leaned across the seat to open the door for Andrea, and she climbed onto the bench seat. Dan got in beside her, forcing her to slide closer to Mike.

The Vidtel film crew, with Connie, loaded into their four-by-four truck, and the band's rented Chevy van pulled alongside. Mike rolled down his window and called to the van driver. "You can't take that thing out to the herd. It's not a four-by."

"We have to get footage for the video," the driver called back.

One of his passengers, the boy who'd greeted Dan, waved an elaborate camera and yelled something Andrea couldn't make out.

The driver interpreted. "Todd's a film major at UCLA. Vidtel's lending him the equipment for the video in return for first television rights."

Mike shrugged. "All right. We have room in the back if you can hang on." He waved them toward the truck. "Climb aboard."

They waited while the members of Rusting Hulkk— Todd, the filmmaker and keyboard player, Stench, the lead singer, Dev, the bassist, and Jock, the drummer—clambered into the truck.

Mike opened the window between the cab and truck bed so the boys could hear him. "We'll take the road instead of going directly across the property," he said, looking down at Andrea. "It's easier when we know where the herd is." They started down the drive toward the main gate, the other vehicles following.

Andrea glanced up at him, tipping her head back to meet his eyes. "How do you know where they are?"

"Radar," he said shortly, flipping a switch on the dash.

"You're kidding."

Dan chuckled. "He's kidding, but not much. The lead bull is tagged with a radio transmitter. We go out and look for the herd, and this—" he tapped what looked like an AM-FM radio set into the dash "—tells us when we're getting warm. With this much land, it takes too long to just drive around and hope you stumble on them. Especially a small herd."

"How long have you been raising bison?" Andrea asked.

"A couple years," Dan said. "I bought the herd just before Mike signed on. He's been a real help, and he's great with the animals. Now, if we could just figure out why we're in this mess."

Mess? What mess? Andrea looked at Mike, hoping for an explanation.

He stared straight ahead, expressionless, and turned the truck through an ungated opening in the fence. The gravel road smoothed out for a few feet, then disappeared entirely.

"Hey, man," Jock, the drummer, called from the back. "There's no gate. What keeps the cows from leaving?"

Mike glanced into the rearview mirror. "We just crossed over a cattle guard above that little gully behind us. Cattle and bison don't like to walk on it, so they stay where we put them. Hang on. It'll get rough from here on out."

Andrea clutched the dash with one hand and the edge of her seat with the other. Hip to hip with Mike, she was thrown hard against him with each bump.

The day was warming up. Tightly wedged against Mike in the front seat, she could feel his heat even through the heavy cotton of her western shirt. The sensation was unaccountably disturbing. She planted her feet firmly against the floorboards to steady herself, all the while struggling to keep from grasping at his arm for support with every bounce.

He smelled of leather and the musky essences of hay and animals, counterpointed by a green, subtle fragrance. The aromas mingled with the grassy breeze from the open windows.

The resulting scent spoke to Andrea of earth and nature, rich, lush and alive. She inhaled deeply, the fragrance a tonic for her strained nerves.

Mike pointed ahead of them. "There they are."

In the distance, the herd dotted the grassland like squat, bulky trees. The truck drew closer and the mounds turned into individual bison, deep brown, woolly and massive.

All the animals were adults.

Surely this late in the spring, she thought, there should be one or two gangly, caramel-colored calves among them. "Don't you usually have calves by now?" she asked Mike.

He looked down at her, his face expressionless. "Usually, but not so far this year. Gypsy's the only pregnant cow, and she was artificially inseminated."

Andrea frowned and glanced at Dan, who looked as if he wanted to say something but thought better of it.

"Wow, this is terrific!" Todd shouted from the back. "Can we get closer?" He rose onto his knees in the truck bed and aimed the camera as they approached the herd.

Mike halted the vehicle about fifty feet from the animals. The Vidtel truck pulled alongside.

"Can we film the band next to them?" Todd asked.

Mike rolled his eyes but remained silent.

Andrea answered for him. "I don't think that would be a good idea. They're unpredictable."

The herd seemed inclined to ignore the vehicles, although Andrea noticed that a huge male, probably the lead bull, was watching them warily. She glanced at the Vidtel truck. Its occupants were busily filming the animals.

As she watched, one of the Vidtel crew switched from his video camera to an expensive-looking thirty-five-millimeter outfit. He began to shoot, the motor advance filling the air with a high-pitched whine and whirr.

The noise agitated the massive bull. No longer content to simply observe his onlookers, he snorted and pawed the ground.

"Great stuff," Todd said eagerly. "Just look at that big guy. I've gotta get closer." He hefted the camera onto his shoulder and, before anyone realized his intent, climbed onto the hump of the wheel well and hopped to the ground to walk toward the huge, angry animal.

"Damn!" Mike swung around to face Stench, who was staring wide-eyed after his friend. "Get him back in here."

Stench moved to follow Todd over the side of the truck, but Mike reached through the sliding window and caught him by his jacket collar. He shook his head, exasperation on his face. "For God's sake, call him. Don't go after him."

Stench turned back toward his friend, but before he could open his mouth, Mike shouted, "Look out!"

The bull lowered his head and charged.

CHAPTER THREE

ANDREA WATCHED THE massive bison thunder toward Todd as the truck vibrated with the animal's pounding hoofbeats. Todd stood frozen in place, camera dangling limply from his hand as he faced the charging bull.

Then Mike moved. The tableau dissolved into a frenzy of motion. He shoved the truck into gear, pushing the gas pedal to the floor. Tires spewed rocks and dirt as he swerved the vehicle into the animal's path.

"Jump on!" he shouted.

With only a heartbeat's hesitation, Todd dropped the camera and leaped onto the truck's running board. He clutched the window frame as Mike accelerated away from the herd. The Vidtel truck followed, both vehicles stopping a short distance away.

The bull took out his anger on the discarded camera, stomping and goring it. One curving horn pierced the casing and stuck. The bull raised his head, wearing the camera at a jaunty angle. He shook his head vigorously, tossing the camera aside, then snorted and trotted back to the herd, apparently satisfied at having taught the intruder a lesson. The camera, a mangled wreckage of plastic and metal, lay where the bull had tossed it.

Todd released his death grip on the truck and dropped to his knees in the dirt.

Throwing open his door, Mike leaped out and stormed toward the boy. "What kind of idiotic stunt was that? Were you trying to get us killed? Do you have any idea how dangerous these animals are?''

''I...I'm sorry.'' Todd stared up at him, his eyes huge below his spiked white hair. ''I didn't think...''

''You're damn right you didn't think. Take a look at that camera. That could have been you out there!''

From her seat in the truck, Andrea watched Mike's reddened face in alarm. The man was completely out of control. She climbed out of the truck and walked up behind him. ''Mike.''

Andrea's voice penetrated the haze of fury that swirled around him. Taking several deep breaths, he counted to ten and slowly regained control before he turned toward her, cursing inwardly that he'd let his temper get away from him. Cursing her because all of this was her fault. If she hadn't been taking the ranch from him...

The shriek that issued from the Vidtel truck kept him from completing the thought. He and Andrea both turned as Connie burst from the truck, roaring toward them, a blue-and-white-fringed tornado.

Todd stepped behind Mike in hope of shelter, but no port offered safety from the coming storm.

''You moron! Look what that animal did to my camera!'' Connie's face, a puffy pink mask of fury, was only inches from Todd's. She looked like a plump army drill instructor in drag. ''Do you have any idea how much that camera cost? A helluva lot more than your hide is worth, let me tell you.''

''Whoa, Ms. Chambers.'' Mike was grateful for the distraction of someone else's anger. ''Todd nearly got himself killed here. I think the camera is the least of our concerns, don't you?''

Connie jammed a finger into Mike's broad chest, her long acrylic nail denting his shirt. ''Don't tell me what to worry about, you...cowhand. I have to account for this equipment. I don't give a damn about some scraggly Eddie Vedder wannabe.''

Mike felt his control slipping. Then Andrea stepped in front of him.

"Wait a minute, Connie.'' Andrea's voice carried an air of authority that surprised him and, from the look on her face, probably surprised Andrea as well. "Mr. Winterhawk is the foreman of this ranch and my employee. For now.'' She shot a quick glance back at him, then faced Connie again. "Don't speak to him that way.''

Mike suppressed a grin as the tall brunette faced down the stubby blond whirlwind. He had to admit, she had guts.

Connie stared up at her, clearly unused to such insubordination. She blinked rapidly several times. "Fine,'' she huffed. "Well, you're welcome to him, *and* this dump of a ranch. And you—'' She spun back to Todd. "You're fired, you and the rest of Dust Bowl. Your salaries and your return plane tickets will go toward the replacement of that camera.'' She started toward the Vidtel truck.

"Hey, you can't do that!'' Todd protested. "We have a contract. Besides, how are we supposed to get home? You can't strand us in the middle of nowhere.''

Connie glanced over her shoulder, her smile poisonous. "I just did. You can walk back to Seattle for all I care.''

She stalked to the truck and clambered in. "Get us the hell outta here,'' she growled at the driver, and slammed the door so hard the vehicle rocked.

The truck roared off in a cloud of dust. Then it slowed, circled back and pulled to a stop beside them once more. The driver rolled down his window and leaned out, his expression sheepish.

"I don't know how to get back to the ranch,'' he said. "I'll have to wait and follow you.'' He rolled the window back up as Connie threw him a look of pure hatred, then slumped in her seat to sulk.

Todd turned to Andrea, suddenly looking like the eighteen-year-old he was. "I'm sorry about the buffalo, ma'am. I didn't mean it." He glanced at the worried faces of his companions. "I don't know what we're s'posed to do. I mean, they haven't paid us yet, you know? We can't get home without our tickets, and we don't have money to buy more...."

Andrea sighed deeply, a frown etching her face.

Mike found himself sympathizing, against his will. When she glanced at him, as if in a silent plea for help, he decided to take pity. After all, she'd stood up to the Chambers woman on his behalf.

"They can stay at the ranch tonight," he said. "I have to go into Minot tomorrow, anyway. I'll take them with me, and they can wire home for money."

Andrea looked at the boys. "Will that work?"

Todd accepted for the band. "Thanks. We'd really appreciate it. I was afraid we'd have to sleep out here with the buffalo tonight."

They loaded back into the truck, Andrea climbing in beside Mike once again. He could smell the soft fragrance of her perfume on her skin, or maybe in her hair, as she positioned herself in the exact center of the seat as though reluctant to touch him. He was grateful for the space, although he'd have preferred to put a lot more distance between Andrea Moore and himself; ideally, the distance between White Thunder Ranch and Seattle.

"What about the camera...carcass?" Andrea asked.

"Let's leave it for now." He looked at the bull grazing watchfully a short distance away. "I'd rather not challenge his territory again today."

She followed his gaze. "Good idea."

Giving the herd a wide berth, they headed back to the house with the Vidtel truck close behind.

When they reached the house, Connie moved to the limo

and sat alone in the wide back seat while the crew loaded their gear. Her secretary checked to make sure Andrea had all the necessary paperwork and an open-ended plane ticket for her return to Seattle. The Vidtel personnel piled into their vehicles, one of Connie's staff driving the van the band had arrived in after first tossing out the boys' belongings, no doubt at Connie's command, and headed toward the gate.

Lena and Dan joined Andrea, Mike and the band on the porch as the Vidtel contingent departed.

"Well, Mike." Lena slapped his shoulder, nearly knocking him off the top step. "I don't know what you said to 'em, but it worked." The redhead arched her eyebrows as her gaze took in the stranded members of Rusting Hulkk. "Looks like they left a few stragglers, though. Did you boys decide to visit a few days and get a taste of country life?"

Todd blushed. "No, ma'am. We didn't intend to stay. She abandoned us."

Lena frowned and glanced at Mike. He nodded.

"Well, the old witch. I knew she was trouble." Lena clucked like a hen rounding up chicks. "No matter. Supper's almost ready, and there's more than enough for everybody." She turned to Andrea. "Are we putting these children up for the night?"

Andrea looked up with surprise. She hadn't expected to be consulted. "Uh, yes. It looks that way. I don't know where."

"They can stay in Mike's trailer overnight." Lena pointed across the yard to the long mobile home near the barn. "It's got two bedrooms. Mike can bunk up here for the night. I'd rather not have strangers staying in the house," she confided in a whisper.

"That sounds fine," Andrea said, relieved and pleased that she apparently wasn't included in that category.

"You fellas gather up your things and take them out there, then come on back for dinner. Oh, and remember to call your families and let 'em know where you are." Lena shooed the boys off the porch toward the pile of suitcases and duffel bags that littered the yard. "I'd better get back to my supper." She turned and went back inside.

Lena's comment about calling home brought Mother and Jeffrey suddenly to mind, and Andrea recalled her promise to get in touch with them once she was settled. She'd been so busy all day, she'd almost forgotten.

She started to follow Lena into the house to look for a phone, but Mike caught her arm and held her on the porch.

She looked up at him, puzzled. Up close, his eyes were gray, an unusual pale shade like a Seattle winter sky, but flecked with hints of green. They sparkled when he smiled at her, and she realized it was the first time she'd seen him in a reasonable temper since she'd arrived.

"Lena likes you," he said. "Before long she'll be bossing you around like any other member of the family."

"Thanks." Andrea hoped she didn't sound as breathless as she felt. She glanced down at his hand on her arm. He let her go and took a step back.

"By the way," he added, "thanks for standing up to Chambers out there. 'You're a better man than I am, Gunga Din.'"

"It was nothing. She's the type who delights in walking all over everyone. I've met people like that before." *And almost married one.*

He said nothing more, and she remembered her intention to call home. "Is there enough time before dinner for me to make a couple of quick phone calls?" And they *would* be quick, she told herself. Their impending supper would at least provide her an excuse to hang up if Jeffrey or Mother got too worked up.

"Sure, I think so." Mike opened the screen door for her. "Phone's in the kitchen, here. Help yourself."

"Thanks." She stepped inside and picked up the kitchen phone as Mike headed into the living room, then started dialing, conscious of Lena's curious gaze.

Good grief, she couldn't do this with an audience. "Do you have another phone, Lena?" she asked, hanging up. "I don't want to be in your way here."

"Oh, you're not in the way…oh." Understanding dawned on the housekeeper's face. She gestured toward the other room. "In my room, the one on the left. It's a little more private."

Surprised, Andrea thanked her. The woman didn't miss a thing, she thought, starting for the back bedroom.

In the living room, Dan sat engrossed in the Minot paper. Mike, pretending to scan the want ads, watched Andrea walk into the bedroom, then heard her voice, low and urgent, on the phone. A few seconds later, Lena emerged from the kitchen and headed toward the bedroom, as well. She stopped short of entering, though, and appeared to busy herself dusting knickknacks on a small console near the door. Mike couldn't blame Lena for her curiosity, but eavesdropping was too much.

He walked across to stand beside her and silently shook his head. Lena scowled at him and put a finger to her lips, catching his arm to hold him by the door.

"That's right, North Dakota," Andrea said from the bedroom. "Yes. A buffalo ranch. No, I'm not joking. No, I'm fine, really."

Lena glanced up at Mike, her eyes wide with curiosity.

"No, honestly, I wasn't kidnapped by a cult. No, not militia survivalists, either. What would a militia want with a veterinarian?"

Mike bit his lip. Survivalists? What was going on here?

Andrea sighed. "Well, yes, I suppose they would have

animals. I just don't think they'd worry too much about medical care.''

Lena stared at him and frowned. She mouthed the word *who?* at him, apparently trying to guess who Andrea had called. He shook his head. A family member, a significant other? From the sound of things, that person wasn't too happy that Andrea was at White Thunder.

Good. Maybe they'd put pressure on her to dump the place and come home.

"Mother, please don't cry. I'm fine." Andrea paused a moment. "No, I haven't called him yet. I will as soon as I hang up. Yes, I know, and I'm sorry. I'm sorry I embarrassed you, too, but it was my decision and I'm not going to change my mind."

Mike lounged against the corner beside Lena, now thoroughly engrossed in the one-sided conversation despite his best intentions. They knew precious little about the new owner of White Thunder, but this call was providing some intriguing hints.

"He can send back the presents," Andrea said. "Well, I don't see it that way. I shouldn't have let it go this far."

Mike heard a soft sniffling sound. Was she crying?

He frowned and turned away from the door, then turned back, took Lena's arm and pulled her with him. He didn't want Andrea Moore here, but whatever she was going through, she deserved her privacy. As he and Lena moved away, he heard Andrea say, "Goodbye, Mother. I love you, too."

Andrea wiped her eyes, took a deep breath and dialed the number of the clinic. The last thing she wanted to do was talk to Jeffrey, but she had no choice. She had to clear the air between them.

The phone rang twice, then a woman's voice answered, "Black River Animal Clinic."

Andrea took a deep breath. "Hi, Patti, it's Andrea. Is Jeffrey in?"

"Andrea?" the receptionist gasped. "Just a minute. I'll see if he's available." The phone clicked and switched Andrea over to classical "hold" music.

She waited, glancing at her watch as her heart pounded out the seconds. What would she say to him? "I'm sorry" just seemed so inadequate. A minute passed, then two. Maybe he was in the middle of a procedure and couldn't pick up. But surely Patti would come back and tell her it would be a few moments.

The phone clicked again, and for a moment the line was silent. Then Patti said, "Um, Andrea?"

"Yes? Is he busy?"

"No." She sounded hesitant. "Um, he just doesn't want to talk to you."

"Oh." The knot of tension in Andrea's stomach dissipated a little at the reprieve, but her guilt didn't. "Well, okay. I guess I can't blame him for that. Take my number here. If he wants to call, at least he'll have it." She recited the number off to Patti, who read it back as she copied it down. "Thanks, Patti."

"Sure, Andrea. I'll give it to him, but, well, I don't think he'll call. You know how he is."

"I know. Thanks, anyway. Goodbye, Patti."

"Bye, Andrea. And good luck."

The phone went dead and Andrea sat staring at it. Well, it was what she'd expected. Jeffrey had his pride, and it was probably too wounded just now to allow him to talk to her rationally. At least he knew how to reach her if he should change his mind. Somehow, though, she doubted he'd call. If there were a first move to be made, he'd expect her to make it.

If he expected her to "come to her senses," though, he was going to be disappointed. She'd made her choice, and despite her uncertainties about White Thunder, she had no intention of returning to Seattle. She took a couple of deep breaths to calm her still-pounding heart and went back to the living room.

Supper at White Thunder reminded Andrea of old television shows where big families gathered around the dinner table, everyone eating and chattering happily. Rusting Hulkk's presence provided unexpected relief. She'd dreaded her first meal alone with the ranch's residents, and her phone calls home had done nothing to ease her tension.

Food was the last thing on her mind, but Lena was a fantastic cook. Andrea didn't realize how hungry she was until she saw the table laden with roast beef, steamed potatoes, vegetables and fresh-baked bread. Comfort food. She ate two helpings of everything; the band ate three plus dessert, homemade lemon bars and brownies, washed down with strong, hot coffee. She pushed her chair back from the table, unable to manage another bite.

"Why don't you folks head into the living room?" Lena suggested. "I'll just get the table cleared off and join you in a minute."

Andrea automatically stood, plate in hand, to help. Before she could leave the table, though, Stench, the flaxen-haired singer, rose gracefully and took the plate from her.

"We'll take care of the dishes for you, ma'am," he told Lena. "It's the least we can do to earn our room and board."

A brief murmur of dissent broke from Dev and Jock, but Stench quashed it with a steely look and the help of Todd's strategically aimed elbow.

Lena protested halfheartedly, clearly torn between delight at his offer and distrust of strangers in her kitchen, but Stench's unlikely charm won out. The housekeeper let herself be dismissed to the living room.

Andrea took a seat on the wide sofa, sensing it was neutral ground. Her instincts proved correct as Dan and Mike settled into two large recliners.

Lena chose an overstuffed chair, pulled a half-finished sweater from a knitting bag and began working rapidly, her needles pausing with each muffled clatter from the kitchen. Before long the noises stopped, replaced by the hum of an electrical appliance.

With a murmur of dismay, Lena dropped her knitting. "Oh, they're using the dishwasher."

Dan gave a long-suffering sigh. "Yah, I should hope so. Dat's what I got it for, you stubborn Swede." Andrea noticed his Scandinavian lilt had intensified.

"I told you when you bought it I was perfectly happy washing dishes by hand. Got 'em cleaner, too." This last she added as an aside to Andrea, then muttered something about extravagant Norwegians.

She looked up as the four young men came in from the kitchen, their chore complete. "You didn't have to use the dishwasher," she said.

"Did, too," Dan muttered.

Todd looked puzzled but didn't pursue the subject. "I hope we put everything away right. It's hard to find your way around someone else's kitchen."

Lena gave up on the dishwasher argument. "I'm sure it's fine. Thank you boys very much." She gestured to the sofa. "Have a seat. Let your supper settle."

Stench, Jock and Dev sat on the long sofa beside Andrea. Todd took the last remaining chair, near Dan.

"We were thinking," he began shyly, "we'd like to provide some entertainment. We have our instruments out in the trailer, but all the electronic gear was Vidtel's and they took it with them."

Andrea just made out a muffled "Thank God" from Lena.

Todd seemed not to hear it. "Do you have an acoustic guitar around, maybe? We'd really like to play for you."

Dan rose. "No guitar, but maybe you could do something with this." He bent behind the sofa and pulled out a medium-size black case, which he set on the coffee table and opened. Black plastic, ivory and chrome gleamed. Dan lifted the bulky instrument from the case and slipped his arms through the straps.

"My God!" Stench gasped in an almost reverent voice. "Lawrence Welk's spoor."

The gray-haired man shot him a sharp glance, followed by a wink. "Don't speak ill of a state hero, boy." He unsnapped the straps that held the bellows of the accordion closed and pressed a valve that allowed them to expand. Then, fingering the buttons with his left hand and the keyboard with his right, he launched into a sprightly version of "The Tennessee Waltz."

The music's richness surprised Andrea. She had always thought of accordions as little squeeze boxes for playing polkas. As if he heard her thoughts, Dan segued into a lively polka, then a slow ballad. At the end of the song, Andrea led the applause.

Dan slipped the instrument from his shoulders and held it out to Todd. "Would you like to give it a try?"

Todd hesitated.

"Go for it, dude," Dev said enthusiastically.

"Sure," Stench added. "It might be the new sound we're looking for."

Even Lena laughed at the idea.

Todd grinned and stood up. He held out his arms, and Dan slid the straps of the heavy instrument over his shoulders. When he let go, the unaccustomed weight doubled Todd over.

He shifted the accordion and regained his balance.

"Got it?" Dan asked. "Okay. Now, slide your left hand

under the strap. Feel the buttons there? Those are the chords. Find the one with the dimple. That's C major.''

Todd nodded and fingered the buttons, playing experimentally.

"When you play," Dan continued, "you work the bellows by moving your arm out with your wrist against the strap. Then your fingers are free to play the chords. You play the keyboard with your right hand."

He laughed as Todd attempted to follow his instructions but kept trying to swing the keys into a horizontal position.

"I've never played a piano on its side before," Todd explained. After several tries, though, he managed to coordinate his efforts enough to force out a few recognizable bars of "Beer Barrel Polka." A few more attempts and he returned the instrument to Dan with reluctance.

Dan strapped the accordion on and began to play. Stench surprised them all by joining in for the chorus of "Red River Valley," his voice a smooth tenor at odds with his leather and studs. He sang along with most of the ballads and folk tunes that followed and even coaxed Todd into singing harmony on a couple of songs.

Andrea relaxed against the sofa cushions, the combination of a good supper and lilting music taking its toll. She glanced at Mike. He seemed relaxed but watchful, his posture curiously straight, defying the recliner's comfortable slouch.

Military. The word leapt unbidden into her mind as she recognized his seated "at ease" position.

Andrea's father had been a veterinarian in the air force, the branch of the armed forces he referred to as "an alternative to military service." Still, his assignments to training bases had offered her ample opportunity to see troops on the parade ground.

Mike's automatic assumption of the position in this setting bespoke years of training, probably army or marines.

So what was a professional soldier doing on a bison ranch? Mike didn't seem like the type to just chuck it all for the quiet life.

As if he sensed her thoughts, Mike looked up and caught her gaze. Andrea glanced away, her face heated, and feigned a yawn. A real one followed unbidden.

Suddenly she couldn't keep her eyes open. Sleep deprivation was finally catching up with her. Dan noticed her sleepiness and wound up the session with a few bars of "Good Night Ladies," then suggested they all call it a night.

Before Dan put the accordion away, Todd approached him hesitantly. "I'd really like to learn to play it, sir. Unusual instruments are kind of a challenge to me."

"Unusual?" Dan snorted. Then he grinned and handed Todd the accordion after strapping its bellows closed. "Go ahead and take it out to the trailer if you'd like to practice with it awhile. I don't get to play too much anymore, so it'll probably be good to get it loosened up."

Todd's thanks were profuse as he headed toward the back door with his burden.

Mike stood up and stretched. "I'll walk you guys out to the trailer and get my gear. Then you can make yourselves at home. Within reason," he warned, then followed the young men out the door.

"Good night, Andrea." Dan grasped her hand. "See you in the morning."

"I think you're all set, but if there's anything you need, help yourself," Lena told her.

"Thank you. Good night." Andrea climbed the steps to her room and closed the door behind her. Downstairs, she heard footsteps on the wooden floor and the click of lamps being turned off. She performed her bedtime preparations, slipped on the most modest of her trousseau nightgowns and turned off the light before climbing into the high antique bed.

Snuggling into the soft mattress, she lay staring at the solid darkness of the room until her eyes adjusted to the starlight seeping in through the sheer curtains. Night was certainly black out here in the country, she thought. And quiet. Only cricket chirps and the musical croaks of frogs joined with an occasional old-house creak to break the silence.

Downstairs, the kitchen door slapped shut; Mike returning from the trailer, Andrea thought. She waited for the sound of footsteps on the stairs, then remembered Dan's comment that the room across the hall was Lena's sewing room. The steps stayed downstairs, and soon the house grew quiet again.

It seemed ages rather than only a day since she'd left Seattle. She already felt as if that portion of her life had been erased forever. Except for the lingering guilt of abandoning Jeffrey.

No matter how many times she told herself that she'd hurt Jeffrey's pride more than his heart, she still suffered for the embarrassment she had caused him.

She also empathized with Mike Winterhawk's situation. She knew how she'd feel if her job, her life-style, her home, were threatened, so it was easy to make allowances for his behavior.

Actually, given the provocations of the past few hours, he'd behaved remarkably well. He had a temper, though; that was more than obvious. Would he finally decide it wasn't worthwhile to stay at White Thunder?

What would she do if he left? She couldn't run the ranch alone. She knew too little about ranching to make a go of it without help.

Andrea yawned again. Even as her thoughts raced, exhaustion began to overtake her.

She turned toward the window, her eyes tired yet craving light. A thin sound drifted over the song of the crickets and frogs. She raised her head from the pillow and listened carefully. It couldn't be, she thought, straining to hear more.

No, she hadn't imagined it. Outside, off in the distance, someone was playing "Highway to Hell."

On an accordion.

CHAPTER FOUR

ANDREA STOOD AT THE BACK of a huge cathedral. Her white gown, the skirt suddenly three times its width, flapped around her in the unexplained gale swirling up an aisle the length of a football field.

Far away before the altar stood Jeffrey, slim and dark, continually raising his arm to check his watch. Pews filled with thousands of people rose like bleachers on either side of the aisle.

I'm dreaming, Andrea told herself. *Who are all these people?*

She scanned the crowd for a familiar face. Hadn't anyone she knew come to her wedding? None of her family? No one from the clinic?

Something pressed into the small of her back like a cold, hard finger through the fine lace bodice. She looked over her shoulder and stared into the angry face of her mother.

Mother wore a simple sheath of mauve silk overlaid with flowing chiffon that fell below her knees in ruffles. Champagne pearls and a pert pillbox hat, à la Jackie Kennedy, accessorized the ensemble, but the item that pulled the look together was the mauve shotgun she held to Andrea's back.

Andrea knew she was dreaming. Mother never wore mauve. It made her look her age and she knew it.

Mother prodded her with the gun. "Get a move on, girlie," she said in a dreadful hillbilly drawl, then in her own voice, she said, "You're not going to disappoint me again, are you, dear?"

Andrea's eyes shot open and the nightmare images dispersed. Cold sweat beaded her brow. She knew if she closed her eyes again she'd see her mother's distorted face.

Lying rigid, she glanced around the room. It seemed brighter than when she'd gone to bed. The music that lulled her to sleep had given way to occasional cricket chirps. She squinted at her watch.

It was 1:00 a.m. Less than three hours' sleep and now she was wide-awake.

Sitting up, she tossed back the covers and swung her legs out of the bed. As if in protest, her stomach rumbled loudly. Andrea had heard that country air gave one an appetite, but this was ridiculous. Supper had been filling. Still, the image of Lena's brownies rose enticingly in her mind.

Feed a cold, starve a fever, she thought irrationally, *or was it the other way around?*

And liberally medicate everything else with chocolate.

Maybe a glass of milk would help her sleep.

She started to climb out of bed, then stopped abruptly. This wasn't her apartment in Seattle. She couldn't go traipsing around in the dark in someone else's house, much less raid the refrigerator.

Well, okay, technically it was *her* house, but she didn't have to be pushy about it. What if she woke someone up? Like Mike Winterhawk?

You'll explain that you couldn't get to sleep and came down for a glass of milk. Surely no one would blame her for that. She'd just grab a quick brownie and milk, then bring it back upstairs.

She rose and shrugged into the pink chiffon peignoir she'd thrown over the footboard. The wavy mirror reflected the fabric's movement, and Andrea paused a moment and regarded herself.

Good grief, she thought, striking a pose that accentuated the fall of chiffon and lace, *I look like the cover of a gothic novel.* She imagined herself in the yard, the farmhouse behind her dark except for a single lighted window upstairs. Or exploring the darkened house, carrying a single candle, approaching an ominous locked door.

She stuck her tongue out at her reflection, breaking the mood. There was no help for it. She had to wear something, and the pink chiffon was the only robe she'd packed.

She stepped into her slippers, then, flinching at every creak of the old wooden floor, opened her door and started downstairs.

At the foot of the staircase, she plunged into darkness much denser than that of her bedroom. Unlike her filmy bedroom curtains, the drawn living room draperies admitted no moonlight.

She hesitated. How had the living room furniture been arranged? All she needed was to fall over a few chairs and break a lamp or two between here and the kitchen. It wasn't enough to drive Dan out of his home. Might as well destroy all his belongings in the process.

She stepped forward, feeling her way. A board groaned loudly.

She sensed motion against the shadows, then a blackness even darker than the surrounding gloom loomed before her.

''Who's there?'' she whispered.

Hands clamped like iron bands around her upper arms, crushing the chiffon puffs. She raised her hands to ward off her attacker, her fingers meeting warm, smooth skin.

Her captor spun her around roughly and wrenched her right arm behind her. He forced her head back, his muscular arm around her throat. She squeaked with surprise as she was half lifted off the ground.

Her flailing left hand brushed something on the wall. A light switch. She felt for it again and flicked it upward. The room exploded into brilliance.

For a heartbeat, nothing happened. Andrea twisted her head to look up at the man who held her so tightly.

Mike Winterhawk.

Mike stared down at his suddenly quiescent adversary and with a choking gasp realized where he was and what he was doing.

Oh, hell.

He held her for another moment, uncertain what to do. His rage subsided, replaced by quite a different, and surprising, response to the warm softness of Andrea Moore.

He dropped her.

Support gone, she crumpled to her knees on the floor, then whirled to stare up at him, eyes wide with shock.

"Damn," he swore as dream images of steamy Central American rain forest gave way to the familiarity of the living room. He crouched to help her to her feet. "I'm sorry. I didn't know it was you." The words sounded lame even to his ears. "Are you all right?"

She nodded, squinting up at him, and he expelled a relieved breath. Another second and he might have done her some serious damage.

Bloody hell, what was the woman thinking, roaming the house in the middle of the night?

She was dressed, if you could call it that, in some kind of fluffy, sheer pink thing over a brief, flowery nightie. Her dark curls were tousled from her pillow, and her green eyes stood in sharp contrast to her pale face.

He blinked a few times, accustoming his eyes to the light and trying hard not to stare. "We get up early out here in the country, but this is a little extreme."

Her face colored to match her robe. "I...I'm sorry. I didn't mean to wake you. I couldn't get back to sleep, so I came down for a snack."

Her gaze dropped briefly to his bare chest, then flashed back to his face. "I thought maybe a glass of milk..."

Mike bit back the urge to comment on her nocturnal wanderings. "No problem. I wasn't asleep, either," he lied.

He'd been asleep, all right, dreaming about the jungle again. The sound of her on the stairs had jolted him into an instinctive and aggressive response. It had been a long time since he'd reacted like that to noises in the dark. Some commentary on his state of mind, he thought.

Damn, I must still be half asleep. The last thing he wanted was to stand here exchanging pleasantries with the woman who was taking White Thunder from him, even if he *had* just attacked her in the darkness.

"Well, I'll just, uh…" Andrea stammered. She darted a glance toward the kitchen like a cornered animal spying an escape route. "I'll just find everything myself."

She scurried past him, the silky fabric of her robe brushing his bare shoulder as she fled. A delicate floral fragrance lingered in her wake.

A moment later, she poked her head out of the kitchen. "Can I get you something while I'm in here?"

Mike blinked in surprise, not sure what to say. "Yeah, sure, I guess." What was she trying to do? It was bad enough that she was taking the ranch from him and disturbing his sleep; now she wanted to have a slumber party. And what was she up to running around in that nightie? If it was some sort of seduction scene, he wasn't interested.

Then again, he couldn't help but recall how she'd felt in his arms.

He shook the thought from his head. *Don't even go there,* he thought as Andrea returned from the kitchen carrying a tray.

Andrea placed the tray on the coffee table. Mike had moved to the recliner, where he sat in gray sweatpants. He'd turned off the ceiling light and switched on a table lamp. The subtle lamplight gleamed on the bronze contours of his muscular chest and arms. He shifted toward her.

Light danced along a white tracery of scars that ran the length of his right upper arm and crossed to his chest, where it spread and blossomed into a pale island just below his right collarbone. She met his eyes, steel gray in the dim light, and looked away, noting that his short dark hair was spiky from his sofa pillow. He looked strangely boyish despite the scars.

They ate in uncomfortable silence. The moist chocolate brownie tasted like sawdust, and she gulped milk to wash it down. Lowering the glass, she glanced at Mike furtively. His gaze caught hers and held it.

"So…" she started, fumbling for something to break the tension. What was she thinking, sitting here trying to make conversation with this man? Not to mention gawking at his admittedly well-muscled chest and arms. She'd just dumped one man; she sure wasn't in the market for another one.

"Well…" Mike began at the same time.

"I'm sorry. Go ahead," Andrea said, self-conscious.

"No. I didn't mean to interrupt."

"Oh…" Andrea realized that she'd forgotten whatever it was she'd been about to say. She grasped for something, anything. "Have you been at White Thunder long?" She grimaced at her lack of originality.

"About two years."

"Oh?" She remembered that Dan had said so. And what was the mess he'd mentioned? When Mike said nothing further, she asked, "Have you known Dan a long time?"

He shook his head. "I met him at a buffalo auction. He knew some of my distant relations from the reservation near here and offered me the job."

"You're from around here, then?" The reservation comment confirmed her earlier guess about his name. She'd seen signs for the Sioux reservation on the drive out.

"I was born here, but I'm an army brat. I went into the

army myself, then when I got out I came back here to, I don't know, find my roots."

So far, so good, Andrea thought. At least they had something in common and he was speaking in more than monosyllables. Still, Mike Winterhawk was leaving far more unsaid. Despite her reluctance to intrude, she couldn't help but ask, "Did you find them? Your roots, I mean."

He watched her a moment, as though considering his reply. He reminded her of an injured wildcat a client had trapped and brought to the clinic. The animal had stared at her through the bars of its cage, yellow eyes narrowed in suspicion as she'd prepared to treat its wounds. No amount of coaxing or baby talk could diminish its hostility, and it fought her violently when she tried to take it from its cage, not understanding that she only wanted to help.

Mike nodded, his look faraway and misty like a distant storm cloud. "I did. That's why I'm still here." He blinked, and his gaze became cool steel again. "So how about you? Any idea what you're going to do with White Thunder?"

The question sounded casual, but his gaze was probing. Andrea forced herself to meet his eyes without flinching.

"No. I didn't even recall entering the contest, much less expect to win."

His expression didn't vary as he waited for her to continue.

"I needed a change, though." She paused, not sure how much to tell this man. She certainly couldn't tell him about Jeffrey—not him or any of White Thunder's residents. They'd think she was horrible.

"Do you have your own practice in Seattle?" Mike asked.

"No, I worked as an associate in a small-animal clinic."

His dark brows drew together in a frown, then he spoke up. "Are you planning to keep the ranch?"

"I don't know," she answered honestly. She could sell

the ranch and use the money to start over somewhere else, but the permanence and history of White Thunder appealed to her in a way she'd never have expected—probably because she'd grown up in one military town after another. Still, it didn't hurt to explore her options. Selling out didn't necessarily mean returning to Seattle.

"Why? Do you know a buyer?"

Mike nodded. "Yep. Me."

"Oh?" His answer both surprised and alarmed her. It certainly explained his hostility. "Why didn't you buy it from Dan in the first place? Did you enter the contest?"

"As a ranch employee, I wasn't eligible. And I didn't buy it for the same reason I probably won't be able to buy it from you. I don't have the money right now." His mouth twisted at one corner.

"I see," Andrea said.

"Look, I won't try to hold you to anything, and I don't know what I'll be able to come up with, but promise you'll give me first shot at buying White Thunder if you decide to sell."

"Okay, but..."

"Thanks." Mike cut her off. He rose abruptly and collected their plates and glasses, then carried them to the kitchen.

When he returned, he dropped onto the sofa, his face betraying none of the tension she'd heard in his voice. His tone was light when he changed the subject. "Tomorrow I'll take the band up to Minot and get them on their way, then pick up some supplies. I suppose you'll want to take a look at the rest of the ranch when I get back?"

"I'd appreciate that," Andrea said, noting the reluctance in his words. "I have a lot to learn about ranching if I do decide to stay."

"No doubt." His voice was taut.

Andrea felt her cheeks grow warm. "Look, Mike," she began. "I realize how hard this is for you."

He cut her off, his face darkening. "No, I don't think you do."

His sudden anger startled her. *Dangerous ground,* she thought. "If it's any consolation, I regret that things had to happen this way."

Mike brushed aside her words. He yawned ostentatiously and studied his watch. "Hey, it's late, and we really do get up early out here. You'd better try to get back to sleep. Go on—I'll get the lights down here."

Feeling like a dismissed child, Andrea rose without argument and headed for the stairs. She paused on the way up and looked back at him. He sat upright on the sofa, watching her go, his shoulders and chest golden in the lamplight, but his face oddly colorless.

"Good night," he said softly.

When Andrea reached the door of her room, the living room lamp switched off. She clutched the doorjamb to get her bearings, then walked across the bedroom to the open window and leaned on the sill to look outside.

The night that had seemed so black took on a silvery glow once her eyes readjusted to the moon and starlight. Above, the sky was indigo velvet scattered with diamonds. She could make out the barns and Mike's trailer in the distance, and even some of the terrain beyond.

Near the corral two figures moved against the darkness, vague shapes without identity. Who would be outside at this hour? she wondered.

Probably a couple of the boys. The band wouldn't be used to early bedtimes.

Her thoughts returned to Mike. The image of him, tawny skin glowing in the lamplight, rose in her mind.

Touchy. Like a wounded animal. You could never be

sure what action or remark might provoke a hostile response.

What would it take to win his cooperation, short of handing the ranch over to him? If she intended to stay and make a go of White Thunder, she needed help. Someone who knew the ranch and all the details of its operation.

She needed Mike. But would he stay? And if he did, how would she pay him, or Lena, for that matter, once Vidtel's payment of their salaries ran out? The video network had paid to keep the ranch staff on during her transition into ownership or until she decided to sell, up to a maximum of two months. After that, any expenses were hers to deal with.

Andrea slid the window down and pressed her forehead against the cool glass.

A flash of light in her peripheral vision caught her attention. She looked toward the northwest. A small round object glowed against the blue-black sky. It hovered for a few seconds, then began to move, slowly, toward the east.

Andrea watched the gleaming sphere drift across her line of sight. Its distance was impossible to judge, as was its size. At a point somewhat east of the ranch house, it flared into a small fireball, bright enough to blind Andrea to the night's stars.

Then it disappeared.

ALONE AGAIN IN THE darkness, Mike lay back on the sofa.

Well, you old devil, he reproached himself, *you certainly handled that smoothly. You'll be lucky if she'll sell you the time of day, much less White Thunder.*

What had come over him to make him behave like such a jerk? He knew the answer without even considering the question.

He was angry that she had won the ranch and was doing his best to take it out on her.

With good reason, he rationalized. After all, she was taking everything he'd come to live for.

When he'd come back from Honduras the wounded hero of a covert operation, there had been no parades for him, just a medal and a medical retirement. The mine that sent shrapnel ripping through his body had torn apart his life, his career, his peace of mind.

He'd spent the next months piecing the bits of his existence back together, like the surgeons who'd stitched together his damaged flesh. But he'd discovered that gaps still remained.

Some part of him that had lain dormant for most of his adult life awakened with his injury. That part of him, conscience, spirit, whatever it was, made him see the lie that was the life he'd chosen.

His sight had turned inward, toward discovery of himself, his heritage and his culture. He'd returned to his father's home, his father's people, to seek his past—and his future.

His father's people might have called it a vision quest, the personal spiritual journey a young man of the Sioux undertook to find his path in life.

He hadn't yet found his vision. The key to his destiny was here on White Thunder Ranch, though, and he knew it was close. For the first time in his life he felt something strong and whole supporting him, surrounding him, something he was part of.

And no one was going to take it from him. Especially not Andrea Moore.

CHAPTER FIVE

ANDREA STRETCHED luxuriously and rolled to look at the clock beside the bed. Glowing green digits read 9:00 a.m.

She bolted upright. Nine o'clock! White Thunder's residents had probably been up since dawn. What would they think of her?

Wide-awake with panic, she leapt out of bed and tripped on the throw rug, then skidded against the dresser, stubbing her toe. She bit back a curse at the pain as she flipped open her suitcase and surveyed its contents.

The island prints and shorts definitely wouldn't do. Neither would the white eyelet sundress chosen to set off the Hawaiian tan she'd planned to acquire on her honeymoon.

At last she settled on jeans and a serviceable T-shirt.

Digging through the suitcase for a pair of shoes, she rejected sandals, dressy pumps and a sparkling pair of Nikes she knew wouldn't stay white for long in White Thunder's dust.

Finally she turned to the green snakeskin boots, abandoned under the edge of the bed, and sighed resignedly. At least they were comfortable. If she got them dirty enough, maybe they wouldn't look so bad.

Andrea showered quickly, then dressed and started down the stairs.

Could she get through the day without making a fool of herself like she had last night? Mike Winterhawk probably wouldn't make it easy.

And what about Dan and Lena? This would be her first

full day at the ranch, and she couldn't shake the feeling that she was out of place here and everyone knew it. She couldn't remember being this nervous since her first surgery at the clinic.

Voices from the kitchen and the aroma of frying bacon interrupted her thoughts, and she paused for a calming breath before entering the room.

Lena stood alone at the stove, but the screen door still vibrated from someone's exit.

"Good morning, Lena," Andrea said, battling a sudden wave of shyness.

"'Morning." The housekeeper grinned and waved her to a chair at the kitchen table. "Sleep well?"

"Yes. Too well. I didn't mean to sleep so late."

Lena poured a mug of steaming coffee and set it in front of her. "I figured you'd need some time to get settled in, so we're having a late breakfast this morning. The men got an early start out in the barn. We'll just call them in when it's ready." Her gaze darted to the green boots, then away quickly, as though she were trying hard not to stare.

The poor woman, Andrea thought. She seemed morbidly fascinated by the ghastly things.

Self-conscious, Andrea took a sip of coffee and smothered a gasp at its potency. She'd expected to miss Seattle's coffee-crazed culture, but it looked as though Lena was more than capable of providing her morning caffeine jolt. She swallowed the stiff brew and, taste buds still stunned, took another sip.

When she regained her voice, she replied, "Thanks, Lena. Sorry to throw off your schedule, though."

Lena waved aside her apology. "It happens to everybody when they first come out here. It's the country air. Anyway, you were up pretty late, too."

Andrea started. Had Lena overheard her midnight encounter with Mike? Had he told her about it?

Dan stepped inside from the back porch before she could probe further.

"Good morning." He took a mug from the counter and filled it with coffee.

Andrea returned his greeting.

"Dan." Lena's voice carried a note of warning.

"Aw, hush, woman. It's my first real cup this morning." He winked at Andrea, a smile crinkling his face. "I'm not supposed to have caffeine. Cardiac arrhythmia," he pronounced carefully, then shot a glance at Lena. "And one cup won't hurt it."

Lena snorted and rolled her eyes.

Dan pulled up a chair beside Andrea. "After breakfast Mike's going to drive those boys to the bus station in Minot and stop for supplies. If you want to go with him, he can stop in Rorvik on the way back so you can see the sights, such as they are. I expect you'll have some business there. We've got one bank and two CPAs if that's any help."

"CPAs?" Andrea asked.

"For the income tax you'll owe from winning the property," Dan explained.

Oh, great. Everything had happened so fast, she hadn't considered the ultimate cost of her prize. She didn't even know how much White Thunder was worth. The taxes would probably be tens of thousands of dollars.

A sinking sensation formed in the pit of her stomach. She'd finally paid off her student loans after working for three years. Now she was in debt again. She'd have to break into the emergency fund she'd set aside, her inheritance from her father. And that wouldn't go far.

She forced a smile at Dan. "Sounds like a good idea. Where is Mike? I should find out when he wants to leave."

Dan cocked a thumb toward the door. "In the barn. Rusting Hulkk is helping him stack hay."

"Really?" Andrea took a last gulp of coffee and stood

up. "That should be interesting." And it meant she
wouldn't have to face Mike alone.

"Tell them to come on in for breakfast, Andrea," Lena
called after her as she headed outside.

MIKE TOOK A BALE from Jock and tossed it smoothly onto
the neat stack in the corner of the barn.

Jock sniffled and rubbed red, teary eyes. "Man, I thought
hay fever was just a figure of speech."

"Nope," Mike said. "You've come to the source. It's
worse than usual this year, too. We've had a dry spring."
He laughed. "Go see Lena. She has it, too, so she should
have something that'll help."

Jock nodded his thanks and started toward the house.
Dev's call of "wuss" followed him from the hayloft.

Mike watched him stop to wish Andrea a stuffy-nosed
"good morning" as she approached, resisting an impulse
to look at his watch. They had been up late, after all.

She looked good this morning, he had to admit. The slim
blue jeans and white T-shirt flattered her tall, slender form.
He wondered what had possessed her to wear that orange-
and-fringe getup the day before, then remembered Connie's
similar outfit. He suspected Ms. Chambers had a hand in
picking Andrea's clothes for the trip.

Fortunately, Andrea probably looked good in just about
anything.

He remembered her last night, swathed in that silky pink
robe. He recalled the feel of her in his arms.

The temperature suddenly seemed to have risen several
degrees. Mike turned away from Andrea to straighten the
newly stacked bales, taking several deep breaths and willing his surging pulse to slow to its normal pace. Had he
been alone so long that the presence of a reasonably attractive woman was enough to get him worked up?

She hasn't even been at White Thunder twenty-four hours and she's already causing problems.

He heard her below, talking to the remaining members of Rusting Hulkk, and pretended not to notice her arrival.

Then she called, "Good morning, Mike. Lena says to tell you breakfast is ready."

He stepped to the edge of the loft and looked down. She stood scuffing her bilious reptile boots in the hay dust.

"'Morning," he said, trying to sound casual. "We're about ready for a break here. Thanks."

When he said no more, she spoke quickly. "I'd like to come with you to Minot if you don't mind. I need to stop in Rorvik on the way back, though. I don't want to inconvenience you," she continued. "But I have some business in Rorvik. Dan said it wouldn't be out of your way."

Remind me to thank him for that, Mike thought, but he answered, "No problem. Where do you need to go?" *Besides home where you belong.*

"To the bank, for a start. Is there anyone in particular you work with?"

Mike climbed down from the loft and brushed the dust from his jeans. "You'll probably want to talk to Bert Petersen. Dan's worked with him for years."

He glanced at Dev, Todd and Stench, all collapsed and sweating on hay bales. "Can you boys be ready to go after breakfast?"

Stench laughed. "With what Connie left us, are you kidding? We're ready now."

Mike smiled. "Fine, but wouldn't you like some of Lena's bacon and eggs first? I've waited long enough for breakfast." He glanced at Andrea.

She reddened at the implication, and he was surprised to find himself regretting his remark. The realization irritated him. It wasn't as if he had any reason to be friendly, under the circumstances. He stepped past her and followed the boys toward the house.

Andrea noticed the sweat that glistened on his arms as he passed, the dampness that made his T-shirt cling to his chest and flat stomach. She'd never seen Jeffrey break a sweat from hard work, other than a workout at his expensive gym. Somehow this was different; honest labor compared to, well, recreation. Mike even smelled different, warm and musky, his own scent blending with the fragrance of hay and wood.

She counted to ten silently, fighting the urge to heave a pitchfork at his retreating back. What was the man's problem? All she wanted was a lift into town on ranch business. Wasn't that sort of thing his job?

After what he'd told her last night, she understood his anger, but that didn't excuse it. If it kept up, she'd...

Well, she didn't know what she'd do. Maybe she should talk to Dan.

No. Dan had his own troubles to deal with. He needed to see that White Thunder was in secure hands. Showing him that was the least she could do.

Maybe she'd have a chance to talk it out with Mike today, once they dropped off Rusting Hulkk. Minot was eighty miles away. They'd have to talk about something.

She followed Mike and the boys into the house. As they took their places at the table, Lena shot a quick glance at Dan, then back at Andrea, turning a shade of pink that clashed violently with her hair. "Andrea, you had a phone call while you were outside. From a Professor Hale."

"Who's Professor Hale?" Andrea asked.

"She's a lady scientist," Dan said. "Calls herself a ufologist, whatever that is. She wants to talk to you about investigating White Thunder. She's been calling here almost every day since she found out about the contest, wanting to talk to the new owner." He scratched his head. "We've managed to keep her at bay till now, but I suppose you'll have to talk to her eventually."

"Wow!" Stench tore his attention away from the plate he'd loaded with scrambled eggs, hash browns, bacon and biscuits. "Clarissa Hale is coming here? I watch her show all the time."

"You've heard of her?" Andrea asked.

"Yeah, she's a famous scientist. She's got this TV program, 'Visitors.' It's great."

"'Visitors'"? Dev said. "That show's lame. It's all 'the aliens are among us' and 'your dog may be a Martian' and stuff."

Jock rubbed his finger across his throat and warbled in a sitcom alien voice, "'We mean no harm to your planet, earthling.'"

"'Live long and prosper.'" Todd added with an uncoordinated attempt at a Vulcan greeting.

"Happy b-b-b-birthday, you thing from another world, you."

"Silence, earth creature, or I'll use my Alludium Q-35 atomic space detonator." Todd aimed a bacon strip like a ray gun.

Jock didn't answer but slowly began sculpting his scrambled eggs into a miniature, if somewhat lumpy, replica of the Devil's Tower, sending Todd into gales of laughter.

Andrea laughed, too, then glanced across at Mike to see his eyes sparkling with unexpected mirth. He'd relaxed his usual taut, intimidating military bearing. He was quite good-looking when he smiled. Hell, he was even good-looking when he scowled. Her gaze was drawn to the sensuous curve of his lips, and warmth suffused her cheeks. Her thoughts were taking a dangerous turn here; one she definitely didn't want or need.

He looked up and caught her staring. She blinked and turned her attention to the boys.

"That's enough, you guys. You don't even watch the show." Stench scowled from the end of the table. "It's really a good program." He turned to Dan. "She always goes to these places where aliens are supposed to be visiting. Usually they're off in some desert somewhere."

Todd laughed. "Yeah, I guess space aliens don't like cold weather."

"Seems like North Dakota is the last place they'd want to come, then," Mike said. "There's a saying around here. Forty below keeps out the riffraff. Human or otherwise."

Dan leaned forward. "I've seen that 'Visitors' show. I guess lots of folks believe in those things." He shook his head pityingly. "I can't think of any reason space aliens would come here."

"Maybe they're looking for the secret recipe for Lena's *lutefisk*." Mike winked at the housekeeper. "To use as a weapon of mass destruction."

"Well!" Lena gasped in mock indignation while Andrea and Dan grimaced in unison.

"What's *lutefisk*?" Todd asked.

Stench looked at him as if he'd sprouted two heads. "You haven't heard of *lutefisk*? How long have you lived in Seattle, anyway?"

Todd shrugged. "A couple years. Why?"

"Most people who've lived around Seattle for any length of time have heard of *lutefisk*," Andrea explained. "It's a Scandinavian, uh, fish delicacy. It's supposed to be pretty noxious, gray and gelatinous, and I understand it smells really bad." She looked at Dan for assistance.

"*Lutefisk* is codfish cured with lye," the older man said.

"Lye?" Aghast, Todd glanced at Mike, who nodded solemnly. "If that's the cure, what was the disease? And people actually eat it? On purpose?"

Lena gave him a curt nod, the laughter in her eyes belying her pout of wounded pride. "Of course. You should try it sometime. It'll put hair on your chest."

Mike grinned wickedly. "And on your back, and on your toes, and on the plate and on the table, and anywhere else it touches."

"Gross." Todd shuddered.

"The smell alone could attract aliens, not to mention flies," Dan said. "She doesn't fix it too often, but when she does, I get out of the house. That stuff peels the plaster off the walls."

The housekeeper shook her head. "You just don't know what's good. It's healthy, too."

"No amount of health is worth that, Lena." Mike laughed.

"Really, though, why would this professor want to investigate the ranch?" Andrea steered the conversation back to the subject at hand.

"She investigates a lot of different things," Stench said. "Ghosts, aliens, any kind of spooky scientific phenomena." He leaned forward, his eyes bright. "She travels around the country with electronic equipment and a team of researchers, and they do all their own monitoring and observations. Then she presents it on her show. She says the purpose of her research is to prove the existence of paranormal phenomena. Have there been UFO sightings out here?"

"Here? At White Thunder?" Andrea asked, glancing at Dan, then at Mike. Even as she asked, though, the image of a bright, slow-moving light came sharply to mind. The light she'd seen last night. She caught her breath, remembering its steady course across the blackened sky.

Oh, no! It couldn't be!

"Actually, some pretty sophisticated research has been conducted into the possibility of extraterrestrial life," Stench was saying, his boyish face earnest.

Andrea could only stare at him.

"Is this a sideline of yours?" Mike asked. "Rock star and rocket scientist?"

"Just a hobby." Stench shrugged. "These ongoing studies, like SETI, the Search for Extraterrestrial Intelligence, use huge radiotelescope arrays to pick up transmissions from other planets. It's really high tech and all privately funded, too, so there's obviously a lot of interest. Like they say on 'X-Files,' 'The truth is out there.'"

Andrea shook her head in disbelief, suddenly weak, as though all her blood had drained into her feet. No, there had to be another explanation.

Dan touched her hand and she jumped.

"Are you all right, Andrea?" His hazel eyes were dark with worry. "You look a little pale."

"Yes, I'm fine," she assured him. "It's just that I'd forgotten..."

What had she done that her life was suddenly taking on the proportions of a supermarket tabloid story? She could see the headlines now: Space Aliens Menace North Dakota Ranch.

"What did you forget?" Dan's soft voice brought her back to the present.

"Nothing. Really." She shook her head in dismissal.

He watched her patiently, as though he knew something more lay behind her denial, and waited for her to continue.

She concentrated on buttering a biscuit, trying to appear casual. "I just saw a strange light in the sky last night, that's all. Probably a meteor or something." *Or something—meteors didn't follow straight paths across the prairie.* "I don't believe in UFOs," she finished emphatically.

Dan and Lena exchanged concerned glances. *Oh, no,* Andrea thought, *something is going on here.* She was certain it meant another unpleasant surprise. Probably worse than the taxes.

"Well, I don't believe in them, either, strictly speaking. That is, I've never seen..." Dan cleared his throat, reddening, then took a deep breath and spoke quickly. "Some folks around here, they've seen t'ings in the sky at night. In the daytime, too, some say."

Lena snorted. "There's nothing strange about that. After an evening down at the Sons of Norway Hall, lots of people see things."

Andrea laughed, but her concern didn't diminish. "So somehow this professor has gotten the idea that we're being invaded by little green men, and she wants to look for them here?" she asked with a bravado she didn't feel.

Dan nodded. "She wants permission to investigate the ranch. Said she already had some sort of study going on out on government land, but she didn't want to enter the ranch without permission. Must've gotten her hand slapped for trespassing or something. She's going to stop by to talk to you, from the sound of t'ings."

"I can hardly wait." Andrea slumped in her chair, her appetite fading fast. She'd hoped the worst was over with the departure of Connie and company. The cost of her freedom was beginning to rise higher than she'd imagined.

"SORRY, BOYS." The grizzled ticket agent at the Minot bus station tipped his cap higher on his forehead and jabbed a thumb in the direction of a milling group of sign-carrying men. "You aren't goin' nowhere. 'Least not by bus."

"I didn't know bus lines even had baggage handlers," Andrea said.

"Well, this one does," the agent replied. "And they're on strike. That wouldn't be so bad, but the drivers won't cross the picket line. So we're as good as shut down. Don't know for how long."

Todd dropped his backpack and slumped against the wall with a sigh. "Man, we're never going to get out of here."

"Yeah," Dev agreed. "Hey, maybe that Vidtel woman, Connie, paid them to strike."

Todd rolled his eyes.

"The fiend," Stench intoned melodramatically. "Is there no end to her efforts to thwart us?"

Jock and Todd laughed, but Dev simply looked confused.

They'd reached Minot and gone in search of the Western Union office. There, Stench picked up the money his family had wired for bus fare after he called from the ranch to let them know the band was stranded.

"Just a loan," Stench reminded them. "Do you know how many hours I'd have to put in at Dick's Drive-in to pay this off?"

Then they'd driven to the bus station. The boys were subdued and more than ready to head for home after their adventure at White Thunder.

"So, now what?" Andrea turned to Mike. "We can't just leave them here."

Mike glanced at the band, the members of which were staring at him, wide-eyed and forlorn. Like stray puppies, Andrea thought, grinning.

He shrugged. "I guess we could take them back to the ranch till the strike's over. I can probably find something to keep them busy."

"How long do you think it'll be?" Dev asked. "I promised my folks if this gig didn't work out, I'd be back in time for summer quarter at the U."

"Well, you've got some time," Andrea said. "Classes at the University of Washington don't start for a few weeks."

"Yeah." Dev flipped his wavy, dark hair out of his face, his eyes worried. "But these bus strikes can last months. Years, even."

"I don't think you'll be here for years," Mike said. "It's up to you, though. Can you get home another way?"

"I could hitch, I guess." Dev's expression was uncertain.

"Man, that might take you longer than waiting out the strike," Stench said. "Look, I have an idea, but we've all got to agree on it."

"What is it?" Jock asked. "We're all for one and one for all, you know."

Andrea hid a smile she knew the boys wouldn't appreciate. For all Rusting Hulkk's hard-core metal band aspirations, they were really a nice bunch of kids. They just didn't want to make it too obvious.

Mike cocked an eyebrow. "The Four Rustketeers?"

Stench grimaced while the others groaned loudly. "We have enough money for four bus tickets, right? Well, we could probably get one plane ticket for the same amount."

"Sure," Todd agreed enthusiastically. "One-ways are pretty cheap."

"Wow, dude, you'd do that for me?" Dev was clearly touched by the group's generosity. "But what about the rest of you?"

Andrea spoke up. "They can stay at the ranch a few days till the strike's over."

"Or until another option presents itself," Mike added.

"And you can pay me back for the ticket when I get home," Stench said. "Since our folks will have to spring for bus fare again, eventually."

They climbed back into the car for the trip to Minot's airport and escorted Dev to the airline ticket counter.

The agent at the counter, a pretty blonde, laughed when he asked for a nonstop to Seattle.

"There's no such thing," Mike explained. "We're kind of off the beaten path as far as airlines are concerned. You have to fly from here to a hub city, usually with a couple stops in between."

The blonde nodded. "This flight goes to Minneapolis, then Seattle."

The band's contributions covered the cost.

After Dev's flight departed, Andrea and Mike climbed back into the car with the remaining members of the band. She sensed his tension and forced back the urge to apologize. She had nothing to apologize for.

Their next stop was Minot Feed and Farm, a big farm-supply store flanked by towering grain silos. Andrea started to follow a silent Mike inside, when behind her Jock gasped loudly, stopping the band members in their tracks.

"Look. Across the street," Jock whispered, and pointed to the window of a small café just opposite them. "It's Connie." He kept his voice low, as though the sound might attract the woman's attention.

Through the plate-glass window, the Vidtel producer was clearly visible, sitting at a booth across from a small, plump bespectacled woman who resembled a myopic sparrow. Andrea recognized the startling fringed blouse. It was Connie, without a doubt.

"What do you suppose she's still doing here?" Andrea wondered aloud. Connie had been more than eager to get as far from the ranch as possible. Surely nothing would keep her in Minot.

"I don't know," Stench said, "but it's probably best if we don't run into her."

Todd nodded. "She's probably still pissed about the camera." He grimaced and ducked into the feed store, with Jock and Stench close behind.

The store held enough distractions to make them forget Connie. The band members trailed Andrea through the cramped aisles, picking up items and examining them with interest. Stench and Todd made a game of guessing the uses of the more mysterious implements.

"This is just like a hardware store," Jock said, wrinkling his nose. "Except it stinks."

Andrea smiled, surprised to find her earlier irritability fading. The store was dusty and cluttered and smelled of grain, animal feed and agricultural chemicals. Jock was right. It did stink, but in a warm and comfortable way, if such a thing were possible.

Mike smiled at the remark, as well.

He seemed somehow less forbidding than he had earlier. Perhaps because he was doing errands for the ranch, for something he cared about deeply. Andrea had never been tied to one place for long. The very idea was foreign to her, and yet somehow appealing. Perhaps whatever he'd found at White Thunder would grow to hold the same meaning for her. If she stayed.

"Do you grow hay on the ranch or buy it locally?" she asked, suddenly eager to learn as much about her new life as possible.

He looked at her curiously. "We grow alfalfa hay for our own use and to sell. That and wheat are our main source of income. And Lena has a vegetable garden for our own use."

She nodded, her unease returning along with the certainty that she'd never be able to do this alone. As little as she knew about ranching, she knew even less about farming.

Mike collected rope and wire, then paused to study a row packed with bags and bottles of livestock vitamin supplements. He selected a bottle and turned to her, hesitating a second before asking, "Think these would be good for Gypsy?"

She took the bottle from him and read the label, surprised he would ask her opinion. "Has she had any health problems prior to the pregnancy?"

Mike shook his head. "Uh, no. Not that I know of." He

shrugged. "I just want to do all I can to get her through this in good condition."

His concern for the animal touched her. "I'm not much of an expert on bison nutrition," she admitted. "But if they're like other bovines, they don't need supplemental B vitamins. Their ruminal bacteria synthesize it for them."

Mike gave her all his attention.

"They make their own vitamin C, too," she continued, studying the bottle to avoid his intense gaze. "But it wouldn't hurt to give her additional vitamin A if she hasn't been on green feed through the winter. Vitamin E and selenium would probably be a good idea, too, for the calf." She handed back the bottle. "This one seems to have everything she'd need. You might need one of these, though."

She pulled a large metal syringelike object from the shelf next to the vitamins. "Do you already have a balling gun?"

Mike looked warily at the device and shook his head. "I haven't had to give her pills very often. Usually I just hide them in a marshmallow."

Andrea bit back a smile at the thought of the big foreman feeding marshmallows to the even bigger bison. Mike's expression was serious. "Well, I'm sure that's less stressful for her. We can try that first."

"Good. Um, thanks." His gaze held hers a moment as a look of genuine gratitude softened his cool gray eyes.

Someone tapped her on the shoulder.

She jumped and turned quickly to face Jock. The Rusting Hulkk drummer held up a tool that looked like a long, heavy pair of pliers. Wide jaws curved out from the handle and met at the tip of the instrument in a flat crushing plate.

"We can't figure out what this one is," he said. "Stench thinks it's pliers for pulling branding irons out of the fire. Todd thinks it's used on barbed wire for making fences."

Andrea glanced at Mike. He arched his eyebrows at her

and eased away from the group. She was on her own with this one. Her face grew warm, and she knew she was blushing. *Oh, well, this'll hurt them a lot more than it does me.*

She took the heavy object from Jock and hefted it in one hand. "This, boys, is an emasculator."

Todd and Jock looked puzzled, but Stench's eyes widened in growing and horrified understanding.

"It's used for castrating farm animals," she added. "Young ones, usually. Calves, lambs, you know."

Warming to the clinical discussion, she clamped the device over a hanging bag of large round vitamin capsules. "You just clamp it over the scrotum and squeeze. Hard." She demonstrated. "You crush both the spermatic cord and the blood vessels above the testicles. With no blood supply, they just sort of dry up and drop off. In theory, that is." She looked up at her audience and gave a brief, not-quite-innocent flutter of her eyelashes.

Stench and Jock had gone white, and Todd was a funny shade of green. All stood with their knees tightly clenched and their expressions pained. Andrea held the instrument out to Jock, who backed away, shaking his head. "Any other questions?" she asked.

There were none as she went up to the counter where Mike waited, looking as though he was fighting back a smile.

"I actually hate those things," she told him. "They're barbaric and potentially a lot more trouble than a quick surgery."

"I think you enjoyed the demonstration, though, didn't you?"

"I couldn't resist." Why, he was almost friendly, Andrea thought, amazed. Would it last?

He laughed, a low, pleasant sound. "Well, I was impressed. And thanks again for the advice about Gypsy."

The cashier rang up Mike's purchases. "Will this be on White Thunder's account, Mike?" he asked.

"Yeah, Steve, but I'd like you to meet White Thunder's new owner, Andrea Moore." He turned to Andrea. "Steve owns the store. Guess he'll be addressing the bills to you from now on."

Andrea shook hands with the man. Yet another complication she hadn't considered. "Yes, I guess so," she replied.

They piled back into the car for the drive to Rorvik, Jock and Stench still pale from Andrea's animal husbandry lesson. Todd followed a few moments later. Andrea noticed he held a brown paper bag half hidden behind his back.

"What did you buy?" She had to ask.

"Shh." Todd put a finger to his lips, grinning wickedly, and opened the bag to reveal the gleaming chrome emasculator. "A souvenir. We might need it if we run into Connie again."

Andrea just shook her head and climbed back into Lena's big, woodgrain-paneled station wagon for the ride to Rorvik.

"Wow, it's sure empty out here," Todd remarked from behind her once they'd left the outskirts of Minot to head back across the prairie.

She looked out at the rolling hills covered with pale yellow-green grass that stretched out in all directions, and had to agree.

They'd passed signs pointing off toward towns with picturesque names like Wildrose and Lostwood, but the only indications of civilization they encountered were occasional farms and ranches like White Thunder.

Mike's gaze remained fixed on the road ahead. "Yep. Miles and miles of miles and miles."

Jock stared out at the unobscured horizon. "Don't you

ever get—what's it called—the opposite of claustrophobia?''

Mike glanced at him in the rearview mirror. "Agoraphobia. No, actually I get claustrophobic with too many trees around. I like to be able to see what's coming at me."

His remark didn't surprise Andrea. He was the kind of man who'd sit with his back to the wall to avoid being taken unaware.

"You wouldn't like Seattle, then," she said, feeling obligated to contribute to the conversation.

"No. Probably not." He looked at her steadily.

She flinched under the weight of his stare and turned her attention to the sweeping landscape. She'd hoped that maybe he'd gotten over his mood after the moment they'd shared in the feed store, but apparently not. The man still held a grudge.

"The scenery *is* pretty out here." She directed her comments to the band members. "But I think I'd start to miss the trees back home. Not to mention the mountains and the ocean."

"Then you'll be glad to get back." Mike's remark was a statement, not a question.

"Maybe," she answered, but couldn't resist adding, "I'm pretty adaptable, though. I had to be as an air force brat."

He frowned slightly. Had the remark hit a tender spot because of his own background? Andrea really hadn't decided whether or not she'd stay at White Thunder, but if he insisted on acting like a jerk, she'd just keep him wondering.

CHAPTER SIX

EVERYONE WAS QUIET during the rest of the trip from Minot. The three remaining members of Rusting Hulkk sat silently in the back seat, Mike noticed, either dozing or gazing out the windows. Whether their reticence was due to contemplation of their masculinity after Andrea's vivid lesson or the departure of the fourth Rustketeer, he couldn't tell.

He appreciated the quiet. His own mood certainly hadn't improved since morning. Andrea's advice about Gypsy had both impressed him and eased his mind about the bison. The realization annoyed him. The last thing he wanted was to be grateful to her.

Something in the way her expression softened when he asked her about Gypsy told him she understood what the animal meant to him. If he'd known that would happen, he wouldn't have asked. He didn't intend to start sharing tender moments with the woman.

They *had* shared something in that moment, though. He couldn't deny it. He'd just have to see that it didn't happen again. And the sooner he got her off the ranch, the less likely it would.

He watched her out of the corner of his eye, feeling as if he should say something.

Why? What was it about her that had him struggling for a conversational opening? And not only searching for something to say, but actually trying to find some common ground with her against every instinct.

She was taking White Thunder. He had no reason to make overtures to her.

But what if she stayed?

Could he stay on as foreman under those circumstances?

Worry about that when the time comes, he told himself. For now, until she decided what to do with the ranch, they'd be practically living together, at least as long as the band occupied his trailer. He owed it to Dan to try to be civil. At least until he could get rid of her.

As though she sensed his thoughts, Andrea glanced up.

"Just a few more minutes to Rorvik," he said quickly, and looked away.

Andrea's first sight of Rorvik, North Dakota, was of a high, onion-shaped water tower that sprouted like a mutant mushroom from a grove of shelter-belt elms. The town itself, a sparse handful of buildings, was clustered at the base of the tower along a two-lane main street.

"Wow, this place is sure a wide spot in the road." Todd remarked. "Ow!"

Andrea turned to look at the source of the outcry. "What happened?"

Todd rubbed a spot on his arm and scowled at Stench. "He jabbed me with his elbow."

"Well, watch what you say about people's towns and you won't get jabbed." The musician glanced at Mike apologetically. "Excuse the Tactmeister here, Mr. Winterhawk. You'd think he'd never seen a small town before."

"Not this small," Todd muttered.

Jock nodded from the other end of the seat. "I'd have to agree with that. This is a *really* small town." He turned to Stench. "And just because you're the star doesn't give you the right of corporal punishment, man."

Stench shrugged, contrite. "Well, I just don't want to make a bad impression. Someone has to keep you guys in line."

Todd snorted. "If I want my mom around, I'll invite her along on the next tour."

The comparison to Todd's mother seemed to shock Stench into silence. He sank into the seat, and Andrea bit her lip to keep from laughing. A quick glance at Mike showed that the exchange hadn't been lost on him, either, bad mood or not.

He was almost smiling as he turned the station wagon down Rorvik's "main drag," looking almost cheerful for the first time that day. "Yep, this is Rorvik. One bank, one school, a seniors' center, a gas station, a vet clinic and a Lutheran church. The Catholics meet at the seniors' center for mass. Priest's a circuit rider from Williston, southwest of here."

Houses and trailers spread outward from the center of town, becoming increasingly scattered until they gave way completely to rolling grassland.

Mike pulled to a stop in front of the bank, a tiny cinder-block building painted in crisp white and blue. Andrea started to open her door, but he moved quickly around the vehicle and opened it for her.

"Thank you," she murmured, a little shocked. Where she came from, men who opened doors for women were a dying breed.

Mike just shrugged, moving aside to let her climb out. "No problem."

The boys got out, as well, and stood absorbing the sights of the little hamlet. Around them, the town was quiet. Small frame houses mingled with commercial buildings whose vinyl or corrugated metal siding lent them an oddly temporary appearance. Trees, the ever-present elms, grew out to shadow the sidewalk in places. Along with hearty lilac bushes, now fragrantly in bloom, they all but obscured many of the homes.

Mike nodded across the street while the boys climbed

out of the truck behind him. "We'll be over at Charlie's. Just come and get us when you're ready to go."

She looked where he'd indicated. Bright neon beer signs provided the only spots of color on the low, battered prefab structure across from the bank. Andrea took note of the other two corners of the intersection.

Similar buildings, flat-roofed, prefabricated metal or frame cubes with beer signs, squatted at each point of the compass, with the exception of the one occupied by the bank.

Andrea turned back to Mike.

"And three bars," he said. "That's about one for every hundred and fifty people in town. Typical ratio around here, actually."

He cocked a thumb back toward the bar he'd indicated earlier. "Lena used to tend bar at Charlie's during the summers before she came to stay at the ranch. During the winter, she was principal of the elementary school."

"Are you serious?"

He raised his right hand. "On my honor. Lena always said tending bar was the best way to keep in touch with her former students." He grinned. "Seriously, though, there's not much to do out here for entertainment. Rorvik is pretty typical of other towns in the area. The bars are a place to hang out. We're not all raging drunks."

"I'm happy to hear that," Andrea said, still skeptical.

"We're just going to go over and have a root beer." He looked at the band appraisingly. "This bunch aren't legal drinking age, anyway. Go ahead and talk to Bert, then come get us." He started to turn away but hesitated and turned back to her, his expression grave. "By the way, take anything he says with a grain of salt."

Before she could ask him what he meant, Mike rounded up the band, and the four of them dashed across the street to disappear into the darkened interior of the tavern.

Suddenly abandoned, Andrea stood alone on the side-walk. What was all that about? she wondered. Why shouldn't she believe what Dan's banker told her? Well, there was only one way to find out. She opened the door and walked inside, not sure what to expect.

The building looked just like she'd have expected a small-town bank to look, with its broad, high counter on one side, nondescript desks on the other and heavy vault door at the back. She headed for the reception desk.

Before she could address the Nordic-looking young woman seated there, a short, stocky man whose thin, gray-ing hair was combed over the top of his head to hide a sizable bald spot, rose from behind a large desk and walked toward her, arm outstretched. His smile was radiant.

"You're Andrea Moore." He sounded as if he'd been waiting for her all his life.

"Bert Petersen," he introduced himself without waiting for her reply. He shook her hand vigorously, then ushered her to a seat in front of his desk.

She sat down, noting, as Bert walked around the desk to take his own seat, the numerous certificates, clippings and plaques that decorated the wall behind him. Bert Petersen was apparently involved in everything from the Boy Scouts to the local softball team. One plaque touted his donations to the Rorvik volunteer fire department, while another tes-tified to his activities on behalf of the local church. A news-paper article detailed his efforts to bring a major shopping center to the area. Bert was clearly a big fish in the small pond of Rorvik, North Dakota.

"Please forgive me for not being at the ranch when you arrived, Andrea," he said. "We have a lot to discuss, and I'm sure you have plenty of questions."

His eyes were small and bright behind wire-rimmed glasses. She'd almost have called them beady, except that beady eyes conjured up a sinister impression, and nothing about Bert was sinister.

With his tidy but inexpensive suit, neutral shirt and inoffensive tie, Bert looked the soul of respectability, exactly as a conservative, small-town bank officer should.

He leaned forward, smiling. "So, what do you think of White Thunder Ranch? Is it all you expected?" He pulled a file from a drawer and opened it.

Andrea shrugged. "I didn't know what to expect. It's a lovely ranch, though, and Dan has been very nice."

"Good old fellow, Dan," Bert said. "Place was getting to be too much for him, though. He was lucky to sell out to Vidtel. The ranch was just what they were looking for— big, lots of atmosphere and reasonably priced."

He pulled several documents from the folder and spread them out before her. "Here's the deed to the property, various insurance forms, utility paperwork, loan documentation, just about everything. I've kept track of it all for Dan. We can continue that arrangement if you'd like or turn everything over to you."

Andrea studied the papers. This was more than she could absorb at a glance. One figure, a recent tax assessment of the ranch, stood out. Over three hundred thousand dollars! She stifled a gasp. Before White Thunder, the most expensive property she'd owned was a beat-up Honda.

"I haven't decided yet whether I'll be keeping the ranch or selling it." She struggled to keep her voice calm. "I suppose it would be best if you kept everything for now."

Bert nodded understandingly. "I know this has been a big step for you, Andrea. Have any problems come up? Or can we do anything for you now?"

"Well, there is something I should check into," she replied. "If I keep the ranch, it'll boost me into a new tax bracket." *And how,* she thought. "Can I use the ranch to secure a loan for the amount of the income tax?"

Bert rocked back in his chair and considered her question. Then his forehead crinkled and he leaned forward. "Andrea, I'd be happy to accept the ranch as collateral, but there are some problems." He paused, sighing deeply. "Perhaps you should discuss this with Dan. Or maybe Mike Winterhawk."

Andrea frowned. *What was going on here?* "Discuss what with Dan or Mike?"

Bert pursed his lips. "I suppose if no one else has informed you, it's my duty."

He reached out and patted her hand. Andrea noticed that his nails were well manicured, but his skin was surprisingly rough.

"What is it, Mr. Petersen?"

He took a deep breath and let it out slowly. "White Thunder has had some serious troubles. That's part of the reason Dan sold out. His deal with Vidtel was fortunate for him. He'd never have found a local buyer. The ranch's reputation was too bad."

"What are you saying, Mr. Petersen? That I won a worthless piece of property?"

"Oh, no." Bert shook his head, disturbing his carefully combed-over strands of hair. "I wouldn't say worthless. There might be something you can do with it. But as ranchland, it's no good. Those bison Dan brought in haven't taken hold. That cow Gypsy, the one that's pregnant, she's the first cow to carry a calf this near to term in well over a year. And she didn't get pregnant naturally. They had to have her inseminated."

No wonder there'd been no calves with the herd yesterday. What had Mike said when she'd asked about them? Not so far?

Not for more than two seasons was more like it. Why had Mike lied to her? He would have been at the ranch last spring. Surely he must have been aware of what was going on.

Bert patted her hand once again. "I see no one told you."

Andrea shook her head, unable to speak. Why *hadn't* anyone told her?

"They aren't sure what the cause is," Bert continued. "Dan's run just about every known test, and nothing has turned up. It's a mystery." He leaned forward again and lowered his voice. "Some folks in these parts think that forces beyond human understanding are the cause. There's been a lot of talk. This area is known for strange phenomena."

Andrea stared at Bert in disbelief. What was the man saying, that the problems at White Thunder were caused by some sort of supernatural activity?

Suddenly Mike's comments outside made sense. He must have known Bert had strange ideas. No wonder he'd warned her.

Still, there was no denying White Thunder's problems. There were no calves where the fields should have been dotted with miniature bison, or at least pregnant cows.

Something strange was going on, and she had to find out what it was.

"So," Bert continued, "I can accept the ranch as security on a loan for your taxes, but if you need to sell quickly, you might have problems. Do you have any income right now to make payments on the loan?"

Andrea shook her head. "No. I plan to get my license to practice here, but it'll probably be a while before I have a regular income." She slumped in her seat. How was she going to come up with the money? Her inheritance would cover the payments for a time, but that wouldn't last forever.

"Andrea, I'm sorry." Bert rose and moved around the

desk to her side, his expression all sincere concern. "I'd
hate to make you the loan only to have to foreclose on you.
Is there anyone who could lend you the money? A family
member, perhaps?"

Andrea shook her head. "No. No one." Her mother and
Jeffrey were the only ones who might have the money
she'd need, and there was no way she could ask either of
them.

"I don't want to see you lose White Thunder. You're
just what the place needs, I'm sure of it."

Andrea clenched her teeth. A lot of good that did if she
lost the ranch because she couldn't pay the taxes.

"Look, your tax bill won't be due for some time," he
said. "Why not go ahead and get settled in, then see where
you stand. Once you're working, come back and we'll get
this taken care of. I know it would be good for Rorvik, as
well as for White Thunder, for you to stay, and I only want
what's best for both."

Andrea rose quickly. "Yes. Well, thank you." That was
the best idea, she thought. Her situation was too uncertain
at this point. Especially given Bert's comments about the
ranch. She had to talk to Mike. Now.

"I'll have the paperwork ready if you'd like to have an
accountant go over everything with you." Bert followed
her to the door. "But you'd be wise to talk to Mike or Dan
in the meantime."

Outside, Andrea shuddered involuntarily despite the
warm sunshine. The man had seemed so pleasant, but he'd
actually hinted that White Thunder's problems were caused
by…

How had he put it? Forces beyond human understanding?
What exactly was that supposed to mean?

And why had he suggested that Mike might know something?

Andrea's breath caught in her throat. Was Bert actually

suggesting that Mike was somehow involved in the problems at the ranch?

It couldn't be true.

Or could it? She'd only known Mike a day. How did she know he *wasn't* at fault? He wanted the ranch for himself. He'd said as much. Could he possibly be that desperate?

She started across the street to Charlie's, suddenly recalling the statement printed on a tiny plaque on Bert's desk: The Truth Is Out There.

Hadn't Stench said the same thing when they talked about UFOs on the ranch? The thought sent a chill through her. Was Bert hinting that aliens were responsible for the troubles at White Thunder? And that Mike knew something about them?

The idea was ridiculous, but the statement on the plaque made sense.

The truth *was* out there.

And she intended to find it.

CHAPTER SEVEN

THE INTERIOR OF CHARLIE'S tavern was astonishingly dim after the bright sunlight outside. Brown wood paneling covered the walls and matched the planked pine flooring almost seamlessly. The mirrored surface of the mahogany back bar reflected the room's wood-grained murk.

Neon in the windows and a Wurlitzer jukebox belting out country tunes from the corner provided the only spots of color. Surely the place had been livelier when Lena worked here, Andrea thought.

The dreariness added a layer of gloom to her anger over the interview with Bert.

Mike and the boys sat at the bar, a row of soft-drink bottles empty before them. He glanced up as she entered, and his expression hardened as he caught the look on her face.

Her anger flared. How could he have kept White Thunder's condition from her? She deserved to know what was going on with her ranch. And the foreman, still her employee as long as Vidtel paid for his services, was the one who should have told her.

"Mike, can I see you outside a moment?" She managed to keep her tone neutral.

He nodded and rose. "Stay here, boys. I'll be back in a few minutes." He flagged the bartender. "Another round, Jack."

Andrea stepped outside and waited, relieved to be in sunlight once again. Mike joined her a moment later.

"What's up?"

She spun to face him. "I think you know the answer to that. Why didn't you tell me about the problems White Thunder is having? Didn't you think I had a right to know what's going on?" She couldn't keep her voice from carrying and thought she saw faces inside the bar look their way.

Mike seemed to notice, as well. He took Andrea's arm firmly and steered her around the side of the building.

She shook herself free of his grip, annoyed at him for the gesture and at herself for the way her heart raced at his touch. The sudden breathlessness she felt was anger, she told herself, nothing more.

Mike studied her. "What exactly did Bert say to you? I told you not to take him seriously."

"It doesn't matter what he said," Andrea snapped. She didn't believe Bert Petersen's hints that some kind of supernatural force was responsible for the ranch's problems, but something was obviously wrong, and she'd be damned if she'd let Mike patronize her. "What matters is what you're keeping from me."

"Can we discuss this later? In private?" He glanced back toward the street as though expecting to see someone peering around the corner.

Andrea shook her head. "I want answers. Now."

"All right." He slouched resignedly against the side of the building, hands on his slim hips. "What do you want to know?"

Andrea took a deep breath to calm her anger and spoke slowly. "I want to know what problems White Thunder is having and why the bison aren't breeding. I want to know why Dan had to sell the ranch."

"Ask Dan."

I can't, Andrea thought. She was still too self-conscious about winning the place to pry into Dan's personal life on top of it. She raised her chin defiantly. "You're still an employee of White Thunder. I'm asking you."

"Dan has some medical problems. If you want more details than that, you'll have to talk to him. He decided to sell when he heard about Vidtel's interest and made a good deal. Now he'll be able to retire in comfort."

Mike hesitated a moment as though considering her other questions, then went on. "Dan had cattle on the property earlier. When they got to be too much for him, he sold them off and went into partial retirement, then decided to try bison."

The decision made sense, Andrea thought. Bison were hardier than cattle. They'd thrive on rough rangeland with less work. "But the bison haven't done well."

"No. They aren't breeding. We haven't had a bison calf brought to term in a couple of seasons. That's why I've been so concerned about Gypsy. She's our first attempt at artificial insemination." He ran a hand through his short dark hair, his eyes deep gray with worry.

"Any ideas what the problem might be? Could it be the rangeland they're grazing?" Andrea asked. Bert had said they'd done numerous tests on the property, but they might have missed something.

"I don't know. That's one reason I have Gypsy corralled. I can control her feed and keep an eye on her."

Andrea met his gaze. "I suppose you've had a veterinarian check them out."

"First thing when we started seeing problems. He didn't find anything unusual."

"I want to talk to the vet. Is he nearby?"

Mike nodded. "He's here in Rorvik. Doc Coggins. He seems to know his stuff. Dan's used him for years."

"Good. Let's stop by. I can at least find out what kind of tests he's done and whether he has any ideas."

"We can swing by there now, but I don't know if he'll be in." He paused.

"Well let's give it a try, since we're here." She stood her ground, refusing to let him intimidate her. "If he's not available, I'll make an appointment and you can bring me back."

He gave a curt nod, his mouth curled slightly at one corner. "You're the boss. Anything else?"

"As a matter of fact, there is." She forced herself to meet his gaze. "Why didn't you tell me all this sooner? Didn't you think I had a right to know what was happening?" Frustration and disappointment had replaced her anger.

"What should I have said, 'Welcome to White Thunder. By the way, the land's worthless and the bison aren't breeding'?" He raised an eyebrow enquiringly.

"That wouldn't have gone over too well," Andrea admitted. "Can you imagine the look on Connie Chambers's face?"

"That would almost have made it worthwhile," he said. "Anyway, later there just wasn't time. Dan and I agreed it was better to let you get settled before we started in with the serious stuff. This is nothing new. A few more days wouldn't have mattered."

He was right, Andrea knew. She couldn't cure White Thunder's problems overnight. But if he'd just told her before she spoke to Bert. Like last night.

Mike straightened up. "Doc's clinic isn't far. Of course, in Rorvik nothing is."

They walked back to the street, and Mike ducked into the bar to tell Rusting Hulkk to wait for them, then he met Andrea outside once again and they started up the sidewalk.

The May sunshine had banished the chill from the air, and Mike turned his face upward to feel its warmth on his skin. This was his favorite time of year on the plains, when the frost and cold gave way to life once more.

Strange that it'd taken so long for him to notice the cycle of life and death and rebirth that was the change of seasons. Since coming to White Thunder, he'd grown closer to the land than he'd ever thought possible. Not long ago, he'd have scoffed at the idea that he even had a spiritual side.

Now it was so much a part of him that he marveled he could have been unaware of it before.

Funny, he thought, *what you don't see unless you look.*

He'd have to ask Tony Gray Elk if there was some Lakota teaching to that effect. The shaman, an instructor at a nearby community college where he'd taken classes, had become his mentor in his studies of his heritage and was an inexhaustible source of knowledge about his people.

Mike glanced at Andrea. She had her head tipped back slightly, letting the sunlight bathe her face, but her brow was knotted in concern. Maybe she was having second thoughts about just what she'd gotten into with White Thunder.

She tilted her head, and the sun sparked coppery highlights in her hair. He wondered whether, if he pulled a strand of the curls caught up at the back of her neck, it would spring back into place. Was it as soft as it looked?

He shook himself abruptly to change the disturbing direction of his thoughts. The sunshine must be getting to him.

"Is spring always this nice here?" Andrea asked.

"Usually," he said, grateful for the distraction. "Once it gets here. Sometimes it comes a little late in the year. Like August."

"Seattle springs can be that way, too," Andrea said. "Sometimes we go a whole year without seeing one. But, of course, our winters are a bit milder than yours."

"Most places' winters are milder than ours. They say the

snow doesn't actually melt here, it just blows around until it wears out."

She raised an eyebrow. "Sounds grim. What do you do with the animals?"

"The bison weather the cold really well. They're made for it. But we do take feed out to them, since there's not much to graze on unless they burrow through the snow."

"Bison burrow? What do they do, carve out giant dens in the prairie, like prairie dogs?"

"Well, not quite." Mike had to smile at the idea of bison tunneling their way across the plains. "They use the big muscles in their necks and humps like snowplows to shove the snow out of their way so they can graze."

He rounded the corner, and Andrea followed him to a large frame house with a low, rectangular addition, flanked by covered pens and an empty corral.

"This is it," he said. He opened the door and they stepped inside.

The earthy smell of animals blended with other scents—alcohol, disinfectant and odors Mike couldn't identify. The aroma made his nose itch, but he noticed Andrea breathed deeply, seeming more relaxed than she'd been all day.

She led the way to the front desk. "Hi," she said to the receptionist. "I'm Dr. Andrea Moore. I'd like to speak with Dr. Coggins if he has a few minutes."

The receptionist, another blonde—*Do they clone them here?* Andrea wondered—looked up at her, blue eyes bright with undisguised interest.

"The Dr. Moore who won White Thunder?"

Andrea nodded.

"Welcome to Rorvik." The girl glanced at Mike, and a pretty flush rose in her cheeks. "I'll get Doc. Just a moment." She dashed through the doorway to the back of the clinic.

Andrea glanced at Mike, who was looking after the girl with a puzzled expression.

Good grief, she thought, it certainly couldn't be the first time a girl had reacted to him like that. He was incredibly attractive. His khaki shirt, almost military in style, molded to his muscular arms. His eyes, in his thoughtful state, were the clear, silvery gray of clouds after the storm has passed and no threat of thunder remained.

Her gaze was drawn to his mouth, and she noticed its sensuous shape, his upper lip deeply bowed and lower lip full.

She realized it wasn't the first time she'd noticed. Last night, when he'd held her as the light switched on, she'd been perilously close to his lips.

"Dr. Moore!" A deep voice boomed from the doorway.

Andrea jumped and looked up as a tall, solidly built older man approached, arm outstretched.

"I'm Jim Coggins." He enveloped her hand in his massive paw and gave it a hearty squeeze. "Everyone round here just calls me Doc, though." He nodded to Mike, and his broad grin widened farther. "Mike, how's it going? Givin' the new boss the grand tour, huh?" He released Andrea and shook hands with Mike.

"Showing her the sights, Doc." Mike smiled wryly. "Next, we're going over to the market so she can get postcards of the water tower for the folks back home."

Doc laughed. "I'm afraid Rorvik *is* a little shy of tourist attractions, Dr. Moore. May I call you Andrea?"

"Of course, Doc," she replied, charmed by the man.

He stood at least six-foot-six and appeared to be solid muscle. His thick hair was a rich salt-and-pepper shade, and he could have been anywhere between forty-five and sixty-five. His face was tanned and lined with character, but engagingly so with brown eyes that sparkled with boyish humor.

"Come on back to the office." Doc led the way from the waiting room. "Can I get you some coffee?"

Andrea and Mike both declined the offer as they entered Doc's office.

The room matched the big veterinarian—warm, open and friendly. A massive desk and chair dominated the space, but a seating area across from it was comfortably filled by a pair of leather wing chairs and a low table.

A rhythmic thumping caught Andrea's attention. She glanced down as a large yellow dog squeezed from beneath one of the chairs and ambled toward them, tail wagging fiercely and a look of sheer delight on his homely face.

"Ole, be polite," Doc said.

The dog sat and raised a paw in greeting. Andrea bent and took it in her hand. "Pleased to meet you, boy."

Ole, clearly thrilled with her attention, stayed seated, but his bannerlike tail swept the floor behind him.

"I don't think I'm familiar with this breed, Doc," Andrea said. "What is he?"

Grinning, Doc gestured her and Mike toward the chairs. "An Abandonese. I found Ole dumped by the highway. He was about six months old." His expression turned serious and he shook his head. "People still haven't gotten it through their heads that they shouldn't just dump their unwanted animals. Ole was lucky."

Taking a seat, Andrea nodded. She'd seen the same thing at Jeffrey's clinic, even though it was in an urban area. Someone once abandoned a dog on the front porch of the clinic, tied to the doorknob with a piece of rope. The only thing that had kept her from adopting him herself was the fact that her apartment, in the same building as Jeffrey's and which she'd moved into at his urging, didn't allow pets. One of the clinic technicians took him home instead.

She ruffled Ole's ears, and he groaned with pleasure, collapsed at her feet and rolled on his back. "Well, I can tell you have a hard life, big fella,'' she said, obliging him with a tummy rub.

Doc pulled his office chair around the side of the desk and sat down. "So, Andrea,'' he began without preamble. "I expect I know why you're here.''

She nodded. "I need to find out what's wrong with the bison. I figured this would be the best place to start.''

The receptionist entered and handed Doc a thick manila folder.

"Thanks, Amy.'' Doc thumbed through the file, then leaned forward and passed it to Andrea. "These are the records for White Thunder. All the exam findings and test results are there.''

Andrea opened the file. The most recent records showed the history of Gypsy's pregnancy. All her tests appeared normal, but as Andrea paged back through the file, she noted a pattern of infertility and the loss of calves at various stages of pregnancy for other animals in the herd.

"I've tested them for just about every disease that can cause fetal loss,'' Doc said. "Brucellosis, lepto, BVD, you name it. All negative.''

"BVD?'' Mike asked.

"Bovine viral diarrhea,'' Andrea explained. "You see it more in calves than adults, but it can cause a pregnant cow to lose a calf if she's infected early in the pregnancy.'' She looked back at Doc. "What about some kind of poisoning?''

Doc shrugged. "That would be my guess, but I haven't found anything unusual in the blood work. If it's some kind of toxin, it's at low, chronic levels. That can be a bitch to detect. If you had high-tension power lines across the property, we could possibly even consider electromagnetic effects, but White Thunder doesn't have any. It's kind of a controversial issue, anyway. A lot of respected authorities don't believe there's any connection between electromagnetic fields and health problems, but who knows? Some stores even sell aprons you can wear to shield yourself from EMF, especially during pregnancy.''

"I've heard of higher incidences of cancer near power lines, but nothing like this. Seems to me I read something recently about animal studies, too, but I can't recall much about the article.'' Andrea examined a page in the file. "Necropsy results on the calves look normal, too.''

"Yep. It's been hard to find aborted calves soon enough to get good results on them, though.'' Doc's eyes reflected frustration and genuine regret. "I'm sorry. I wish I had more to tell you.''

She nodded, hiding her disappointment. She'd hoped something might stand out from the animals' histories but realized she'd been overly optimistic. "From the look of these records, you've tried everything. May I borrow these for a day or so to give them a thorough reading?''

"Sure.'' Doc turned to Mike. "How's Gypsy doing, by the way?''

"Just fine,'' Mike replied. "She's eating well and she looks great. I'm trying not to get my hopes up, but everything seems normal so far.''

"Good. I have some calls out your way next week,'' Doc said. "I'll stop by and take a look at her while I'm in the neighborhood. But feel free to call me before that if you notice anything unusual.''

"Thanks. We will.'' Andrea started to rise, then hesitated as an idea occurred to her. "Doc, are you in the market for an assistant by any chance?'' Before he could answer, she continued, "I'll need to look into getting my license to practice in this state, but I'd really like to help out to get a little refresher on large-animal work in the meantime.''

Doc looked thoughtful. "Actually, I *was* considering hiring a technician. I suppose I could postpone that for a while, though, if you'd like to help out. I wouldn't be able to pay you as much as you'd make as a vet, of course."

"That's all right," Andrea said, relief sweeping through her. "I'd really like to learn about more than family pets." And earn some money.

She wouldn't make enough to pay off her income taxes from winning White Thunder, she thought, but it was a step in the right direction. After all, she didn't have to worry about rent now.

"Good," Doc said. "Why don't you come in Monday, and we can work out the particulars."

"That sounds fine. Thanks." She rose with Ole still lying across her feet and held out her hand.

Doc took it with a grin. "Thank you. It'll be nice to have more help around here." He looked down at the dog, who had deigned to sit up and was now leaning heavily and possessively against Andrea's legs. "Come on, boy. She'll be back soon." He gestured with his hand, and the dog reluctantly left Andrea to resume his spot under the chair.

As they walked back to Charlie's in silence, Mike watched her out of the corner of his eye.

Damnation. She'd asked Doc for a job. What was that all about? The ramifications were clear. *She's staying at White Thunder.*

The realization irritated him, but on the positive side, it meant he wouldn't have to compete with another buyer for the property right away. Now all he had to do was convince her to sell to him.

"So why do you want to work for Doc?"

Andrea looked at him a moment. "I need the money," she admitted at last. "For income tax. I'll have to make a partial payment in a couple of months. I expect there'll be property taxes, too."

"You asked Bert for a loan." The realization struck him.

"He turned me down. The ranch isn't good enough security in its present condition.'' She paused and looked at him, her eyes narrowed. ''He said something strange about unknown forces at work, things beyond human understanding.'' She raised one brow.

Mike gave a derisive snort. ''That's Bert, all right. He has some funny ideas.''

''What did he mean? He said you might know something.''

Hell, Mike thought. He really didn't want to get into this now. Bert had always had the town's best interests at heart, but the man couldn't seem to keep his strange notions to himself. He looked at Andrea, who patiently awaited his reply. She clearly intended to move no farther till she had some answers.

''You wouldn't picture him as the local flake, but Bert thinks he's seen UFOs around here,'' he said flatly.

Andrea's eyes widened. ''Really? Maybe he's a friend of that professor Dan mentioned. I should have asked him about that light I saw last night.''

She sounded flip as she said it, but Mike didn't miss her strained expression.

He shrugged. ''It doesn't sound like something you'd hear from a banker, but he claims it's true. It's strange, actually—he's usually occupied with all sorts of civic-improvement projects and business plans, but he's always been a little on the strange side. Still, he doesn't seem like the UFO type.''

''Is there a UFO type?'' she asked, studying him. ''Bert seemed to suggest *you* knew something about the problems with the ranch. About the cause, maybe even the 'forces beyond human understanding.''' She let the unspoken question hang between them, then continued, ''I didn't believe him, of course. The whole conversation was just too weird.''

Mike could only stare at her. He'd done nothing to de-

serve her trust—quite the contrary—yet she believed in
him. Admittedly, believing him over Bert didn't take a huge
leap of faith, but still. He felt a twinge of guilt that she
should have taken his side when his only interest was in
getting her off his ranch.

CHAPTER EIGHT

WHEN THEY RETURNED to the ranch, the band unloaded their gear and headed back to Mike's trailer to unpack. Andrea and Mike walked in silence to the house to let Dan and Lena know they still had guests.

Lena wasn't disturbed in the least by Rusting Hulkk's return. "Good. It'll give me a chance to put some meat on those boys' bones. They're way too skinny." She reached for her recipe box. "Let's see. I think I can get an apple pie in the oven in time for dinner tonight."

Andrea grimaced. If she kept on eating Lena's cooking, she'd soon have to make a trip into town for larger clothes.

"I'm going to check on Gypsy before supper." Mike directed his remark toward Lena.

The housekeeper rested a hand on Mike's arm and glanced at Andrea. "It'll be a little while till we eat. Why don't you drive Andrea out to the homestead for a look around?"

"We could do that," Mike said slowly. He looked at Andrea. "What do you think?"

She hesitated, surprised that he hadn't rejected Lena's suggestion outright. Was this some sort of overture? If so, she should probably accept it for the sake of maintaining peace. She nodded. "Okay. But I'd also like to see Gypsy."

"Sure." Mike turned to rummage in a kitchen cabinet and pulled out two big marshmallows. "Maybe I can get a vitamin into her."

He took a couple of hefty tablets from the bottle he'd gotten at the feed store and pressed them into the marshmallows. When he finished doctoring the candy, they walked together out to the corral.

Gypsy trotted over to the rail, clearly delighted to see Mike. He reached up to stroke her woolly head.

"Will she let me touch her?" Andrea asked.

"I think so. Just move slowly."

She reached out to lay her hand on the big animal's muzzle. The short hair near Gypsy's nose looked coarse, but felt surprisingly soft. It grew longer the farther up her face it went, reaching several inches at the top of her head, where it was dense and frizzy.

Andrea rubbed the bison between the eyes. The cow tilted her head back and thrust her long tongue toward Andrea's hand.

"She likes you."

She glanced at him, uncertain whether she'd heard approval or disappointment in his voice. His eyes were unreadable. "I think she's probably just looking for marshmallows," she said, self-conscious.

He held the vitamin-stuffed candy for Gypsy to see. "Let's see if she'll take it."

The animal stretched her neck forward, sniffing the marshmallow, then mouthed Mike's hand until he gave her the treat. She swallowed it and looked for more.

"Want to give her this one?" Mike offered Andrea the second marshmallow.

She nodded and took the candy, her fingers brushing his warm, callused hand.

Gypsy strained at the fence rail as Andrea held out her hand, the marshmallow in her open palm. The big animal tickled her hand with velvety lips, then slurped up the treat with a swipe of her broad, wet tongue.

Andrea laughed and wiped her hand on her jeans. Bison

spit didn't bother her. In her line of work, she'd encountered far worse. She glanced up to find Mike gazing thoughtfully at her once more.

She looked out toward the prairie. "How far is the homestead from here?"

"Not far in miles, but cross-country in the truck is the best way to get there, so it takes a while. The terrain's pretty rough." He gave Gypsy a final scratch under the chin. "Are you ready?"

Andrea nodded, and they headed for the truck.

"Should we invite the band?" She looked around for them, knowing she'd feel more comfortable with the boys along.

He shook his head. "No. Lena'll put them to work if they need entertaining. It can be dangerous out there. They might get hurt." He opened the door for her and she climbed in.

Mike didn't seem predisposed to talk further, and once they started bouncing across the ranch, Andrea was too busy holding on to make conversation.

When Mike pointed out the Amundson place ahead of them, Andrea couldn't tell how far from the main house they'd come. The drive had taken fifteen or twenty minutes across the rolling rangeland.

The house itself, a cabin, really, was a low ruin alongside a fast-flowing creek. The dilapidated wooden structure's whitewash had weathered to a rusty gray. A portion of the shingled roof had collapsed, and the whole thing swayed to one side as though perpetually under attack by a stiff easterly wind.

They pulled to a stop beside the creek, and Andrea jumped out.

"Watch your step," Mike called. "The herd likes to graze around here." He looked around. "I'm surprised they aren't out here now on such a warm day."

"Maybe they found some trees to shade them. Or do you have trees anywhere besides next to the house?"

"One," he replied. "It's about a mile that way." He pointed at the prairie, then looked puzzled and turned in the opposite direction. "Or was it that way? It's been so long I've forgotten."

Andrea laughed. "In other words, you don't have an overabundance of them."

"No. The trees around here were planted to provide wind breaks for the crops." He started toward the old house and Andrea followed. "You can tell where the farms and old homesteads are by the trees. The whole area was originally open prairie."

They stopped a few feet from the cabin steps, and Andrea surveyed the old building with interest. The breeze had risen, stirring the knee-high grasses around them and filling the air with a rushing murmur and the warm, sweet scent of blooming alfalfa.

She imagined that if she stood very still, she'd hear the sounds of life that had once filled the little house. She closed her eyes, seeing children running across the yard yelling happily, chickens scratching in the dirt, a woman hanging laundry to dry.

"I can almost picture them here."

"The place always affects me like that, too," Mike said. "Would you like to go inside?"

"Yes, but…" She started to ask if they'd mind the intrusion. Instead she asked, "Is it safe?"

He eyed her curiously but seemed to understand. "I think so. Careful, though. The floorboards are rotting, and some of the roof timbers are hanging pretty low."

She stepped cautiously onto the porch, wobbling as a loose board flexed underfoot.

Mike was there immediately to catch her arm in a firm grip. "Watch it," he said, steadying her.

He held her close beside him for a moment longer than it took her to regain her balance, and she was all too aware of his size and strength. He could probably pick her up and carry her into the cabin, a task few men would dare since she was anything but petite. The idea made her suddenly giddy.

His gaze was full of concern. "I'm sorry. I should have warned you about that board."

"That's okay. I'm fine." Her words sounded breathless even to her own ears. Mike let go and she took a quick step toward the door, away from his disconcerting nearness. She looked inside.

The porch roof at one end of the cabin sagged forward dispiritedly, partially blocking the entry. The front door was missing, and no glass remained in the single front window. Andrea ducked under the drooping beams and entered the dimly lit cabin.

The fallen roof made half of the structure impassable. The remainder consisted of a single open room. A second window on the back wall was boarded over, but light filtered in through chinks in the boards, casting bright beams on the wooden floor.

At the end of the room stood a dirt-encrusted but nonetheless impressive stone fireplace, its rough-hewn mantel still in place. Thick dust coated everything.

The structure was so primitive, offering only minimal protection from the elements. Andrea marveled that people could have survived the harsh conditions of pioneer life in such a place. She realized how comfortable and sheltered her own life was, even now.

The pioneer woman who made this cabin a home had been constructed of sturdier stock, braving incredible hardships to make a new beginning far from her home and the life she had known. But she had persevered and, with her husband, had made a place for herself on the inhospitable plains.

Back then, a woman could not have survived alone on the plains. The work would have been backbreaking, the conditions harsh and dangerous. She'd have needed a man, someone to protect her, to offer companionship, to share the hardships and the joys of their challenge.

Andrea glanced up. Mike stood in the doorway, watching her with a bemused expression.

"How did the roof collapse?" she asked to fill the awkward silence. "Was it age?"

He shook his head. "A tornado. Killed one of Dan's great-uncles when the roof caved in."

Andrea glanced toward the damaged portion. *Someone had died here.* As often as she'd seen death in her work, it still gave her pause.

Mike touched her arm and she jumped. He'd moved close without her noticing. She could smell the cool scent of his aftershave over the odors of dust and musty wood.

"Are you all right?"

She nodded, feeling foolish. "Just lost in thought."

"My people believe in spirits," he said. "In a place like this, you can almost feel them."

His words echoed her feelings. "I wouldn't be surprised if they lingered here, after they put so much of themselves into the land," she said. "It's amazing that they had time for anything besides sheer survival."

"I know," he said. "Nothing came easily back then. They were always at the mercy of tornadoes, drought and blizzards. Not to mention Indians." He leaned against the sill of the front window and took a deep breath, catching and holding her gaze.

"You mentioned your people," Andrea ventured, sensing an openness in him that hadn't existed before, as though he were inviting her questions. "Is that part of the roots you were looking for? What led you to search for them?"

"My father believed our heritage was best forgotten. I disagreed."

Andrea frowned. "Why? I know several Native Americans at home, and they're all very proud of their origins."

"My father had it rough. He was a Lakota Sioux born near here. His parents died, and he was raised in a state orphanage. He was treated badly by the other boys because he was Indian. He was very young and only wanted to fit in and be part of the group. As a result, he learned to despise everything Indian about himself."

He paused and turned to stare out the window. "As soon as he was old enough, he joined the army. He married a white woman, my mother, and never spoke to me about my background. She told me his story and tried to educate me a little about my heritage."

He turned back to Andrea. "It was part of what she fell in love with, after all. She took it upon herself to learn as much about the Sioux as she could for my sake. She knew more than my father did.

"I came here after leaving the army to learn about my background. I found some of my father's family, and I met Dan through them. He needed a hand around here, and, well, he sort of adopted me. So I stayed on." He shrugged. "I've found my culture here, the missing part of my life."

His words were matter-of-fact, but the pain they hid cut her to the core. She moved to stand beside him, instinct driving her to offer comfort. She touched his arm gently. He turned and met her gaze, his expression searching.

She wanted to say something, to thank him for telling her about his life, but the moment passed.

Mike studied her, stunned at the way he'd opened up to her. Damn, he thought. What had he done?

He tore his gaze from hers to glance at his watch. "We

should probably get back. Lena will have dinner on before
long. We don't want her to turn the boys loose on it or
there'll be nothing left but scraps.''

''Oh. Yeah, I guess so.''

He stopped himself from wondering if it was regret he
heard in her voice.

In the truck once more, he started the engine as a kernel
of an idea occurred to him. He hesitated, then turned off
the key and turned to face Andrea.

''Look, I just had a thought, and, well, I know this may
not be the best time...'' He shifted his gaze to the floor,
then back to her. ''But you need money and I might be
able to help.''

''Oh?'' she said warily. ''How?''

''I've saved some cash for a down payment to buy White
Thunder. It's not enough yet.'' He paused. ''But it should
be enough to pay your taxes.''

''Wait a minute. You want to give me money to pay my
taxes?'' She frowned at him.

He shook his head. ''No. I don't want to *give* you the
money. That is, not exactly.''

She waited, watching him.

''I want to trade it to you in exchange for an interest in
the ranch. If you end up selling me White Thunder, the
money can be a partial down payment. If you sell to someone else, you can pay me back from the proceeds of the
sale. And if you decide to keep the ranch yourself, well, I
guess we'll be sort of unequal partners, until or unless you
buy me out.''

Andrea wondered if she'd heard him right.

Partners?

Well, it *would* solve her money problems, at least for
now. And ensure that she had someone around the ranch
who knew what he was doing. On the other hand, it meant
a closer relationship with Mike than she'd considered.

The way her pulse sped up at the idea annoyed her.

Okay, so he's attractive, she admitted. Attractive, hell, he was drop-dead gorgeous.

But emotional involvement with a business partner—well, she'd been in that situation before and knew how badly it could turn out. Her response to Mike was just a combination of rebound and nerves, she was certain, but it disturbed her nonetheless. If she had any choice, she'd be well advised to stay as far from him as possible.

But did she have a choice?

Mike's offer might be the only chance she had to keep the ranch and her new life. And the more time she spent here, the more she realized that White Thunder was what she'd been looking for. She couldn't let it go when it had taken so long for her to find it. She met his gaze. "I'll think about it."

Whatever she decided, she knew they'd have to remain businesslike or she'd be in serious trouble.

Again.

CHAPTER NINE

ANDREA STUDIED a farm equipment catalog over her morning coffee, trying to shake the cobwebs from her brain. She'd set her alarm to ensure an early start, but White Thunder's day was well under way by the time she rose at six-thirty.

A stack of farming and ranching magazines with titles like *Progressive Farmer, Dakota Rancher* and *Small Farm Today* awaited her perusal—not material she'd normally have selected for early-morning reading, but then, she'd never had to worry about running a ranch before, either.

She flipped through several pages of ads with growing dismay. She'd never realized the variety of machinery it took to keep a farm going. Or the costs involved.

"I can't believe how expensive this equipment is," she remarked to Dan, who sat across from her at the table.

"Yah, they're high, all right. Most small operations rent them seasonally. Between the initial costs and the upkeep, we'd never make a profit if we all bought our own."

"That's one reason we grow alfalfa, too," Mike said from the doorway.

"Because it's inexpensive to grow?" She concentrated on stirring sugar into her coffee as he took a seat at the table.

"It's a perennial. Doesn't have to be planted every year, so it's less labor intensive."

"And we don't need to rent planting equipment every season," Dan added.

"Mike mentioned you grew some wheat, too. How much work does that involve?"

"A lot more. I haven't put in wheat this season, since my health hasn't been so good."

"We'd normally grow spring wheat," Mike said. "It's planted in the spring and harvested in late summer."

"I see," Andrea said, but she felt overwhelmed. There was so much to learn. How would she ever make a go of the place? She'd have to force the issue of participating in the operation of the ranch. She'd only learn so much from reading farming magazines.

"Don't worry," Dan said. "You'll get the hang of it all."

She met his gaze. "Thanks. I hope so." Not without help, though, she thought. Not without Mike.

The realization stunned her. She needed him. For his experience and knowledge, of course, she told herself.

Well, he'd suggested a way to guarantee she'd have them. All she had to do was accept his offer of partnership and she'd be assured of his staying on.

Lena turned away from the counter, where she'd been busy putting the finishing touches on a batch of caramel rolls. "Mike, go wake those boys and get them in here for breakfast. I'm not running a diner here."

Mike glanced at his watch and stood up. "Yeah, I guess they've slept long enough."

Dan rose as well. "I'll head out with you."

Andrea looked up. "Is there anything I can do? Anything you need help with?" She wanted to be a part of things, to feel useful. Sooner or later she'd have to learn all the details of the ranch's operation if she intended to stay.

Lena refilled Andrea's coffee and answered for him. "No, he's just going out to putter. Sit still and finish your coffee." To Dan and Mike, she said, "The buns will be

done in twenty minutes. Get yourselves back in here by
then.''

She watched the men leave, then pulled up a chair next
to Andrea. "I know it seems pretty overwhelming, but
don't worry, you'll catch on fast.''

Andrea studied the older woman's open face. "Do you
think so?''

"I'm sure of it.'' Lena patted her arm. "So, tell me about
yourself. Do you have family in Seattle? What do they
think about all this?''

"My mother's back there. It was quite a surprise to her.''

Lena nodded. "Especially since you were about to get
married, I guess.''

Andrea looked up, shocked. "How did you know about
that?'' Good grief, what must Lena think of her? Probably
just what she thought of herself.

The housekeeper's expression was sheepish. "I, uh,
overheard you talking on the phone that first night. You
mentioned telling him to send back the presents. What else
could it be but wedding presents?'' She fixed Andrea with
a curious gaze. "So why didn't you marry the guy? Was
he a jerk?''

Andrea couldn't help but laugh at the woman's blunt-
ness. "No, not really.'' She thought about it a second.
"Well, maybe a little. But mostly I just realized I wasn't
in love with him. That is, I knew it all along, really, but
didn't have the guts to do anything about it till I found out
about the ranch. It was a way out.'' A coward's way, she
thought ruefully, but she'd had no choice.

"So now you're going to start all over?''

"I guess so.'' If she'd expected blame or accusation from
the older woman, it didn't come. Lena seemed to accept
her explanation with equanimity. "What about you, Lena?
What are your plans once the Vidtel allowance runs out?''

Lena's clear blue eyes crinkled thoughtfully. "I don't

really know. I'd be happy to stay on if you'd have me," she ventured almost shyly.

"Really? You'd want to stay?" Andrea was touched and pleased, but, as always lately, the specter of money reared its head. How would she pay Lena if she stayed?

"Of course. I've been living here awhile, now. I'd just keep doing what I've always done."

"I'd love to have you stay, Lena," Andrea said. "But I don't know how I'd pay you."

Lena laughed. "Lord, I haven't been paid in ages. Not till Vidtel bought us out. Dan arranged for the deal to include wages that I would have gotten plus the two months' worth to get you settled in, but heck, I've always gotten room and board here and that's about it. I have social security and my state retirement, so it's not as though I have no income. I do all right."

"You mean you haven't been a paid employee all this time?"

"No, I guess I'm more like family," Lena said.

To Andrea's immense surprise, the older woman blushed. "Oh, you mean you and Dan..." Andrea trailed off, understanding dawning as she felt her own cheeks flush.

Lena nodded, looking almost girlish.

"So what are you and Dan going to do now?" If Dan moved in with his relatives, would that mean the end to his and Lena's relationship?

Her concern must have shown in her face, because Lena patted her hand. "Don't worry, hon, it's not your fault. We've talked about it. We'll work something out."

Andrea heard angry voices outside in the yard. She glanced at Lena, who raised a curious eyebrow, then she rose and hurried to the door to look out. Todd lay trembling on the lawn, his face contorted. Stench stood over him, scowling.

Something was wrong!

Andrea shoved the door open and started outside before she realized Todd was laughing. The uncontrollable, rolling-on-the-ground, clutching-your-stomach kind of laughter.

Standing over him, Stench raised his arm menacingly, waving a long silver object—the emasculator.

Jock poked his head out from around the side of the house, laughing as well, and crept toward his companions.

Stench rounded on him. "That wasn't funny, man. You almost gave me a heart attack."

Andrea had never seen Rusting Hulkk's unflappable lead singer so distressed. She couldn't contain her curiosity. "What happened?"

The boys jumped apart, apparently unaware of their audience. Todd stood up and brushed the grass off his pants, still laughing too hard to speak. Stench threw him a disgusted look and turned away.

"Todd put that thing in Stench's bed," Jock explained, fighting laughter himself. "In a compromising position, if ya know what I mean." He winked.

Todd collapsed once again in gales of laughter. "I told you it would come in handy."

"Well, it looks like you boys are ready to get to work." Mike stepped up behind them.

"I think you'd better confiscate that thing for safekeeping." Andrea gestured to the emasculator. "Before someone gets hurt."

Stench handed the tool to Mike. "Yeah, someone like Todd or Jock. They might end up with it wrapped around their necks."

Todd started to protest, but Mike stopped him with a raised hand.

"You'll get it back before you leave," he said. "In the

meantime, Lena's got breakfast on the table. Better get in there while it's hot."

The boys raced into the kitchen, followed by Mike and Dan as the oven buzzer sounded and the phone rang simultaneously.

"I'll get the phone, Lena," Andrea said, reaching for it. The phone seemed to be ringing a lot since she'd been at the ranch; probably with calls from Dan's friends asking about the contest.

The housekeeper looked thoughtful a moment, then nodded and went to the oven for her rolls. "You boys have a seat. Breakfast is just about ready."

"Hello," Andrea said loudly into the phone over the general din of the kitchen. It was too early in the morning for anyone from back in Seattle to call, fortunately.

"Hello, my dear." A voice pitched somewhere between a bad imitation of Julia Child and a Monty Python falsetto sang in her ear. May I speak to Dr. Moore, please? This is Professor Clarissa Hale."

Professor Hale? Then she remembered. The ufologist. *Oh, great.* "This is Dr. Moore," she said warily.

"My dear, it's urgent that we talk," the scientist warbled. "I'm in Rorvik, and I'd like to come out to see you this afternoon. Would that be convenient?"

Convenient? Hardly. She glanced at the group at the kitchen table. Rusting Hulkk were concentrating on demolishing Lena's caramel rolls. Only Mike watched her with interest.

What would he think? Bert had hinted that he knew something. Would Clarissa Hale's visit disturb him?

Well, she could always just say no, she thought. From Dan's and Lena's comments, though, Clarissa Hale sounded pretty persistent. Perhaps the best thing to do would be to talk to the woman and put the whole issue to rest once and for all.

If she could, she thought, recalling the light she'd seen her first night on the ranch.

"Dr. Moore?" Professor Hale asked tentatively from the other end of the line."

"Yes, I'm here. This afternoon would be convenient, I suppose."

"Outstanding. I'll see you in a couple of hours." She hung up.

Andrea replaced the phone and took her seat at the table. "That was Professor Hale," she said, watching Mike for any sign of reaction. "She's coming out to talk to me."

"Cool," Jock said around a mouthful of roll. "Hey, maybe we'll get on TV. That would be great publicity for the band."

"Why do you suppose the professor wants to come here so badly?" Andrea wondered aloud. *Did Clarissa Hale know Bert Petersen? Perhaps the bank manager had contacted her about his suspicions.* "Could someone have told her there were—" she hesitated, unsure whether Dan knew Mike had told her about White Thunder's situation. Well, he had to know she'd learn about it eventually. "Problems here?"

Dan shook his head. "I don't know. Lots of folks in town knew about our problems. I suppose someone might have said something."

"But for most rational people, aliens aren't going to spring immediately to mind as the cause." Mike looked at her meaningfully.

Jock sat upright in his chair. "You mean UFOs are visiting the ranch? Is that why Professor Hale is coming here? Cool."

Stench leaned forward, his eyes bright with excitement. "I just read about a UFO sighting recently. It happened in Texas. These people were driving one night when a spaceship almost landed on them. They got out of the car for a closer look and the blast from the ship, maybe its exhaust, heated up the metal of the car so much they got burned touching the door handles. One woman ended up in the hospital because of the burns and other problems that showed up from the exposure. Nausea and stomach problems, I think.''

"That sounds like radiation poisoning," Andrea said. "Did she recover?"

"I think so. But the really neat thing was that a bunch of helicopters appeared while they were watching and chased after the ship. That means the government knows about it. They had to."

"And they've kept it a secret?" Mike's question dripped skepticism.

"Woo-woo-woooo-ooo," Jock hummed. "Sounds like a conspiracy to me."

Bert's remarks came back to Andrea. "I've always wondered why the government would do that." She directed her comments to Mike. "Keep information about UFOs a secret, I mean." He was ex-military, after all. He might have some insight into government motivations.

Stench spoke up first. "Supposedly they're afraid of inciting panic if the word gets out that aliens really exist. That's why they've kept that base in the desert a secret. The one where they're supposed to have those alien bodies from a crashed spaceship."

"Area 51 and Hangar 18." Mike made a derisive sound. "Those stories have been around for years. And no one's proved a thing. You've been watching too many of the professor's shows."

Andrea studied him. He didn't seem to be hiding anything. Even she had heard of the Hangar 18 stories. She turned to Dan, hating the need to ask his advice but not sure what else to do. "What do you think, Dan?"

"I think she sounds like she's got a screw loose, but you

decide yourself. You can always tell her you're not interested."

"Depends on what she has in mind as far as investigating, too," Mike added. "It better not include disturbing the animals."

Andrea nodded. "I'll talk to her. Maybe I can convince her there's nothing going on here. That relates to UFOs, anyway." She looked at Mike. "And I won't let her bother the bison."

"I know," Mike said, and realized he meant it. Whatever had possessed him to tell her all about himself during their visit to the old homestead, he was glad he'd done so. He'd never been one for hunches or gut instincts, but he knew she wanted the best for the ranch and its animals, even if she did decide not to keep White Thunder.

So why *had* he opened up to her like that at the Amundson place?

He watched her from across the table. Tendrils of dark hair had pulled loose from her ponytail and hung in soft little wisps around her face. Her eyes sparkled like emeralds as she laughed at some remark of Todd's. Then she looked thoughtful again, a tiny worry line creasing the space between her brows.

She's beautiful.

Long-forgotten warmth surfaced within him. He took a deep breath, trying to resist the sensation.

This was neither the time nor place to let his hormones get the better of him. He should be doing his best to get her off the ranch. Besides, at the moment, she was his boss. *That* complication he couldn't overcome.

And if she accepted his offer and they became partners? He shook off the thought. What was he doing? He must be insane to even consider romance now. It would make the whole situation worse.

As if it could get much worse than it was already. All they needed were UFOs.

Dan had never said anything to him about seeing UFOs at White Thunder. Surely if the stubborn Norwegian thought that what was going on with the bison had something to do with spacemen, he'd have said something.

No, Dan couldn't really suspect aliens were visiting the ranch.

Bert Petersen was something else again, although his most recent allegations were extreme, even for Bert. Hell, even the banker's plan to build an immense concrete bison on the outskirts of town wasn't as flaky. In fact, there was already a giant concrete bison elsewhere in the state.

The topic of discussion had changed to how to keep Rusting Hulkk occupied, and Mike looked up to meet Andrea's gaze just in time to realize she was talking to him.

"So," she asked. "Do you have any ideas for ways to keep the boys busy?"

"I've put off a lot of repairs until I could bring in a couple extra hands," he said quickly, hoping to cover his inattention. "This would be a great time to get them done." He looked at the boys. "If they're willing to earn their keep around here." Not to mention an opportunity to convince Andrea just how much hard work was involved in running a ranch, he thought. With any luck, he'd give her second thoughts about staying at White Thunder.

Todd looked mildly rebellious, no difficult feat with his spiky white hair. Jock scratched his nose, still reddened by hay fever, and grimaced. But Stench spoke for the group.

"We'd be happy to do anything you need done," he said graciously, shooting a warning glance at his comrades. "Right, guys? It's the least we can do to repay them, isn't it?"

Todd hesitated, staring down at his now-empty plate. "Yeah, I suppose so."

Jock looked sheepish. "Sure, we'll be happy to help." He sounded like a small child coached by his parents to thank a relative for a gift he didn't especially like.

With further prompting by Stench, Todd and Jock stood and helped clear the table. Mike waited, expecting a protest from Lena, but this time the housekeeper seemed to be glad of their assistance.

WHEN MIKE AND THE BOYS rose and headed outside, Andrea followed unbidden. Mike made no argument, but put her to work with the band replacing dry rotted planks in the hayloft floor.

Todd and Jock, having professed woodworking experience, he put to work sawing boards. While they worked, Mike showed Andrea how to pry up the old boards, then Stench laid new ones and hammered them into place.

"We're making good progress," he remarked as she levered a crowbar in an effort to rip up a particularly well-secured board.

"I guess it helps to have a few extra hands." She smiled at him, seemingly enjoying herself despite the difficult job.

He scowled. He hadn't intended this to be fun. "Here, let me have a try."

He took the crowbar, positioning it under the edge of the flooring. "Extra feet help, too," he said. "Stand on this. Carefully."

Andrea tentatively stepped onto the end of the bar to pry the board loose. It didn't budge. "Isn't rotted wood supposed to be a little weaker than this?"

"It's weak, just not right here. Put more weight on it." He gripped her elbow to steady her as she stepped onto the bar with both feet and bounced slightly in an effort to force the plank free.

It came loose all at once with a rending creak. The crowbar dropped out from under Andrea, rolling beneath her feet to trip her. She lost her balance, stumbling toward the edge of the loft.

Mike was nearby, but she caught herself and waved him away before he could reach her. The last thing she needed when she was trying to prove herself was to be rescued.

"Damn. You okay?" He folded his arms across his chest.

"Fine. Thanks." Pulse racing, she glanced over the edge of the loft to where the boys worked on, oblivious to her near fall.

Mike studied her. "You're pale. Look, we're almost done here. Why don't you take a break and head back to the house?"

"I'm fine. I don't need a break." To tell the truth, she thought, Mike looked a little pale himself.

"And I don't need you falling and breaking your neck," he said softly. "Besides, the professor will probably be here soon. I'm sure you'll want to get tidied up."

She wanted to argue but realized he was right. She did feel light-headed, probably from adrenaline, but it would be stupid to risk a fall just to prove her worth. She climbed down from the loft and headed inside.

IN THE HOUSE, ANDREA SAT alone at the kitchen table, trying to work a small splinter out of her fingertip. Funny that she hadn't noticed getting it. She'd been completely engrossed in her work. And Mike's presence.

For a few moments they'd shared a common goal, a mutual interest in the ranch. Then she'd slipped and everything had changed. He'd become his old self again, and she was the outsider. And a clumsy one at that.

The doorbell rang.

"I'll get it," she called to Lena, who was busy in the laundry room. She walked through the living room to the front door and opened it.

A tiny, round woman perched on the front porch. She blinked up at Andrea through bottle-glass spectacles and bobbed her head in a greeting that made her look like a plump mother hen.

"May I help you?" Andrea asked.

"Yes," the little woman clucked. "You must be Dr. Andrea Moore. I'm Professor Clarissa Hale, and I'm here to save you from terrible danger."

CHAPTER TEN

ANDREA STARED DOWN at the little woman.

"May I come in, dear?" An anxious frown buried the professor's brows behind the frames of her thick glasses. "We have much to discuss."

Andrea opened the screen door, resigning herself. "Of course. Please, come in."

Clarissa Hale stepped inside and Andrea gestured her to a seat. The professor toddled across to the sofa and settled herself onto the cushions like a nesting bird.

She wore a serviceable navy polyester suit, its plain white blouse buttoned high at the throat and set off with a gold-colored brooch shaped like a flying saucer with rhinestone portholes. Her graying hair, worn in a fluffy pageboy, looked as sensible as the black leather oxfords encasing her small feet.

She leaned toward Andrea, her expression earnest. "I want to discuss the sightings of alien spacecraft on White Thunder."

The professor didn't mince words, Andrea thought, dropping stiffly onto the edge of Dan's recliner. She forced a smile. "What sightings?"

Professor Hale's expression was tolerant. "I must inform you that this area has quite a history of alien encounters, Dr. Moore, of which you may be unaware. Perhaps you have not yet experienced them yourself, but many others have. They are real, I assure you, and I wish to investigate them."

Before Andrea could repeat her denials, the woman continued. "I host a television program called 'Visitors.' Perhaps you've seen it?" She blinked up at Andrea, her brown eyes unnaturally large, magnified by her glasses.

"Um, no," Andrea replied, adding apologetically, "I don't watch much television."

Professor Hale waved a chubby hand. "No matter. We deal with paranormal phenomena, mostly reports of alien activity and UFO sightings, plus occasional hauntings. We've known for years about the sightings here, despite the authorities' claims that there have been no official reports." She lowered her voice, tilting her round body forward to add ominously, "We have investigated those claims and discovered that several reports that were filed have *disappeared*."

Andrea knew of at least one sighting that wasn't reported—her own. Not for any amount of money would she divulge that to Clarissa Hale, though. She bit her lip and waited for the woman to continue.

The professor raised one eyebrow above the rim of her glasses and paused for effect. "I strongly suspect a coverup. I tried several times to talk to Dan Amundson about the issue, but he was most reluctant to meet with me. When we learned you were the new owner of the ranch, I decided to come out and make you aware of what was going on here. This area holds the key to a great discovery concerning extraterrestrial visitations, and it's my job to make sure the truth comes out. That's why I'm here today."

Warning bells sounded in Andrea's head. The professor was clearly hinting at some kind of conspiracy. *Great, a paranoid UFO hunter.* Maybe Clarissa and Bert *had* already met. Come to think of it, it was more than likely.

"I'm afraid we wouldn't be of much help, Professor." She rose, hoping a gentle brush-off would be sufficient.

"I've only been at White Thunder a few days, but the residents here tell me they've never seen anything strange."

"You're in an unusual situation here, Dr. Moore. Perhaps the residents of the ranch are too uncomfortable to tell you about their experiences."

Andrea walked to the door, her impatience growing. The woman clearly didn't want to take no for an answer. "I can promise you, Professor, nothing has happened at White Thunder to indicate that anything has been kept from me." *Well, nothing about space aliens, anyway,* she thought, putting aside the thought of the light she'd seen her first night here. "So if you'll excuse me...?" She opened the door and stood to one side.

The professor hauled herself to her feet and moved reluctantly toward the door. "Perhaps you aren't aware of the types of encounters that have been reported. If my staff and I could just spend a few hours here, I'm sure we could determine whether the stories are true. We have considerable experience. We can have our equipment set up in no time, and you'll hardly notice it."

A movement from the kitchen doorway behind the professor caught Andrea's eye, and she glanced up to see Lena's head poking around the edge of the jamb. The housekeeper rolled her eyes emphatically and ducked back into the kitchen.

She agreed with Lena. This whole conspiracy business was getting out of hand. She shook her head. "No, Professor. I can't have a bunch of alien hunters running around the ranch, for your safety as well as that of my livestock. You'll just have to find another place to investigate."

The professor stared up at Andrea, her lips pursed and her eyes swimming hugely behind her lenses. "Surely you don't want to stand in the way of important research, Dr. Moore? We use sensitive electronic instrumentation and scientific techniques. Nothing that would disturb your animals."

"Well, you'll have to use them somewhere else. I can't take the chance. White Thunder Ranch is not a research project." Andrea eased the ruffled ufologist out the door and started to close it behind her.

"Wait...Dr. Moore...Andrea." The professor clutched at the door frame. "My team is out collecting data from equipment we set up some time ago on the federal grassland adjoining your ranch. They'll be here shortly. Please let me show you some of the data we've gathered. I know I can convince you of the seriousness of this study."

She reached forward and caught Andrea's hand in her tiny, plump one, gripping it urgently. "It's important that you learn what's going on out here, Andrea. For your own safety, as well as that of your property and livestock." She pursed her lips into a small beak. "Are you sure you haven't noticed anything unusual or heard of strange occurrences from your employees? I understand one of your employees, a Native American, is a former army officer. Has he said anything about this to you?"

Andrea paused in her efforts to extricate her hand from the smaller woman's grip. How had the professor found out about Mike's background? And what did his ethnic origin have to do with space aliens?

Professor Hale's eyes narrowed to slits behind her glasses as her voice dropped to an urgent whisper. "Has he acted unusual in any way? Has he encouraged you to oppose our investigations? There are those in our government who would prefer that the truth remained hidden. And many who believe that much of the spiritual heritage of Native peoples is tied to the visits of extraterrestrials. Researchers suspect that the biblical description of Ezekiel's wheel is actually an ancient UFO sighting. The medicine wheel of Native Americans is a similar image. It's only natural to suspect a connection. These visitations have occurred for centuries.''

Andrea yanked her hand from the professor's doughy grasp. She couldn't believe what she was hearing. The woman was not only suggesting that Mike was some sort of agent whose mission was to keep her off the trail of the UFOs, but that he had spiritual ties to them. She had to be nuts!

"For the last time, I haven't seen anything unusual, and neither has anyone at White Thunder. And I resent the implication that one of my employees is involved in some kind of conspiracy.''

"You wouldn't necessarily see flying objects,'' the professor rambled on as though Andrea hadn't spoken. "The visitors might manifest themselves as strange patterns in your crops or medical phenomena such as unusual behavior or unexplained deaths among the stock—mutilations, radiation injuries, miscarriages and fertility problems, any number of things.''

At her last comment, an icy lump formed in the pit of Andrea's stomach, and for a moment she couldn't respond.

Miscarriages and infertility caused by UFOs? How?

She refused to believe such a thing was possible. As Doc had pointed out, poisoning of some type was the likely culprit, and it could be difficult to diagnose. Just because they had no answer yet was no reason to formulate some bizarre UFO hypothesis. They simply hadn't stumbled on the cause.

Her emotion must have shown in her face, because the professor clutched at her hand once more.

"There *is* something, isn't there? You must tell me, dear. You can trust me.'' She peered earnestly up at Andrea.

Andrea shook her head, both to deny the ufologist's assertions and to clear her own disturbing thoughts. "No.

Nothing. Nothing at all." She hoped she sounded more resolute than she felt.

Professor Hale frowned, her brows dipping behind the top edge of her glasses. "At least let us set up our equipment here so we can monitor the area. We can help. You must believe that. You don't know what grave danger you may be in."

Andrea almost believed the professor was sincere in her concern, as well as in her desire for a scientific discovery. But there was too much at stake. The woman was clearly a wacko. She couldn't risk the chance that they'd injure the animals, especially Gypsy.

"I'm sorry," she said firmly. "It's just too dangerous, for you and the bison. I'm afraid I can't allow it."

The woman pursed her lips once more. "Well, I see I'm not going to change your mind. But please be careful and promise me you'll call if anything unusual happens." She dug through her massive handbag and pulled out a business card, which she handed to Andrea.

Andrea glanced at the card. "I will." She tucked the card into her jeans pocket. *If the Martians land, you'll be the first to know.*

Around them the house shuddered. For half a second, Andrea wondered if Martians had indeed landed. Then she heard the familiar rumble of a heavy truck. She leaned past the professor and looked toward the road.

A semi with a long black trailer pulled into the yard and stopped. Andrea could feel the deep-throated hum of its engine vibrate all the way through her before the driver switched it off. She glanced at the professor.

"My equipment," the older woman said, bobbing like a plump blue hen.

Two white-coated men climbed out of the truck and went around to the back of the trailer and disappeared inside. They reappeared carrying pieces of scientific-looking equipment, moving in unison like Tweedledum and Tweedledee in lab coats. Andrea recognized a satellite dish, cameras and recorders, but other pieces were unfamiliar to her.

"You may as well have them reload that stuff." Andrea kept her voice calm, despite her growing annoyance. "They can't set it up here."

The professor must have hoped she'd relent when presented with the test equipment. Her face fell in disappointment, and she toddled down the porch steps. Andrea followed.

The noise had attracted other attention, as well. Mike and the band, along with Dan, approached from the barn, and Lena gawked from the kitchen window.

"What's going on here?" Mike stopped beside her, his expression wary.

"Nothing," Andrea replied. She had to get the professor and her people out of here before they descended on Mike and started accusing him of who knew what outlandish schemes. "They were just leaving."

One of the technicians, who had begun stacking material beside Gypsy's corral, glanced at the professor for confirmation.

Clarissa Hale nodded stiffly and the man shrugged, then started hauling things back to the truck. The other man had donned a pair of headphones, which were plugged into a large metal box beside him. The first technician tapped him on the shoulder and the man jumped, pulling the headset free from its jack.

A loud, shrill wail filled the air.

In the corral, Gypsy raised her head in alarm and looked around quickly. Seeking a means of escape, she darted first one way, then the other in panic.

"Turn that damn thing off!" Mike shouted. He leapt onto the fence rail and called to Gypsy, trying in vain to calm her.

The frantic animal shied away from him and charged toward the opposite side of the corral. For a moment, it appeared she was going to leap the fence. She balked at the last minute, but not soon enough to avoid striking the railing.

The wood splintered under the impact of nearly a half ton of bison. The instrument's shriek stopped abruptly, and Gypsy, apparently stunned by her encounter with the fence, halted her escape attempt.

Mike and Andrea raced to the far side of the corral. The bison stood placidly enough, but her wide eyes showed white at the corners. The splintered wood had cut a deep gash across her chest, and blood dripped down her leg, pooling red-black in the dust.

Andrea shot a quick glance at Mike. His jaw twitched with anger, and his eyes, meeting hers, flashed like lightning. He spun back toward the professor and her technicians. Andrea reached to hold him back, but to her surprise, he didn't move.

The professor faced him, her plump cheeks pale. "Oh, my. I'm sorry. If you'd only allowed..."

Mike cut her off. "I'd advise you all to leave. Now." His voice was dangerously low.

Tweedledum and Tweedledee hurriedly repacked their equipment, and in a few moments, the truck was rumbling off down the drive. The professor's car followed close behind.

"Do you have a handkerchief?" Andrea glanced at him, then returned her attention to the bison. A sick feeling welled inside as all her professional detachment fled. She breathed deeply, fighting panic.

Mike swung back toward her, took a quick look at Gypsy and dug inside his jeans pocket. He handed her a square of white cotton.

"Have Lena call Doc Coggins." The calm in her voice

amazed her; inside she was trembling. She squeezed through the demolished rails to the inside of the corral and approached Gypsy slowly, letting the animal become used to her presence.

Mike reached for her arm. "Be careful. She was hand-raised, but I don't know what she might do while she's upset like this."

Andrea nodded. "Don't worry. I plan to be *extremely* careful." She met his eyes and their gazes held. His concern, she realized, was as much for her as for Gypsy. "There's a medical kit in my room, in a black case." She silently thanked the impulse that had made her throw the bag into her suitcase before she left Seattle. "Could someone get it?"

He nodded, then waved Stench over and conferred quietly with him, after which Stench took off for the house.

Dan stepped up to the fence rail, followed by Jock and Todd. "What can we do?"

She looked up at the big animal, who stared back at her placidly. Gypsy seemed to have suffered no serious effects from the impact. *Let's just hope the wound isn't too bad.*

She turned to Dan. "Do you have any way to restrain her? A halter or a squeeze chute?"

"We've got both," Mike said. "If we can get the halter on her, we can lead her into the chute. Are you going to try and stitch her up?"

Andrea released a shuddering breath. "If she'll let me. If not, I'll wait for Doc, but we don't know how long he'll be. I'd rather take care of it so we can minimize her stress."

"I'll get the harness." Dan turned to Jock and Todd. "Boys, give me a hand with the chute."

The three of them set off for the barn.

"What can I do?" Mike asked.

Andrea glanced at him. "Do you have any more marsh-mallows? This might take a little coaxing."

Mike shook his head. "Not on me, but I told Stench to bring some. How does she look?"

"I'll need to get in closer." She stepped nearer to the animal. "Easy, girl. I just want take a look."

Mike climbed through the railing behind her and eased up to Gypsy, stroking her nose as he talked to her softly. Andrea smiled. The distraction would make her job easier.

The bison nuzzled Mike's hand and pawed the ground beside the splintered rail, but made no attempt to evade Andrea as she moved alongside.

Gypsy turned her head away from Mike and nudged Andrea's knee. Andrea slowly worked her right hand, holding the handkerchief, along the bison's neck, then forward and down to her chest.

She crouched to examine the wound, keenly aware of the huge animal standing over her. Even with Mike's calming presence, all Gypsy had to do was toss her head or move quickly and she'd be lucky to come away with only a few broken bones. The animal stood calmly, though, not even twitching as Andrea probed the area around the wound in order to judge its depth through the thick fur.

Blood still oozed from the cut, but seemed to be slowing. *Thank God,* Andrea thought. A few inches to one side or the other, and the bison might have severed a jugular vein. Her dense coat had helped to provide some protection.

"How is it?" Mike looked down at her from his position beside Gypsy's head.

Andrea noticed that his left hand was clenched deep in the dense wool of the bison's neck in case he had to turn the animal away from her quickly. The realization gave her a measure of comfort.

Moving slowly, she pressed the handkerchief against the laceration. The bison took a half step forward. Andrea stumbled slightly to keep the compress in place, but the animal made no further move. Instead she turned her head and regarded Andrea with one chocolate brown eye.

"That's a very good girl, Gypsy," Andrea cooed, her voice low and soothing as she stroked Gypsy's shoulder with her free hand, hoping the cow couldn't hear her racing heartbeat. She knew animals could sense fear in humans and wondered if fear *for* the animal counted. She glanced up at Mike. "It doesn't look too bad. A few stitches should take care of it."

Her attachment to Gypsy, as well as the knowledge that the bison might be the last hope for the ranch, tempered the normal sense of exhilaration she felt when helping an animal.

Without Gypsy's calf, White Thunder was as good as worthless. She'd lose her chance for a new start.

And more, she'd lose Mike.

Some distant part of her mind tried to argue that she didn't care what happened to Mike. But even as the thought formed, she knew it was a lie. There was a bond between them now. She could feel it even as they worked on Gypsy. She could sense his presence, feel his concerned gaze and his trust in her.

She kept her voice soft, crooning nonsense to the bison, telling her what a wonderful, precious girl she was. Her pressure on the wound was steady, the caressing motion of her free hand rhythmic.

Stench returned first. He slowed from a run to a walk as he approached the corral, his eyes wide. "Doc's on his way, but he'll be about a half hour. He's stopping by the clinic for his ultrasound unit." He handed the medical bag and marshmallows to Mike. "Is she okay?"

"She's fine," Mike said, handing Andrea the bag. "Looks like she'll only need a few stitches." He took a marshmallow from the bag and held it out for Gypsy, who gulped it down eagerly.

Andrea patted the animal's woolly neck, aware of Mike's gaze resting on her like a warm cloak. "I'm glad he's bringing the ultrasound to check the calf," she told him. "Just to be sure."

She hadn't liked the idea of increasing the bison's stress with an internal examination. The calf had probably suffered no ill effects from its mother's accident, but she was relieved that Doc didn't want to take any chances.

She darted another look at Mike. His face was grim, but his actions were restrained, as though he didn't want to let her know how worried he was, how much he'd pinned his future on Gypsy's offspring.

"I'm sure the calf's fine, Mike," she offered reassuringly. "The wound is fairly minor and the impact shouldn't have had much effect."

He nodded, a look of surprise and gratitude softening the deep crease between his brows.

A loud, metallic creak sounded across the yard. Gypsy flinched nervously, and they glanced up. Dan and the boys approached, rolling a large contraption of metal tubing. Mike and Stench moved to assist them.

Dan handed Mike a set of long leather straps, then turned to help wheel the squeeze chute into the corral.

Mike caressed the bison's face and eased the halter up over her head. "I don't know if she'll let us lead her, but we can give it a try."

He buckled the halter in place around her muzzle and took the straps in his hand.

"Move slowly," Andrea said. "I need to keep up the pressure on the wound." She threw a glance over her shoulder. "Stench, grab that case and bring it along, would you?"

"Me?" Stench's eyebrows shot up in alarm. Underneath, though, his eyes were bright with excitement.

"You're drafted," Andrea said. "Don't worry, you won't have to do anything gross."

Stench picked up the case and followed as Andrea and Mike moved in tandem with Gypsy to the far side of the corral, where Dan and the boys were setting up the chute.

Gypsy walked up the ramp into the metal cage without hesitation. Dan closed the gate behind her.

"Leave the head squeeze loose so I can get to the wound," Andrea directed. "And don't tighten the sides down hard. I just want enough restraint to get the job done."

Dan and Mike tightened the sides of the cage against the bison, leaving some room between her flanks and the metal bars.

"Let's give it a try," Dan said. "We can always tighten it more if she gives you trouble."

Andrea nodded and took her case from Stench. She opened it on the ground and took out a small glass bottle, a syringe and needle and a package of suture material with an attached needle. Then she stepped to the front of the chute and examined the laceration more closely.

"I really should clip this and clean it up." She looked up at Mike. "Do you have battery-operated clippers, by any chance?"

Todd spoke up before Mike could answer. "Jock's got a portable shaver."

Jock turned on him, grimacing. "Man, you're not suggesting they use my shaver to clip buffalo hair, are you?"

"Oh, come on, man," Stench said. "They need it."

"No way." Jock scowled at them, but the pressure of five pleading gazes, not including Gypsy's, was too much. He scuffed his tennis shoes in the dirt. "Oh, all right."

He turned and dashed across the yard toward Mike's trailer.

By the time he returned, Andrea had used scissors from

her kit to clip away the longer hair around the cut. Jock handed the shaver to her with relative grace.

"Thanks," Andrea said sincerely. "This'll help a lot."

Jock ran a hand through his curly hair, eyeing her efforts dubiously. "Yeah, great. Well, it's about time I tried growing a beard, anyway."

Andrea held the shaver behind her back and flipped it on, then brought the humming device slowly toward Gypsy.

The bison rolled her eyes at the noise but didn't flinch as Andrea held it to the trimmed hair around the wound. After a moment, she set the shaver, gummy with hair and blood, on the lid of the medical kit.

"Here." Mike handed her a bottle of brown liquid and a handful of gauze squares.

She squeezed the iodine solution onto the sponges and used them to cleanse the wound. Her initial assessment had been correct, she noted with relief. The wound looked much worse than it actually was. A little blood went a long way.

She knelt beside the chute and carefully injected anesthetic solution into the skin around the wound. Gypsy snorted at the needle prick but kept still. She'd probably had more painful bites from insects.

"The worst is over, girl," Andrea soothed the bison, her own anxiety waning. She took the suture supplies and concentrated on sewing a neat row of stitches, closing the wound. When she tied the final knot, she turned to Mike. "Got another marshmallow?"

He nodded and leaned close to her to feed one to Gypsy. Andrea felt the warmth of his body as he blocked the cool breeze. His face was close to hers.

"We'll need to take these stitches out in a week or so," she murmured, focusing her attention on her patient. She ducked past Mike to her kit to draw a syringeful of white liquid from another bottle and inject it into the muscle of Gypsy's thigh.

"Antibiotic?" he asked.

Andrea nodded. "Doc will probably want her on something for several days, too. Good thing she takes pills easily." She turned to Dan. "Let's keep her here till Doc's had a chance to check her over and do the ultrasound. She's taking it calmly enough."

The older man ambled forward and stroked the bison's nose. "Yup, she's a good ol' girl. Thank you, Andrea." His eyes were moist, and he glanced toward the road, as if embarrassed by the emotion that shown clearly on his face. "There's Doc now."

A big Suburban pulled up the driveway and stopped beside the corral. Doc Coggins climbed out, carrying a medical bag and what looked like a medium-size suitcase.

He entered the corral and greeted them. "How's she doing?"

"Pretty well, I think," Andrea said. "She's stitched up and I gave her a dose of Terramycin."

Doc checked the wound. "It looks good. I'll give you some tablets for her until the stitches come out. Have you had a chance to check on the calf?"

Andrea shook her head. "Not yet. Stench said you were bringing an ultrasound unit, so I didn't want to stress her out with an exam if it wasn't necessary."

Doc set the suitcase down and opened it to reveal a video screen and a bank of electrical switches and knobs. "Well, with any luck, we won't have to do any more than this. And she shouldn't have any objection to it."

He pulled out a rounded object that resembled a computer game joystick with a long cord, which he plugged into a socket on the front of the unit. Then he handed heavy-duty clippers and a plastic bottle to Andrea. "Shave her side, then spread that gel on there."

"What is it?" Mike asked. Dan and the band members

had also gathered around, watching the proceedings with interest.

"Conduction gel," Andrea replied as she shaved the dense hair from Gypsy's side, then spread the thick bluish liquid over the shaved area. "It helps conduct the ultrasonic wave and keeps the transducer, that joystick thing he's holding, in contact with the area he's examining."

Doc slid the case closer to the chute and crouched beside Gypsy.

"Do you have enough room, Doc?" Andrea asked. "We can take her out of the chute if that would make it easier."

"No. This should be fine." He flipped a switch on the instrument and started to move the transducer slowly over Gypsy's side.

Andrea and the others watched as flickering images appeared on the monitor inside the case. She hadn't had a lot of experience with ultrasounds. The pictures had always looked like amorphous blobs to her until someone pointed out the features of the subject on the screen.

This time, though, she could make out the nose and head of the calf inside Gypsy, probably because the baby was so large.

Doc moved the transducer back and forth over the cow's abdomen as though tracing the shape of the calf within her. The pulsing view of the heartbeat was strong and steady. Then the calf rolled and shifted, blurring the image on the screen.

Doc watched closely for a moment, then glanced up at Mike and Andrea. "Everything looks fine. Position's normal. I'd say you have a healthy little girl in there."

The worry that had clouded Mike's face fled, replaced by a grin more radiant than Andrea had ever seen. "A female?" he asked. "Are you sure?"

Doc nodded. "As far as I can tell from the pictures, I'd

say it's a heifer." He gave a wink. "Bulls are pretty easy to recognize at the angle we're viewing."

Mike spun to face Andrea. "A girl!" he shouted. "We're going to have a girl!"

"Oh, Mike," Andrea managed to gasp as tears sprang to her eyes. The calf was fine. Mike's dream for the ranch was still alive. As was her own.

Before she had time to consider what she was doing, she threw her arms around his neck and pressed her lips to his.

After a moment's stunned surprise, Mike enfolded her in his arms.

CHAPTER ELEVEN

MIKE HELD HER, feeling her soft and yielding against him. For a moment all his resentment disappeared, along with his resolve to maintain his distance. He wanted nothing more than to keep holding her while the world stood still around them.

But his rational mind wasn't ready to give in. This wasn't the time, he told himself. He couldn't let himself get carried away simply because she had helped Gypsy. White Thunder was his, and he wouldn't let misguided gratitude and raging hormones threaten it.

He released her.

"Sorry," he murmured. He turned abruptly back to Gypsy.

All around Andrea, silence had fallen. She glanced at Dan and Doc and was annoyed to see twin glimmers of amusement in their eyes. Amusement and something more—approval?

When she looked at Stench, Todd and Jock, all three quickly found something else to focus on and refused to meet her gaze.

What had she done? Her pulse was still pounding from the brief contact. She stole a glance at Mike. He'd turned away to busy himself cleaning up after the procedure on Gypsy, careful not to look her way. He mumbled something about taking things to the barn and strode off quickly in that direction.

Doc directed Stench in shutting down the ultrasound

unit, while Dan put Todd and Jock to work releasing Gypsy from the chute and wheeling the contraption out of the corral.

Free of the confining metal cage, Gypsy darted around the corral, snorting and tossing her head.

Andrea grimaced. "I hope my sutures will stand up to that kind of treatment."

Doc grinned. "They'll be fine as long as she doesn't try to jump the fence. She'll settle down in a few minutes. You with the hair—Stench, is it?" he called over his shoulder. "Get her some hay, would you? That'll keep her occupied."

Stench looked momentarily puzzled, then nodded and ran to the barn. He returned a couple of minutes later carrying a mound of hay at arm's length. Dust and bits of dried grass fell from the pile of hay to coat the front of his jeans like oversize lint.

"Do buffalo actually do that?" he asked. "Jump fences, I mean."

"Oh, sure," Doc said. "You wouldn't know it to look at them, but they're excellent jumpers."

Dan nodded. "I once heard tell of a bison that got out of its pasture and jumped over a parked pickup that got in its way."

Andrea raised an eyebrow. "Yeah, right."

The rancher met her gaze and laughed, raising his right hand. "Honest. At least that's what the fella told me."

Doc shook his head. "I don't know about jumping over trucks, but they do occasionally jump out of corrals and pens. They can be difficult to load into trailers, too." He rested a hand on Andrea's shoulder. "They're wild animals, no matter how tame they may seem." He held her gaze, his expression serious. "Don't take any chances with them. Even with Gypsy. Be sure to have someone help you with her treatment."

Andrea nodded. She was fairly certain Gypsy wouldn't do anything to intentionally hurt her, but she wouldn't take the chance. A nine-hundred-pound animal could do plenty of damage accidentally.

Doc loaded his equipment back in his truck. "I have a couple surgeries I put on hold to come out here, Andrea. Would you like to come back to the hospital and give me a hand? It's nothing glamorous, but I'd appreciate the help. I'll give you a break on the house-call charge as a trade."

Andrea jumped at the chance. "I'd be glad to." A couple of hours away from the ranch, and Mike, wouldn't hurt.

She turned to Dan. "Did you have anything around here for me to do? I hate to take off on short notice if there's something you need me for."

Dan shook his head. "No. Go ahead. Make sure you hold him to the deal about discounting his fees, though." He winked at the vet, who grinned back. "Give us a call when you're done, and I'll send Mike over to pick you up."

From the barn, Mike watched them drive away with a sigh of relief that quickly deepened to a groan with the memory of his response to Andrea's impulsive kiss.

He was glad she'd been here to take care of Gypsy. It didn't mean he wanted her to stay, but for the first time, he realized he could live with it if she did.

Not that he had much choice. She didn't seem inclined to leave.

But he hadn't planned on anything like this. *Damn!* He pounded the side of his fist hard against the barn door frame and got a handful of splinters for his trouble.

He could still see her expression of shock when he'd released her. Not to mention Dan's, Doc's and the band's, which indicated all too clearly the depth of his mistake.

He'd be forever in Doc's debt for getting her away from the ranch awhile. She wouldn't mention it when she returned, he was sure. They could both just forget that it had ever happened.

At least she could. He would never forget.

He glanced up to see Todd, Stench and Jock sauntering over from the corral.

Just let one of them mention it, he thought belligerently. White Thunder didn't have stalls to muck out, but he was sure he could find something equally distasteful to occupy the boys.

ANDREA WAS GRATEFUL that Doc didn't mention Mike on the drive to the clinic. She'd half expected he would, given the expression on his face when she'd kissed him. Instead, the veterinarian talked about the afternoon's workload.

"I have a couple cat spays, one dog neuter and two dental cleanings." He glanced at her and grinned. "On a pair of old poodles owned by the editor of the Rorvik paper."

They arrived at the clinic and went inside. Amy, Doc Coggin's blond receptionist, greeted Andrea warmly. So did Ole. The big dog trotted out, his bannerlike tail waving fiercely. He sat and raised his paw in welcome.

Andrea shook it. "Hello, Ole. I'm glad to see you again, too."

The dog glanced up at Doc as if expecting a translation. "Good boy," the vet said enthusiastically, then turned to Andrea. "Not too long ago he'd have jumped up and barked in your face. His manners have improved considerably."

Apparently this praise was what Ole had been expecting. The dog gazed at Doc and Andrea adoringly, then turned and squeezed back into his spot under the chair.

"I've been meaning to ask, Doc, why aren't there any dogs at White Thunder? Don't ranches usually have a bunch of them running around?"

"Most of 'em do," Doc said. "Bison don't care for

dogs, though—probably some sort of instinctive reaction left over from when they were hunted by wolves. Dan used to have a couple old dogs, but once they passed on, he didn't replace them because of the bison."

"I see," Andrea said. "It's interesting that they've retained that instinct as domestic animals."

Doc nodded. "That's probably why they're still so unpredictable. Their wild characteristics haven't been bred out of them like they have in cattle. Well, let me show you around the place and we'll get started."

The afternoon passed quickly. Andrea helped anesthetize the patients, then scrubbed up and assisted with the surgeries.

She watched Doc operate, noting the small differences in his technique from her own and Jeffrey's. Doc worked at a steady pace with meticulous attention to detail. It was a style she sought to emulate. She was always careful, even with the most routine procedure. And she never let herself forget that her patient was someone's beloved pet.

The thought of Jeffrey brought a fresh wave of guilt. Would he call her now that he knew where she was? She doubted his pride would let him. Her relief at the thought only aggravated her guilty conscience.

"Why don't you close this one?" Doc said, wrapping up the last surgery, a neuter on a big shepherd mix.

Andrea did so, distracting herself by concentrating on her task. She stitched the incision closed with a practiced hand, then removed the sterile drape from the surgical site. Doc peeled off his gloves and bent to examine her work.

"Looks great." He gathered his instruments and placed them in the sink to soak before cleaning and sterilizing, then gave the dog an injection of antibiotic.

Andrea disconnected the dog's endotracheal tube from the anesthetic vaporizer and turned off the machine. Within a few moments, the dog began to move its mouth and tried to swallow. She deflated the cuff that held the tube in place, then pulled the tube carefully out of the animal's mouth. The dog licked his lips and moved his head slightly.

They wheeled him back to the kennels and together lifted him off the gurney and into a large cage.

"If you'll keep an eye on him for a few minutes, I'll get the surgery cleaned up," Doc said.

"All right." Andrea always preferred to watch her surgical patients closely until they were fully awake. She knelt beside the cage and talked soothingly to the groggy animal until he was able to raise his head and roll himself onto his chest.

When Doc returned, the dog was groggy but alert, and wagged his tail in greeting. "I've checked on the other cases." He crouched to pet the dog. "Everybody's looking good. Why don't we duck across the street for a sandwich? My treat."

"That sounds great," Andrea replied. It had been hours since breakfast.

They washed up and stopped by Doc's office on the way out.

"Come on, Ole." Doc slapped his thigh. "Walkies."

The dog crawled out from under his chair, tail waving, and led the way to the door. They started down the street, Ole leading the way.

"I hope you don't mind having lunch at a bar. We don't have any actual restaurants in town. Charlie's has decent food, but the Viking's better."

"Not at all," Andrea said. "Anything's fine."

From outside, the Viking Tavern looked about the same as the other Rorvik bars, a low, square building with neon signs in the windows. The building seemed older, though, with wood-frame construction instead of the ubiquitous corrugated metal. Doc opened the screen door and they entered, along with Ole.

Inside, the bar was lighter and airier than Charlie's. Woodwork abounded, but the heavy oak back bar and plank floors were stained in a rich golden shade. Booths along the walls were upholstered with bright reds and blues in a Scandinavian print offset by dark blue vinyl. Flags of Norway and Sweden hung over the bar, flanking an enormous, horned Viking helmet on a shelf at the back.

A free-standing green-enameled fireplace glowed cheerily in the far corner. Beside it, four elderly men sat playing cards.

"Afternoon, Doc," a slim brunette behind the bar called brightly. "Late lunch today?"

"Afraid so, Margie." Doc flashed her a brilliant smile. "We'll have a couple menus with everything on them."

The bartender handed him a pair of printed sheets of paper. "Just have a seat anywhere. I'll be right with you." She looked over the bar at Ole. "Hello, big fella."

Ole stood on his hind legs with his front feet on the bar, and Margie reached over to pet him. "I can probably find you a nice bone."

Doc and Andrea took a booth across from the bar. Ole seemed inclined to stay where he was, soaking up Margie's attention.

"Ole," Doc called once.

Three of the elderly card players looked up and responded, "What?" while the dog dropped to all fours and trotted over to his master.

Margie followed him, laughing. "You came in on Ole day, Doc. Ole Olson, Ole Andersson and Ole Janssen all play cards with Gus Johansen a couple days a week."

"That must get confusing," Andrea said.

Margie grinned at her. "Not really. They all call one another by their last names just to keep things clear."

Ole the dog crawled under the table and lay across Andrea's feet while she and Doc Coggins ordered burgers and fries.

The food came promptly, and it was delicious. While Andrea and Doc ate, Ole rested his head on Andrea's lap, peering up at her beneath the edge of the table, his brown eyes wistful.

"Doc, your dog is begging."

Doc leaned under the table for a look. "He's not begging, Andrea. He has better manners than that. He's just using his pitiful-me expression in the hope that you'll feel sorry enough for him to share your food. Hamburgers are his favorite."

"I'll save you some," Andrea promised, meeting the dog's adoring gaze. "After I'm done."

She finished her burger, setting aside a few bites for Ole. Doc, who had finished already, was watching her speculatively, and Andrea was uncomfortably certain it wasn't because she had something caught in her teeth. "What is it?"

For a moment Andrea thought he was going to deny that he had anything on his mind.

Then he spoke up. "It's awkward for you at White Thunder with Mike, isn't it?"

"Yes," she admitted, but awkwardness was only part of the issue now. How much had Doc observed on his visit? He was clearly a man who could sum up a situation easily. "Mike wants to buy White Thunder. Did you know that?"

He nodded. "He's become very attached to the place. You should have seen him when he first came out here. He was a wreck. I think he might not have made it without Dan and the ranch. That's why this is so hard for him."

"What happened to him?" She stifled a nagging voice that told her she shouldn't become involved.

"He's told me a little. But Mike's a man who plays his hand close to his chest. He doesn't talk about himself much. I know he was an army ranger before his medical discharge.

He was injured on some type of training mission in Central America. I suspect there was more than training involved, but he's pretty tight-lipped about it. It's probably classified.''

"How was he hurt?"

Doc grimaced. "A land mine. He was lucky it wasn't worse, although I reckon he didn't feel too lucky at the time. He'd been engaged, apparently. The girl left him while he was recovering."

Andrea started. Mike's fiancée had left him because of his injury? Oh, God, what would he think of her if he knew about her leaving Jeffrey?

But it wasn't the same at all, she rationalized. She certainly hadn't left a wounded man in his time of need. She could never have done such a thing. Somehow, though, she doubted Mike would see the situation her way.

Well, she thought, he didn't have to know. She had no reason to tell him. It wasn't like they were involved, an impulsive kiss notwithstanding.

She glanced up to see Doc studying her curiously and realized she'd dropped the thread of their conversation. "So he came here to recuperate after getting out of the army?" she asked.

Doc watched her a moment longer, looking thoughtful, then nodded. "He came to look for the other part of his heritage, I think. The part his father abandoned." Doc looked at her. "You know about his father?"

She nodded. Mike had told her that much, at least. "I feel guilty, taking the ranch from him. I wish I could do something to help."

"Give him time. The adjustment is hard, now that he's come to depend on White Thunder, but I think things will work out. Do you want him to stay on?"

"Oh, yes," Andrea replied without thinking.

The speed of her response wasn't lost on Doc. He grinned.

"Mike's a good man, Andrea. You could do a lot worse." He paused, then added quickly, "Than to have him as an employee, I mean."

"I know what you mean," Andrea said wryly. "Thanks." Once again, she mentally weighed her options, but realized she'd already made her decision. Mike wanted to be her partner, and she needed his expertise to keep the place going. More to the point, the due date for the taxes would be here before long—she needed his money. Theirs would be a business relationship; there was no need to drag their pasts into the open.

Accepting his offer was her only choice.

"Dr. Moore!" a voice called from the doorway.

She looked up. Bert Petersen walked toward them, looking the picture of a small-town politician in an off-the-rack suit that bore a striking resemblance to the one he'd worn the other day.

"I didn't know you were in town, Dr. Moore." He stopped at their table and smiled down at her. "Afternoon, Doc."

"Bert," Doc acknowledged.

Bert returned his attention to Andrea. "How are things going at White Thunder? Have you had an opportunity to think about our discussion?"

Andrea glanced up to meet a quizzical look from Doc. She could almost hear his questions already. Never mind that they hardly knew each other. Without ever appearing to be nosy, Doc seemed to know the business of the entire town.

She wondered how he'd react to questions about UFO sightings at White Thunder.

Bert rocked from one foot to another with an air of expectation, and Andrea looked up at him.

"Yes I have, Mr. Petersen." She took a deep breath to calm the fluttering in her stomach. Was this the right choice? Once she made her decision, there'd be no backing out. "I have a partner in the ranch."

The banker's smile remained fixed, as though painted on his face. "A partner? Anyone I know?"

Andrea nodded and took another deep breath. "Mike Winterhawk, my foreman." There, it was out. She'd made it public; there was no undoing it. If only she knew whether she'd just made a dreadful mistake.

Bert's eyes widened in surprise. "Are you sure that's wise, Andrea? After our discussion? I know you're worried about the tax deadline, but shouldn't you give this a little more thought?"

"I appreciate your concern, but I think we're on the verge of solving the problems at White Thunder." Andrea glanced quickly at Doc. He was listening quietly, his expression carefully neutral, but she had little doubt he was as familiar with Bert's idiosyncrasies as Mike was.

Bert opened his mouth as if to protest, then closed it again. His smile returned, if anything brighter than before. "I hope so. I pray you're doing the right thing."

If he'd come to the Viking intending to have lunch, Bert must have forgotten about it. He turned and strode to the door.

Andrea watched him leave, frowning. *Darn*, she thought, she should have asked him about Professor Hale. She might have found out if Bert had tipped her off to the problems at White Thunder. She glanced back at Doc to find him studying her. "What?"

"You've met Bert before, I gather."

Andrea nodded. "He's Dan's banker. He had some interesting theories about White Thunder's problems."

Doc rolled his eyes. "No kidding. He's become our resident conspiracy theorist in the past year or so. Lately he's into flying saucers. It's kind of a change from his usual entrepreneurial activities.''

"So I've heard. He suggested that White Thunder's problems have something to do with UFOs.'' She took a deep breath and plunged ahead. "And hinted that Mike might know something about it.'' She waited for his reaction.

Doc just shook his head. "Well, I guess you can't have UFOs these days without a government cover-up to go along with them. Don't worry about Bert. His intentions have always been good. I don't know what's set him off in this direction, but I'm sure he doesn't mean any harm. We'll get to the bottom of White Thunder's problems sooner or later.''

"I know.''

Doc looked as though he wanted to say something further, but a shrill beep interrupted. He pulled his pager off his belt and read the message. "HBC dog coming in.'' He rose and waved to Margie, who was already on her way over with the check. "We've got a dog hit by a car coming in, Margie. We have to run.''

"Go ahead, Doc,'' the woman said. "I'll put it on your tab.''

"Thanks. You're a doll.'' Doc turned to Andrea. "I hope Mike doesn't mind driving out late to pick you up. This may take a couple hours.''

"I'm sure he won't mind,'' she replied as they hurried back to the clinic. A few more hours apart wouldn't hurt either of them.

CHAPTER TWELVE

NIGHT WAS FALLING by the time Mike received Andrea's message that she was ready to be picked up.

He headed out onto the dark highway that wound across the prairie toward town. Alone with his thoughts, he felt an oppressive and unfamiliar anxiety. Facing Andrea was going to be awkward.

It had just been a little kiss, he told himself. He'd just reacted more strongly than he'd expected. So why was he so nervous about it?

Because deep inside, he hoped it wouldn't be the last.

If that were the case, then he was a fool. He'd been alone this long, and it suited him just fine. He had White Thunder. It was all he needed.

Haven't you been hiding out here long enough?

He gave a short, derisive laugh that sounded hollow in the empty truck.

I'm not hiding.

If anything, he'd stopped hiding when he came to White Thunder. This was his home. Here he had nothing to hide.

Much.

He broke off the thought. That was the trouble with starry nights and wide-open spaces. They left a man alone with his conscience and his past.

He turned on the radio, loud, and listened to blaring country music for the rest of the drive into town. Somehow, though, the tales of lost loves and misplaced trust did nothing to ease his mind. When the lights of Rorvik came into view he was almost relieved.

The clinic was locked when he tried the door. He rang the emergency bell and stood on the porch, trying to look casual with his arms clenched in front of him to stifle an urge to shift restlessly from one foot to the other. He heard Ole bark once in response to the bell, then quick footsteps approached and the door swung open.

Doc blinked at him with weary, red-rimmed eyes. "Mike! Come in. I was half afraid we had another emergency."

Mike stepped into the bright waiting room and glanced around. Andrea was nowhere in sight. "Rough day?"

Doc yawned, nodding. "Evening, too. I'm glad Andrea was here. She's a good woman to have around. Bet you're glad she was at the ranch this afternoon." He paused and looked meaningfully at Mike for a moment.

Mike scowled, refusing to take the bait, and Doc went on unfazed. "She'll be ready to go in a few minutes. Can I get you some coffee while you wait?"

"Sure." Mike followed him back to the office, where the veterinarian poured him a steaming mug. He took a sip and grimaced slightly at its potency.

"Too strong?" Doc asked. "I'm afraid I live on the stuff, so it can be a shock if you're not expecting it."

Mike shook his head. "No, it's fine. I'm used to strong coffee. Lena believes that if you can't stand a spoon in it, it's not worth the bother."

Doc laughed. "She's a practical woman." He gestured to a chair. "Have a seat. Should be just a few minutes."

Mike sat stiffly in one of the armchairs, cradling his mug. Ole, sprawled out behind Doc's desk, rose slowly and sauntered over to lay his furry head in Mike's lap.

"What's the matter, boy?" Mike stroked the animal.

"Everyone been too busy around here to pay attention to you?"

"Doc says Ole doesn't like busy days because he has to stay up here out of the way." Andrea walked in carrying a file folder. "He's afraid he'll miss something." She placed the file on Doc's desk.

Mike's breath caught in his throat. He could smell her soft floral scent even over the medicinal odors of the clinic, and the white lab coat she wore over her jeans and T-shirt somehow managed to accentuate the gentle curves of her body.

She turned to Doc. "The collie's awake but still groggy. I put an Elizabethan collar on him to keep him away from the cast." She glanced at Mike. "The dog was hit by a car. He had internal injuries and a broken leg that had to be pinned."

"Will he be all right?" Mike asked, genuinely interested and also relieved to keep the conversation on a professional level.

"If there are no further complications," Doc replied. "I'll stay up with him awhile, then check on him through the night. Go on home, Andrea." He glanced at his watch. "It's late."

"All right. If you're sure you won't need me." She slipped out of her lab coat and handed it to the veterinarian.

"We'll be fine. And thanks again for your help." He held out his hand, and Andrea took it. "By the way, have you checked into getting your license to practice here?"

She nodded. "I've called the Department of Licensing. They're sending me the paperwork." After saying their good-nights to Doc, she and Mike walked to the truck.

The cool night made her tremble as Mike unlocked her door. She reached for the handle at the same time he did, and his fingers brushed hers. Both pulled back quickly, self-conscious.

"Sorry," she murmured, and let him open the door for her. He said nothing and she climbed into her seat, feeling his gaze on her, but not meeting his eyes.

She waited, staring into the darkness beyond the lights of Rorvik, while Mike climbed in and started the vehicle.

"I guess you were busy today." Mike's remark took her by surprise. She'd expected the usual tense silence.

"Yes. Mostly routine stuff, though, until the collie came in. Then we were really busy."

Mike turned the truck toward the highway. "I hope the dog pulls through."

"He has a good chance." Andrea relaxed into the routine of shoptalk. She didn't expect Mike to mention the morning's events but couldn't help wondering if they weighed as heavily on his mind as they did on hers.

He sat silhouetted against the night sky, watching the road ahead. The straight, strong line of his nose and the curve of his lips stood out in sharp relief. The memory of those lips on hers returned to her so clearly she could almost feel their warmth.

She hadn't meant to kiss him. And his response had been unintentional, she was certain. She'd seen the regret on his face the moment he released her. He could hardly stand to have her around. Kissing her would have been the last thing on his mind.

What would it feel like to be kissed on purpose?

Oh, God. She had promised herself she wouldn't do this, but now he was all she could think about. Supposedly people on the rebound were susceptible, but this was ridiculous.

Sinking against the seat back, she stared out the window, noticing for the first time how her back and arms ached. The aches and fatigue felt good, though, as if she'd accomplished something today. And driving home next to Mike, sharing the events of their day, seemed almost—intimate.

Was this the time to tell Mike about her decision? If so, there'd be no going back. They would be bound together by the ownership of White Thunder.

Andrea took a deep breath. If she was going to make the leap, now was the best time, before she had a chance to chicken out.

"Mike," she began hesitantly.

He glanced at her. "Yes?"

"I've thought over your offer, about the taxes on the ranch."

He looked at her more closely, one brow arched. "And?"

"I've decided to accept." The words spilled out in a rush. "We'll be partners."

A smile lit his face. "Really? That's great." He looked at her intently. "You agree, though, that if you decide not to stay, I can buy out your share?"

"Of course. *If* I decide not to stay. We can work out the details. I just need to pay the partial taxes by the end of the quarter."

"No problem. Dan can probably help us work out the particulars. Then I'll make out the check." He faced the road once more, a pleased expression curving his lips.

Andrea settled back in her seat, an unexpected sense of peace washing over her. Suddenly sleepy, she closed her eyes and relaxed to the sounds of the road. Her mind drifted and soon she was asleep.

A painful jolt brought her instantly awake.

She looked around, disoriented, and realized she was still in the truck, her head resting against Mike's arm. She shot upright. "What's wrong? Where are we?"

"At the edge of the ranch." Mike's voice was barely a whisper. "I stopped to get a better look at that." He pointed to a spot just above the horizon.

A bright light shone across their field of vision, hovering close to the ground and moving steadily past them.

"How far away is it?" Andrea asked. Distances were hard to judge out here, especially in the dark. She recalled the light she'd noticed from her bedroom window. This one seemed different somehow, but perhaps it was simply closer than the one she'd seen that night.

"Not too far. Maybe a quarter mile."

"Is it a..." She had to ask but couldn't bring herself to use the term *UFO*.

"I don't know, but I intend to find out."

He drove along the fence line until he came to a spot where the wires looped around the post to form a makeshift gate, then halted the truck and climbed out. He opened the fence, then got back into the truck and drove through. "We'll close that up on the way out. I've checked the transmitter, and the herd isn't nearby."

He turned off the headlights. The moon was bright in the clear night sky. Within moments Andrea's eyes adjusted to the darkness. A thrumming beat sounded in her ears, and she realized with a start that it was the pounding of her heart.

What were they doing out here chasing UFOs in the moonlight? This was madness! But then, her whole life had taken a very strange turn since she'd impulsively fled Seattle.

Mike's husky voice sounded in her ear. "Ready? Hold on."

She grasped the safety strap at the ceiling with her right hand and braced her left against the dash. "Ready."

The truck lunged forward into the darkness, bouncing over the rolling terrain. Andrea prayed there were no gullies or washes on this part of the ranch. She'd seen several during her travels around White Thunder over the past few days, and any one of them could do serious damage to the truck if they came upon it unaware. She gripped the strap more tightly and reached down to double-check her seat belt, just in case.

Mike accelerated, turning the truck toward the moving light. The ride became bone-jarring, as every shadow seemed to hide a pothole and every patch of grass a hillock or mound. Andrea glanced at the speedometer. It read a deceptively moderate fifteen miles per hour. It felt like fifty.

Ahead of them, the light had stopped moving and grew steadily larger as they approached. Did it know they were following? Maybe it was waiting for them.

Andrea trembled, but another jolt of the vehicle cleared her head. *There's a logical explanation for this,* she told herself, *and it's not UFOs.*

Mike slowed the vehicle to a crawl as they approached the light. He turned to Andrea. "We'd better stop here and go the rest of the way on foot to maintain the element of surprise."

"Are you sure that's a good idea? What if they're armed?"

Mike raised an eyebrow. "With alien death rays?" He reached under the seat and pulled out a long object that glinted in the moon's glow, the emasculator.

"You're going to threaten them with castration?" she asked. What if aliens don't have…"

"Actually," he interrupted before she could finish, "I had planned to use it as a club if necessary. Are you ready?"

"I guess so." She followed his lead, opening her door and letting it swing silently closed without latching.

He crouched and moved quietly through the tall grass like a commando. She followed, staying low behind him. A slight breeze swayed the grasses around her and whispered softly. She hoped the sound would muffle their approach. Mike was probably counting on it.

Now if she could just keep from doing something clumsy like stepping on a stick. Or a rattlesnake.

A tremor ran through her, and she stared at the ground ahead of her, searching for any sign of serpentine motion.

Great, why did I have to think about snakes?

Did North Dakota even have rattlesnakes?

She was still scanning the ground when she slammed into something large and solid. The impact sent her reeling backward, then someone—Mike—grabbed her arm and hauled her upright. He pulled her close, his face within inches of hers.

"They're right ahead of us." He dropped onto his stomach on the slope of a small, grassy knoll and pulled her down beside him.

She lay next to him in the high grass. The odors of earth and vegetation mingled with the clean, musky scent of Mike Winterhawk, and she breathed the fragrances deeply, her anxiety fading despite her racing pulse.

He draped his arm across her shoulders, almost protectively, but she knew it was probably so he could force her head down if they were spotted. Then he parted the grass in front of them to give them a better view of the intruders.

A battered Jeep with a single working headlight sat a few yards away, illuminating several people just beyond it.

The headlight must have been what they saw, Andrea realized. The Jeep was probably moving across the prairie to this site when they spotted it.

She watched the people working in the beam of the light. Most of them crouched on the ground, doing something with the dirt or grass. After a moment, Andrea realized they were filling small vials, taking samples.

"Anything new on the counter?" one of them asked.

"Nope. Just normal background radiation."

A short, rotund figure detached itself from the Jeep and bobbed, birdlike, into the light. It planted its hands on its hips in a gesture of exasperation. "Blast! I was sure this was the area we mapped out."

Clarissa Hale! What was the professor doing out here after she'd specifically told her she couldn't investigate on the ranch?

Another figure moved to stand beside her. "You mean we've been slogging around this godforsaken prairie all night for nothing? Look, Professor, I can't hang around this backwater forever. Either produce some spacemen or I'm outta here."

Andrea didn't need to see the speaker's face or her bleached blond hair to recognize her. It was Connie Chambers.

CHAPTER THIRTEEN

"WHAT'S THAT CHAMBERS woman doing here?" Mike's whisper was nearly lost in the sound of the night breeze.

"I don't know." Andrea remembered their Connie sighting in Minot when they'd taken the band to the bus station. The Vidtel producer had been sitting in the café with a small woman who undoubtedly had been Professor Hale. But why would Connie get involved with the professor's dubious investigations?

Clarissa Hale pulled a map from a camp table set up beside the Jeep and tilted it into the beam of the single headlight. "According to this, we should still be on federal grassland and the site's right here."

"But there's *nothing* here." Connie peered over the professor's shoulder at the map. "We must be in the wrong place." She held her wrist in the beam of the headlight. "Geez, it's past ten. You can stay out here on this wild alien chase if you want, but I'm calling it a night." She collared one of the white-coated technicians. "And you can drive me back to town, Peabody. That motel ain't much, but it beats all this dirt and grass."

Relief warred with disappointment and rising anger within Andrea. She hadn't seriously expected aliens, of course, but stumbling across the professor and Connie was definitely anticlimactic. What on earth were they doing out here?

Mike got to his feet and offered his hand to pull her up, then together they stepped out from the cover of the knoll.

He tucked her protectively behind him, apparently more concerned about their situation than she was.

Surely he didn't believe this strange little woman meant them any harm. If anything, he was going to have to protect the professor from *her*.

"I'm afraid your map's wrong, Professor Hale, Ms. Chambers," she said. "You're on White Thunder Ranch."

The professor jumped, emitting a surprised squeak, and Connie whirled to face them with a gasp, her cheeks reddening in the headlight beam.

"You're trespassing." Andrea's anger surged, and she stepped past Mike. "After I specifically told you I didn't want you investigating here." They had already caused Gypsy's injury. No telling what other damage they might have done. "What the hell are you doing here?"

The professor looked down at the map again, bewilderment in her oversized eyes. "I...I was sure we were in the right location."

Connie took the map from her and waved it at one of the technicians. "Here," she snapped. "Take this and find out where we went off course."

Professor Hale toddled toward Andrea, hands extended in supplication. "We're seeking physical evidence of extraterrestrial visitations." She reached into her coat pocket and handed Andrea a small glass vial. "That is a sample of soil from this site. We plan to have it tested for unusual compounds or radiation."

Andrea held the vial up for closer inspection. It looked like a typical handful of dirt and grass, but in this poor light, anything out of the ordinary would be difficult to see.

"Soil samples from the ranch have already been tested and nothing unusual was found. Besides, you haven't noted any radiation in this area. I heard your technician say so."

"Well, that's true." Clarissa pursed her lips unhappily. "That is, at least so far."

"And you're in the wrong location to begin with," Mike pointed out.

"We'd better be in the wrong location," Connie growled. "'Cause there sure as hell aren't any spacemen here." She fixed the professor with a piercing stare. "And if we don't find some soon, the deal's off."

"What deal is that?" Andrea asked, her suspicions that Connie played a large role in this whole mess confirmed.

The professor waved her hands at Connie. "Now, now, Ms. Chambers, science can't be rushed. I'm certain we're on the right track. It's impossible to say how widespread the alien contamination may be. All we need is evidence."

She turned back to Andrea. "Ms. Chambers has offered us a major network special. It'll provide us an even greater opportunity to get the truth about extraterrestrials to the public." Her voice dropped to a whisper. "It could be dangerous to stand in the way of our investigation. You don't understand what you're dealing with." She shot an accusatory glance at Mike.

In any other setting, the professor's dramatics would be laughable, but Andrea was in no mood for humor. She'd had enough.

"Right now, I'd say I'm dealing with a group of law breakers. You and your team had better pack your gear and follow us back to the house. We'll contact the authorities from there, and they can decide what to do with you."

The professor blinked up at Andrea, then at Mike, who stood implacable beside her. With a sigh of resignation, she and her crew began to gather their equipment. She stood to one side with a sour-looking Connie as her people loaded the Jeep. When they finished, she turned to Andrea.

"We're ready, my dear." She sighed with the air of one who had become used to suffering for science. "Lead on. I must warn you, however, that you're making a grave mistake. We're on the brink of an important discovery, and it is essential that I continue my research.''

"Well, you'll have to do it elsewhere." Andrea glanced at Mike and rolled her eyes. "Let's go."

"Our truck is a few yards back," Mike told the professor's driver. "Follow us out to the main road and we'll head up to the house from there. It's faster, and you'll do less damage that way."

"Less damage to the property or to themselves?" Andrea asked as they walked back to the truck.

"Both," Mike said. "They don't seem the four-wheeling type, and this terrain can be rough-going in the dark."

"No kidding." She massaged a sore spot on her arm, certain she'd have a whole new crop of bruises between the ride out from the road and the crawl through the underbrush.

Strangely enough, though, she'd never felt better in her life. She took a deep breath of crisp night air and felt her blood race. She was exhilarated, as though she'd never been truly alive before this night.

Mike opened her door for her. His earlier tension appeared to have dissolved, as well. Did he feel it, too? Perhaps this was what he meant when he talked about finding his place here.

Maybe for the first time, she, too, had really come home.

Mike started the engine and waited as the Jeep pulled up behind them. "What are we going to do with them, boss?"

"What would you suggest?" She hesitated, then added, "Partner."

His eyes narrowed in surprise, then he glanced quickly into the rearview mirror. "They didn't damage anything that I could see. I'd like to find out how they got onto the property. We must have some fences down along the boundary with the grassland." He met her gaze once more.

"I'd just toss 'em off the place with a threat of legal action if we see them around here again."

He put the vehicle in gear and started back the way they'd come, the Jeep following close behind.

"Ten minutes ago, I'd have been happy to throw them in jail," Andrea said. "But now, well, I guess they didn't actually do any harm. With any luck, this is the last we'll see of Professor Hale. And Connie Chambers."

The drive back seemed much shorter than the bumpy trip out. Within a few minutes, they reached the opening in the fence where they'd entered. Mike got out to refasten the wires before they continued on to the ranch house, the Jeep right behind them.

Dan stepped out onto the porch as they pulled into the drive and stopped in front of the house.

"Where have you been?" The older man sounded worried. "Doc said you left his place over an hour ago."

Lena, wrapped in a chenille robe of blazing fuchsia, joined him on the step, followed by the members of the band. "We were afraid you might have had an accident."

"I'm sorry. We didn't even consider that you might wait up." Had they really called Doc to check up on Mike and her? Andrea felt like a teenager coming home from a date after curfew. And poor Doc. The last thing he needed was to sit up worrying about them.

Dan seemed to register the presence of the Jeep. "Who's that with you?"

"We took a little detour on the way home to check out some strange lights," Mike explained as a contrite-looking Clarissa Hale climbed out of her vehicle. "And guess who we ran into?"

"Were they out there looking for the UFOs, too?" Stench asked. He peered into the Jeep, then looked aghast. "Hey, isn't that...?"

Andrea nodded. "Yep. Connie Chambers. She and the

professor have some sort of deal going for a new television program about aliens. But they weren't exactly *looking* for the UFOs out there. They *were* the UFOs."

"You mean they were the cause of those lights Andrea saw the other night?" Dan asked.

Mike nodded. "It looks like it."

"Now wait." Professor Hale scowled at him and puffed herself up to her full four foot eight. "Let's not jump to conclusions here. When did you see lights out there, Dr. Moore?"

Andrea thought a moment. So much had happened since her arrival, the days all seemed to run together. "The first night I was here. And it was just a single light." *Like the headlight on your Jeep,* she thought.

The professor clapped her hands. "Ha!" she shouted triumphantly. "We were in Minot until just yesterday. The light you saw couldn't have been us."

Dan stepped forward. "Well, whatever it was, I'm sure there's a reasonable explanation. But now, I think you and your people should leave. It's getting late, and Andrea and Mike have had a long day."

He took the professor's arm and gently steered the protesting woman back toward her vehicle.

"Wait," she chirped, trying to wiggle loose. She broke free and turned to Andrea, her arms outstretched in one final appeal. "Please, Dr. Moore. Don't let the conspiracy silence you, too."

"Sorry, Professor," Andrea replied. Frankly, she'd take actual aliens over Clarissa Hale any day. They had to be less trouble. "If I find you on my property again, I'll have to press charges."

Clarissa let her arms drop to her sides. "Fine. Well, you've made your decision, then. But something is going on out here, Andrea. Something not of this world. Trust no one." She glared at Mike, then turned abruptly, marched back to the Jeep and climbed in. The vehicle drove away with Clarissa Hale staring out at Andrea, her myopic gaze intense.

"Whoa." Todd jumped off the porch, landing next to Andrea. "That's one spooky lady."

"And more than a little paranoid, I'd say." Mike shook his head as he watched the Jeep drive off. He leaned on the porch rail next to Andrea. "Think they'll be back?"

"It wouldn't surprise me," she said. "I suspect the professor isn't one to give up easily. And I know Connie isn't. My only hope is that she'll get fed up and leave. That might cool the professor down a notch. Otherwise, we'll probably find ourselves on her show, portrayed as part of some big government cover-up."

She looked up at him, wondering how much to say. He had a right to know the whole truth. He was her partner now, after all.

"She accused you of being some kind of secret agent involved in the conspiracy, you know?" She said it flippantly but watched closely for his reaction.

"Is that what she was scowling about?" Mike laughed. "I hope the fact that you're telling me this means you don't believe her."

"Ooh, yeah," Jock chimed in. "Maybe he's part of the Hangar 51 bunch."

"Hangar 18, Area 51," Stench corrected him. "Right. He's helping cover up raids by alien cattle rustlers." He waved an arm over his head, spinning an imaginary lasso. "Head 'em up and beam 'em out."

Mike groaned. "I think you guys just bought yourselves a trip out to mend fences tomorrow. Early." He glanced at Andrea. He had what he wanted from her. They were partners, and if she decided to leave, the ranch would be his.

Another hard day's work might help to give her second thoughts about whether she wanted to stay on. Of course, he'd thought putting her to work in the barn replacing planks would, too, and she'd taken that in stride. The woman was made of hardier stuff than he'd expected. She'd proved that on their wild search for UFOs.

Chances were that a little more hard work wouldn't scare her away, either. The realization should have bothered him more than it did.

Dan laughed. "I think that's a hint that you'd better call it a night, fellas." He turned to Mike and Andrea. "I'm going to do the same myself. Will you give Gypsy her medication?"

Andrea nodded. "We'll take care of it, Dan. Good night."

"'Night," Dan replied, and went inside.

Lena grabbed her in a sudden, awkward hug that could have cracked a rib. "I'm glad you're all right. Don't you dare scare us like that again." She hurried into the house, leaving Andrea staring after her openmouthed.

Stench yawned loudly. "I guess this country air is finally getting to me, too."

Todd followed suit. "I think it's the work, not the air." He glanced at his watch. "Man, do you realize how long we've been up already, and it's not even close to midnight."

"It's terrible." Jock ran a hand through his brown curls. "I hope my parents don't find out that I've been going to bed before eleven o'clock. I'll never live it down."

Andrea laughed. "I won't tell. Cross my heart, Jock. But you're welcome to stay up awhile longer and help with Gypsy."

"No, that would be even harder on my reputation," he replied. "Unless you really need an extra person, that is." He grinned, but his offer was serious.

She shook her head. "We'll manage without you. Go on to bed."

The boys said their good-nights as they struggled to hold back yawns, then headed for their trailer, leaving Mike and Andrea alone on the darkened front porch.

Mike shifted uneasily against the porch rail, his hands in his pockets, feeling he should say something. He was relieved when Andrea spoke first.

"I'll get Gypsy's medication together if you'll get the marshmallows," she said. "I could use a flashlight, too, if you have one handy. To check her sutures."

"Sure. I'll meet you at the corral." He started to turn away, then stopped himself. "You didn't answer my question."

"Question?" She frowned a moment, then her expression cleared. "Oh, about Clarissa's accusations." She stared up at him. "No, Mike. I don't believe her."

"Thanks." He smiled briefly, then forced his eyes away from hers and turned toward the house. "Wait for me before you go into the corral."

"Don't worry, I won't take any chances." She started for the corral as he went into the house.

Inside, everything was quiet except for gentle snoring already coming from Lena's room. Dan was probably asleep, as well.

Mike walked quietly to the kitchen and selected a handful of marshmallows for Gypsy's medicine, wrapped the candy in a paper towel and headed out to where Andrea waited by the corral.

She turned at his approach, the breeze tousling her dark curls. The bison stood beside her at the rail, waiting for her treat. Andrea caressed the big animal's nose while Gypsy snuffled and pressed closer to the fence.

"She's getting impatient," Andrea murmured. "She knows I'm out here for a reason and she expects something for her trouble."

Mike laughed. "I brought them. She can have one as soon as we can squeeze a pill into it."

He walked to the fence rail beside her, conscious of her closeness, her fragrance.

He handed her the marshmallows, and she took one and embedded a big capsule in it.

"Want to give her the first one?" She held it out to him.

Gypsy watched her hand, following it with her nose as Andrea reached toward Mike, and snorted impatiently.

"We'd better hurry, before she comes over the fence after it." Mike offered Gypsy the medicated marshmallow in his palm.

The bison strained toward him and slurped up the treat. She swallowed it and looked around eagerly for another, which Andrea prepared.

Andrea held the candy out to Gypsy and laughed as the pink tongue tickled her hand.

She glanced at Mike. Their eyes met, and this time he found himself unable to look away.

Andrea blinked and dropped her gaze, turning back to the animal. "You're a good girl, Gypsy. One more and we're done," she said.

She was good with the bison, Mike thought. She was good at a lot of things. He'd trust her with Gypsy and with the ranch, he realized, both wounded things that needed a healer's touch.

Could he trust her to heal his own wounds?

He shook away the thought. This wasn't what he wanted. The ranch was his, the key to his future. And there was no place in that future for Andrea Moore.

She medicated the last marshmallow and offered it to Mike. He shook his head. "Go ahead."

She fed the bison its final treat.

Around them, the night was cool and breezy, filled with

the scents of the spring prairie. A gust swirled around them and Andrea, dressed in her T-shirt and jeans, shivered.

Almost without conscious thought, Mike slipped off his denim jacket and laid it over her shoulders. His fingers brushed her throat as he settled it around her.

She gazed up at him, her eyes suddenly questioning, and he realized she was close enough to kiss. All he had to do was lean toward her.

But with his hesitation, the moment passed.

She leaned on the corral rail, watching the sky. "Do you think there really are UFOs?"

Mike released a pent-up breath slowly, grateful for the distraction. "I don't know," he answered honestly. "But I don't think that's what we're dealing with here."

She turned to him, her expression serious. "Neither do I. But if not, what *are* we dealing with?"

He shook his head. "We'll just have to keep our eyes open for anything unusual. We'll find out what's going on, don't worry."

"I hope so," she said. "Gypsy's due soon, and I'd like to have this resolved before we have a newborn calf to worry about."

Mike stared up into the starry sky. A glint of motion caught his eye. A shooting star. His mother had always told him to wish on a shooting star. If the event had any symbolic meaning to his father's people, he had yet to learn of it.

He watched the star fade away, a dying ember against the black velvet sky. All of a sudden he had too many wishes to make. A skyful of stars wouldn't be enough.

CHAPTER FOURTEEN

AT THE KITCHEN TABLE, Mike gulped a mouthful of steaming coffee, hoping the heat, if not the caffeine, would jolt him awake. Todd, Jock and Stench, all eagerly helping themselves to pancakes and sausages, for once looked more awake than he was.

"So we're going to mend fences out on the back-forty, huh?" Stench asked with a cheerfulness that was unaccountably irritating this morning.

"Yep," Mike said shortly, taking in Stench's appearance.

The blond singer had pulled his long hair back into a serviceable, if not exactly conservative, ponytail. He wore a T-shirt tucked into jeans that, while they had seen better days, weren't pocked with the strategically placed holes Mike had noticed in some of the young man's other clothes.

Todd and Jock looked almost normal, too, at least by Rorvik standards. Todd's white-blond hair, ordinarily plastered into spikes, lay naturally atop his head. Jock, the least outrageous of the bunch, had run a comb through his mat of brown curls and slicked them down into a semblance of order.

Whatever was going on with them, and Mike didn't want to ask, it was certainly an improvement. Andrea would be shocked at the change in Rusting Hulkk's appearance.

The thought of Andrea brought back the image he'd struggled with through the night: her standing beside the corral wrapped in his denim jacket, dark hair tossed by the breeze. She'd left the garment lying across the sofa when she went upstairs for the night. When he'd picked it up to put it away, her floral scent had lingered on the fabric like a breath of summer.

He'd held it for just a moment, breathing in her fragrance, then he'd hung the jacket in the closet and retired to his makeshift bed on the sofa.

Doc's early-morning phone call had awakened him, and he'd lain in the dark listening to Andrea in her room. She'd crept past him and out through the kitchen, careful to stay quiet, not knowing he was already wide awake.

He took another careless swallow of hot coffee, grateful for the brief pain as it burned the image of her from his mind. He had to get her off the ranch. It was his only chance for his future—and for his sanity.

"Where's Andrea this morning?" Stench asked.

Mike threw him a sharp glance, wondering for a moment if his thoughts were etched on his face. But the singer's expression indicated only curiosity.

"Doc called this morning to ask her help with an emergency calving," Lena said, replenishing Stench's stack of pancakes. "She headed out around four-thirty."

Stench grimaced. "Four-thirty? That's the middle of the night."

"Yeah, I thought about rousting you boys out then," Mike teased. This was the Stench he knew. Apparently the band's changing attitudes didn't extend to adopting ranchers' hours. At least, not yet. "But I figured you'd do a better job on the fences if you could actually see them. Barbed wire's hard to work with in the dark."

Stench raised one eyebrow. "Thanks. We appreciate your concern."

"Yeah," Todd said. "Especially since Jock kept us up half the night looking for aliens."

"I did not." Jock wadded up a paper napkin and tossed

it at his friend's head. "I just…wanted to look at the stars, that's all. You don't see them this clearly back home." He blushed, reddening to the tips of his ears.

Dan came in through the back door. "Morning, Mike, boys." He looked at Jock. "Hopefully all the aliens left with that professor woman and her friends." He took off his hat and hung it on a rack beside the door, then, ignoring Lena's threatening look, poured himself a cup of coffee.

"I've given Gypsy her medicine, Mike, so don't worry about it this morning." He tossed a folded newspaper on the table. "Strike's still on, too, fellas. They're expecting it to last through next week, but you're welcome to stay on as long as you want."

"Good," Lena said from the stove, where she was frying eggs. "These boys are just starting to fill out. If they left now, they'd undo all the good I've done."

She carried a platter to the table and served eggs to Mike and the band. Dan watched with a hungry expression, but she shook her head. "You've had your egg allowance for the week, Dan Amundson. I've got pancakes and turkey sausage coming for you. If you want eggs, I can whip up some of the substitute stuff, but that's it."

Dan scowled. "Darn it, Lena. I can take care of myself."

Lena snorted. "Since when? You'd have been dead a year ago if it wasn't for my cooking and your own orneriness."

"Better dead than trying to survive on that imitation food you keep trying to feed me," Dan snapped. "What kind of life am I supposed to have with that stuff, anyway?"

"A long one." Lena plopped a stack of pancakes in front of him. "Now eat that so you can get out of my kitchen."

Mike hid a smile. Dan and Lena went through this every morning. He was glad to see her mothering the older man. She was right—Dan needed someone to take care of him.

Everyone did. He wondered what would become of them once Andrea took over the ranch for good.

"Well, maybe the boys will still be here for the Memorial Day weekend. It's only a couple of weeks away." Lena said. All traces of her previous annoyance had disappeared.

"Ya, sure," Dan said over a forkful of pancakes and syrup. He, too, had apparently forgotten their argument. "You'll enjoy that. And it'll get you off the ranch for a few hours."

"What do you do on Memorial Day?" Todd asked.

"Well, there's a memorial ceremony, then a picnic at the lake," Dan replied. "There are usually booths set up with games and baked goods. Then there's a white elephant auction and a dance."

"A dance?" Stench asked. "Do they have a band?"

"They got a group playing polka music this year," Dan said.

Reaching across for the platter of pancakes, Todd grimaced. "If you call that music. Hey, maybe if we brought our instruments, they'd let us play if they have amps and stuff."

"They might," Dan said. "I suppose the younger folks might appreciate something new. You're welcome to my old accordion, though, if that'll help." He gave them a teasing grin.

"Uh, gee, thanks, Mr. Amundson." Stench sounded almost sincere. "We'll let you know if we need it."

They all laughed, and Mike rose from the table. "Well, if you fellows are done, why don't we head out and mend some fences before we get any more unwelcome guests."

The boys stood, too, looking less than anxious for the work to begin now that it was actually time to start. They thanked Lena for breakfast and followed Mike out of the house.

Andrea met Mike and the boys as they were on their way out. "Going out to look for wherever the professor got in, huh? Do you need to mend fences a lot?" Like everything else around the ranch, it was something she needed to learn about. She was tired from her early morning and the exertion of the calving but was still eager to get to work on her ranch.

"Not too often," Mike replied. "I get out and check them periodically, just to be on the safe side, but after last night's guests, I wouldn't be surprised if we have some down." He smiled crookedly and asked, "Do you want to come along? We can wait a bit while you get freshened up."

"Thanks. I'll just be a few minutes. No sense getting too cleaned up if I'm just going out to get dirty again." She trotted into the house and dashed upstairs for a quick wash that eliminated the worst of the morning's stickiness.

When she came down again, the boys were loaded in the back of the truck, next to a stack of boards and a bale of barbed wire from which they were all careful to keep their distance.

Mike flipped open the lid of the storage compartment in the bed of the truck and pulled out a pair of rawhide gloves. "Here. You'll need those." He tossed them to her, then looked over her jeans and T-shirt, frowning. "Don't you have a jacket? You'll need some protection from the wire for your arms."

She shook her head. "Nothing I can really work in," she said, feeling like the worst sort of city slicker. She'd never considered that she might need to dress for barbed wire.

"No problem," he said. "Wait here." He dashed into the house and reappeared a few moments later carrying his denim jacket, which he tossed to her. "Put that on. It'll be big, but it's better than nothing."

She slipped on the jacket he'd loaned her the night before. It bore his scent like a memory. "Thanks."

He gave a quick nod, his eyes bright in the morning sunlight. "Okay, load up," he said.

The drive across the property gave Andrea a chance to see a great deal of the ranch for the first time, though she had to admit that once out of sight of the house and barn, one part of White Thunder looked pretty much like another to her uneducated eye.

Rocky, rolling grassland was punctuated here and there by knolls too small to actually be called hills, or by gullies created by flowing streams. Occasionally they passed marshy areas dotted with large white birds.

"The marshes are drier this year because we've had a dry spring," Mike explained. "There's usually a lot more water out there. It's almost a lake in wet years."

"What are those birds?" Andrea asked.

"Pelicans. They like the wetlands out here."

"I've always thought of pelicans as seabirds," Andrea said. "Strange that they'd migrate inland like this."

Mike nodded. "Sometimes we have dozens of them. They're worse around the big lakes. They've even been known to deplete the fish supply in some areas."

"That's amazing." She settled back and watched the huge birds until they were out of sight of the marsh.

This land was incredible, she thought, fresh and open and unspoiled, as though man had never discovered it. She was amazed that such places still existed. It was different from home, of course, but beautiful in its own way.

Home.

This was home now, she realized. How long before she started thinking about it that way?

Mike started along the fence line, scanning the wire and posts for any sign of a break. At last he found what he was looking for. "Here we are," he said, pulling the truck to a stop. The post next to them marked the end of the fence for several hundred feet. "It's worse than I thought," he said, climbing out of the truck to survey the damage.

Andrea and the boys followed.

"Wow!" Todd said. "Is it normal to have such a long stretch down?"

Mike shook his head. "No. It looks like that professor and her bunch just barreled right on through here."

"No wonder they had a headlight out," Andrea said. "Do you think they knew what they were doing?"

He shrugged. "Who knows? I'd like to think they didn't do it on purpose. It's likely some of the fence was down already and they just pulled the rest with them when they went through. In any case, it's going to keep us busy the rest of the day."

Andrea looked out across the prairie beyond the fence line. "What's out there?" she asked.

Mike followed the direction of her gaze. "Federal grassland."

"And what are those?" she asked, pointing to a series of towers beyond the fence line a few hundred yards away, near a rare clump of trees.

He came to stand beside her at the fence. "Radio transmitters or receivers of some kind. Antennae, maybe? They've been there for years." He frowned, staring at the tall steel structures. "The feds apparently change them periodically, though. Those smaller antennae, the ones aimed toward the ranch, were installed just a couple years ago." He shrugged dismissively and turned back to the truck, where the boys were already busy unloading the wood. They'd left the bale of wire for him, though, Andrea noticed. She glanced back at the towers. Cell phones, probably. A threat to low-flying aircraft, maybe, but not to White Thunder. Still, something nagged at the back of her mind....

"So, ready to get started?" Mike asked.

For the next several hours, Andrea worked like she'd never worked before. She took her turn with the saw, cutting posts to length to repair rotted or broken ones along the expanse of downed fence. Mike showed her how to handle the wicked-looking barbed wire without ripping her hands to shreds and how to cut long sections to join to the posts once they were secured in the ground. Some older areas of the fence were board, not wire, and these they replaced as needed where the wood had become too decayed.

"Are these fences actually strong enough to keep the bison inside?" Stench asked, testing one old timber that flexed dangerously under pressure.

"Not if they really want out," Mike said. "Not much would hold them then. These are more a deterrent than anything else. Bison tend to head in the path of least resistance, so they'll usually turn away from a fence rather than going through."

"Have you tried electrified fencing?" Andrea asked.

"We have, but it's too expensive for this large an area. Besides, with the bison's heavy coats, the shock isn't too convincing."

After handling Gypsy, Andrea understood. Few physical measures would deter a bison from going wherever it chose. On the other hand, as long as the animals had enough to eat and sufficient territory, they were unlikely to wander far. At White Thunder, the bison had pretty much everything they could want and then some.

So why weren't they breeding? The question nagged at her as they worked through the day, breaking only briefly for the sandwiches and cookies Lena had packed.

By late afternoon, the fence was whole again. Andrea crawled into the truck, sore, sunburned and exhausted, to collapse against the seat. The boys were similarly arranged in the back. She noticed for the first time that they'd started to acquire healthy tans since their arrival at the ranch.

She smiled at Mike as he climbed into the truck and started the engine.

"Tired?" he asked, studying her with an expectant expression.

"I've never been more tired in my life."

"Well, uh, you did a pretty decent job out there." He turned his attention to the drive, then added, "I just wanted to let you know."

For the first time since coming to White Thunder, Andrea felt that maybe she was home after all.

CHAPTER FIFTEEN

FOR THE NEXT COUPLE of weeks, Andrea stayed busy working with Mike and the band doing repairs and various chores around the ranch, when not helping at Doc's. She'd wanted to be a part of the work around White Thunder. Now she found herself up to her neck in it.

Amazingly, she enjoyed it. Nothing she'd done in her life matched her sense of accomplishment at caring for this land and its animals. The work increased her sense of belonging at the ranch, and her sense that the others believed she belonged here. Even weeding Lena's vegetable garden gave her a feeling of achievement and kinship with the land.

And with Mike. Andrea was honest enough to admit to herself she enjoyed his company and enjoyed sharing the day-to-day events around White Thunder. As never before, the ranch was a common ground on which they could meet, and he seemed to be thawing toward her.

In her spare time, Lena gave her cooking lessons, teaching her to make *lefse,* thin Scandinavian potato pancakes that reminded her of tortillas, and other traditional dishes for the Memorial Day picnic.

Memorial Day dawned bright and sunny with just a lingering hint of crispness. The day's activities, Lena had told her, would begin with a ceremony at the Amundson family cemetery. The picnic and dance would follow later in the afternoon.

For the ceremony, Andrea selected one of the dresses

from her trousseau, a lightweight floral in shades of jade, white and fuchsia, topped with a jade jacket she hoped would keep her warm enough. Even at the end of May, North Dakota's weather was a far cry from Hawaii's.

She took the stairs carefully, out of practice with the high heels and smooth soles of her strappy jade sandals. Dan, Mike and the band waited in the living room.

The boys had either been shopping or had kept their good clothes hidden since their arrival at the ranch. Jock wore pleated tan trousers and a collarless white dress shirt. Todd was dressed in black pants with a shirt of bronze-colored linen, his white hair gelled down for the occasion.

Stench wore unrelieved black, a look that Andrea felt achieved its dramatic intent, especially given the contrast with his long blond hair, which was pulled back and tied Colonial-style with a thin satin ribbon.

"Wow!" she said. "I'm impressed. You guys clean up nicely."

All three, even the worldly Stench, beamed with obvious pleasure.

"So do you, boss," Mike remarked from the kitchen doorway.

Andrea looked up with a start, and her intended retort caught in her throat at the sight of him. His light tan tweed sport coat, worn over an open-collared cream shirt, molded to the broad lines of his shoulders and the muscular shape of his strong arms. Beneath it, slim black jeans accentuated his long legs.

His well-worn brown boots had been abandoned for a polished black pair. He looked like a cross between a cowboy and a college professor.

"You look great," he said, his voice low.

"You, too," she replied, feeling as if they were the only people in the room. Then she caught a quick exchange of raised brows between Stench and Todd, a knowing look that had her suddenly flushing warmly.

"Whew, you fellas look fantastic! You, too, Andrea." Lena exploded from the back bedroom in a cloud of purple crepe that made her look like an overgrown violet with a bright red center. Her pantsuit ebbed and flowed around her as she swept into the room.

After the initial moment of stunned surprise, Andrea had to admit the ensemble suited the flamboyant older woman. Lena clearly knew how to take a fashion chance and make it pay off.

Dan stepped out of the kitchen and stared at Lena. His eyes widened with first shock, then admiration, and he stepped forward to take her arm.

"Are we ready?" In his tan chinos and plaid sport shirt, Dan looked like a dapper moth next to Lena's butterfly splendor.

Mike reached out to take Andrea's arm. She struggled to ignore the tremor within her that his touch induced. Why on earth was she reacting this way to the man? She'd left Jeffrey only a couple of weeks earlier. So where was her self-control?

"Are you cold?" Concern darkened Mike's eyes. "Will that jacket be enough? It's not very warm out."

"I'm fine," Andrea said as they headed out the door. She tried to recall any time in her relationship with Jeffrey when she had responded so ardently to his touch, but not a single instance came to mind.

But she'd been engaged to him! Had she really felt nothing?

They all loaded into the station wagon. Andrea climbed in and fumbled with her seat belt as Mike took the seat next to her.

The air around them seemed charged, electrical, and she found herself edging toward the window as she tried to

resist her attraction to him. Did Mike sense it, too? She
stole a glance at him. He appeared calm and relaxed. The
observation annoyed her but at the same time brought her
back to reality.

She took several deep breaths and stared out the window
to distract herself.

It was working, she thought, feeling herself relax. If he
didn't smell quite so good, she'd hardly notice him next to
her.

Dan turned out of the driveway onto the gravel road to
the highway. The car lurched sharply to one side, then back
again, the force throwing Andrea hard against Mike's
shoulder. He flinched as if burned by the sudden contact,
then grasped her arm to steady her.

"We have to do something about that pothole." His
hand still gripped her forearm and his voice was husky.
"Are you okay?"

"Yes, I'm fine," she replied, unaccountably breathless.

He loosened his grip, but his hand remained where it
was, resting lightly on her arm where her slightest movement away from him would dislodge it.

He was offering her the choice.

Move! her mind shouted at her. *You don't want this!*

But her mind was no longer in control. She didn't look
up for fear of meeting Mike's gaze but stayed where she
was, knowing she was probably making a mistake.

Mike fought to relax, forcing his breathing to slow, med-
itating as Tony Gray Elk had taught him. He recognized
the exhilaration. He'd felt it last just prior to his mission in
Honduras.

He almost laughed. He was taking a chance, sure, but
this wasn't like going into combat. That he should feel the
same heady mixture of exultation and terror in response to
this woman surprised him. He'd told himself he didn't need
anyone else, and he'd almost managed to convince himself.

But something about Andrea was different. The moments they'd shared already had touched a chord in him that had lain dormant for a very long time. He'd tried to show her what she was up against, hoping to scare her off, but she'd stood up to every task. Suddenly the realization that she planned to stay no longer held any fear for him.

To Andrea, the drive seemed to last both forever and no time at all. The sudden halt of the car brought her out of her reverie. Mike's hand left her arm and she felt momentarily chilled, the spell broken.

"Hey, where the heck are we?" Todd asked from the back seat.

"Boy," Jock said, "this really is the middle of nowhere."

Mike opened his door and stepped out, then turned to help Andrea. She met his eyes as she put her hand in his. His gaze was intense. She climbed out quickly and turned her attention to their surroundings.

Jock wasn't far wrong about the middle of nowhere. Rolling green-and-tan prairie stretched away from them in all directions as far as she could see. They'd stopped beside a low stone wall, the only manmade feature visible in the sea of grassland. Other cars were parked nearby, and Andrea watched several small groups of people walk into the stone enclosure through a narrow opening flanked by wildly blooming lilac bushes.

Dan led them inside to join the others.

Around them, set into deep green and carefully maintained grass, stood numerous small headstones, engraved brass plaques and memorial statues. Lilacs grew randomly around the little cemetery, some of them a dozen feet tall, their perfume mingling with the clean scents of fresh-mowed lawn and dewy morning air.

Several people, a few of whom Andrea recognized from Rorvik or from her rounds with Doc, wandered among the

markers. Some stopped to place flowers or tokens on the
graves, others to reflect or to read the epitaphs, their soft
voices indistinguishable from the gently sighing breeze.

Todd and Jock read some of the gravestones, talking quietly but nervously, clearly somewhat uncomfortable with
the surroundings.

Mike apparently sensed their nervousness, as well. "The
service will start in a few minutes, guys." As for himself,
he became aware of the peace of this place and embraced
it.

Andrea was in no hurry, either, despite the cool dew
soaking her nylons through her light sandals. She breathed
the fragrant air, her turmoil fading as an overwhelming
sense of peace settled over her.

Dan and Lena moved around the growing crowd, greeting friends and chatting as though this were any ordinary
social event. The observation brought home to Andrea once
again how death was such a part of life out here.

The rumble of an engine broke the stillness. Andrea
glanced toward the sound to see a ramshackle yellow
school bus lumbering up the road toward them. It squealed
to a halt just outside the cemetery.

The milling crowd inside the walls coalesced to form an
audience as the doors of the bus creaked open. A squad of
men, mostly elderly and all in uniform, shambled out, bearing gleaming rifles.

Their leader, in a uniform of World War II vintage,
yelled "Fall in!" His voice, though hoarse with age, still
carried the tone of authority and strength.

The men formed up in a single line, their backs straight
and heads held erect.

"Forward, hunh," the squad leader half yelled, half
grunted in the familiar military command.

An unexpected shiver ran along Andrea's spine. She
hadn't heard that sound in years—not since the last training

base where her father had been stationed. Memories came flooding back, not all of them pleasant. Her lonely adolescence spent moving from one place to another, her conflicts with a mother she could never seem to please.

But there were memories of happy times, as well; her memories of her dad, the Fourth of July picnic at the base the year she turned fourteen, the places she'd visited and the people she'd met. She looked at Mike. Their backgrounds were similar. Was he feeling the same conflicting emotions?

He stood at attention as the squad passed, his expression unreadable. Then he met her gaze and smiled, and Andrea knew that he was recalling a past much like her own. White Thunder wasn't the only thing they shared.

A chaplain accompanying the party gave a solemn invocation, then asked for a moment of silence from the attendees. When heads were raised once more following the prayer, the commander of the rifle squad ordered, "Present arms."

The old soldiers raised their rifles.

"Ready, aim," the commander ordered. The men angled their weapons upward to their left.

"Fire!" shouted the commander.

The simultaneous blast of seven rifles pierced the morning stillness, then was repeated on the officer's order.

Andrea felt goose bumps prickle her flesh as the echoes faded across the plains.

"Order arms!" the officer commanded.

The riflemen lowered their weapons, returning to attention, then right-faced on their officer's order and marched slowly and ceremoniously back to the old school bus.

"Now what happens?" Todd asked Mike softly.

"They'll drive on to the next little cemetery for another ceremony," Mike answered. "They'll probably do six or eight of these this morning."

"I've never seen anything like that," Stench said.

He wouldn't have admitted it to anyone, Andrea knew, but she could tell he was deeply moved by the event. They all were.

"Now we'll go back to the ranch and change for the picnic," Mike said. "It's not quite as solemn as this. More like a Fourth of July picnic. It's kind of a kickoff for summer."

He was right. The picnic was held at a small lake near Rorvik that was unlike any Andrea had ever seen. It looked as if a water-filled depression in the green prairie, fed by snow melt and early spring rains, had somehow taken on a life of its own. Concrete picnic shelters stood at intervals around its perimeter, offset with a few small nursery trees that had clearly been planted for the purpose of providing future shade.

"Is the lake man-made?" she asked Mike as they climbed out of the truck near a shelter hung with red, white and blue bunting.

"No, it's natural. The climate just doesn't support the forest area you usually see around lakes in other parts of the country."

Around them, other arrivals unloaded hampers and dishes from their vehicles. Others carried strange objects, bowls and vases, birdhouses on tall posts, quilts and hand-stitched pillows and a whole variety of items, some attractive and many less so.

"What's all that stuff for?" Todd asked.

"For the auction," Dan said. "We use the money for upkeep on the picnic area and lake."

Lena handed him a box. "That's my donation," she told Todd. "It's some doilies and things I've crocheted over the past couple months. Mostly folks bring crafts or white elephant items. Sometimes people bring surprises in sealed bags and you have to bid without knowing what you're getting." She grinned in anticipation.

They helped unload Lena's contributions to the massive potluck dinner spreading out across the center tables. She had brought *lefse,* along with butter and sugar to put on them, caramel rolls, potato salad and fried chicken. These offerings joined other salads, more chicken, ham, a variety of casseroles or "hot dishes," deviled eggs and an incredible array of cakes, cookies and dessert bars. The boys immediately headed for the buffet.

"Leave a bite or two for everyone else," Lena reminded them, watching them fondly. She shook her head. "And I thought grown men were bad. Those three are eating machines."

Andrea looked at the line forming at the tables. "Well, they have some competition," she noted.

Lena grimaced. "You're right. We'd better get over there or there won't be anything left but bones. If that."

A cacophony of tuning instruments filled the air.

Dan's eyes lit up. "That's my cue."

Lena looked at him disapprovingly. "Don't you think you should eat first? It's nearly one o'clock."

He scowled. "Nope. I have more important things to do." He snapped open his accordion case and hefted the instrument onto his hip. "Relax, woman. They've never run out of food at one of these things yet. I'll eat later." With that, he headed over to the spot where a group of several men were warming up fiddles, banjos and accordions.

Within a few minutes the sound of a lively polka filled the air. Children gathered, clapping and dancing, far too excited to follow their parents' admonitions to sit and have lunch first.

Several couples, preferring to whet their appetites with some exercise, cleared space on the smooth concrete to create a dance floor. They stepped and whirled to the music, providing an enjoyable show for those who had chosen to eat first.

Among the older picnickers, two camps developed as the men and women separated to discuss their mutual interests. Andrea joined Lena at a table with a number of women, most of them older than she, and sat eating quietly as they talked about domestic issues. Every so often one of them would throw a polite question her way, as though they wanted to try to include her in the conversation but weren't sure how to go about it.

She had little in common with these women, she thought self-consciously. They were part of her new community, though, and while she knew she might never be completely at ease with them, she wanted to make the effort to fit in as best she could.

Mike seemed to have done it. From everything she knew about his background, he had come to Rorvik in much the same situation as she, with very little in common with the locals. Yet now, although he'd been here a relatively short time, he seemed to be accepted and well liked by the community.

She searched the crowd and found him in the center of the men, talking animatedly with a dark-haired youngish man she didn't recognize. He appeared completely at ease.

Her resolve strengthened. If he could do it, she thought, she could, too.

"Who's that with Mike?" she asked Lena.

Lena glanced at the man. "Oh, that's Tony Gray Elk. Tony's a shaman, but he teaches Native American history at the community college. He's a good friend of Mike's."

A shaman? With his casual brown cords and tan sport coat, he looked nothing like Andrea's conception of a tribal medicine man.

Mike glanced up as he felt Andrea's gaze. He seemed to

have a sixth sense about her, as though they were linked through their thoughts.

She looked a little uncomfortable sitting there with the local ladies. He knew the feeling. Never having been a highly social person, anyway, he'd felt like a terrible outsider when he first came to White Thunder.

Dan and Lena had helped a great deal during those rough months simply by involving him in the day-to-day operation of the ranch and giving him some common ground on which to meet the people of the area. And his association with Tony had helped give him his spiritual connection to the land.

He could see that Andrea was already starting to fall in love with the place. He'd realized that when he'd seen her during the memorial ceremony. In a few months she'd be right at home here. So what would that mean for him? He could no longer deny his attraction to her, despite the fact that every instinct told him to keep his distance. It was becoming increasingly clear that she had no intention of leaving the ranch.

He watched her across the picnic area. She had traded her dress for dark blue jeans and a crisp white linen blouse. She wore her hair down today, and the dark curls cascaded loosely around her shoulders.

Once more he imagined twining his fingers in those soft tresses. He recalled their drive this morning, the smooth skin of her hand beneath his, and his pulse quickened.

"That must be the new boss, eh?" Tony asked with a nod toward Andrea. "You want to introduce me?"

Mike gave a wry smile and led the way across the picnic ground to where Andrea sat.

"I'd like to introduce a friend," he said. He gestured to Tony. "Meet Tony Gray Elk. He teaches at the community college in Williston."

She offered her hand. "How do you do?"

"Fine, thanks," Tony said. "Welcome to Rorvik. I've heard a lot about you." He glanced at Mike. "All of it good."

Andrea's eyes met Mike's, then returned to Tony. "I'm happy to hear that."

"He tells me Gypsy's calf is a female," Tony said. He turned to Mike. "Have you told her the story of White Buffalo Woman, Mike?" He looked at Andrea. "It's an important legend of our people."

Mike shook his head. "No, I haven't. Not yet."

Tony grinned. "Well, see that you do. Consider it a homework assignment. The telling of stories is almost as important to our culture as the stories themselves." He glanced back at Andrea. "If you'll excuse me, I have to corner Doc before he gets away. Pleased to have met you, Andrea. And you," he said to Mike, "tell her the story."

"Well?" Andrea looked up at him expectantly.

Mike rolled his eyes. "Later. I tell stories better on a full stomach." He took her arm and led her toward the laden tables.

BY LATE AFTERNOON everyone had eaten their fill, though plenty of food remained. Some of the young people played ball in the open field by the lake; others were still dancing to the tireless efforts of the musicians.

Mike, well fed and feeling surprisingly content, glanced at his watch, knowing what was coming next.

As if on cue, Lena rose. "All right," she bellowed. "Who's ready to spend some money for a good cause?"

People seated around her started clapping as others whooped their agreement.

A farmer sitting next to Mike rose. "Yah, Lena, let's get this show on the road."

Lena headed to the tables where auction items had been laid out for inspection before the bidding started.

"Okay, everyone," she shouted in her most piercing schoolteacher voice. "Gather round. It's time for the auction."

The musicians lowered their instruments and joined the people gathered around the tables.

Lena picked up the first item and held it up for the prospective bidders.

"Okay, what am I bid for this lovely, um..." She held the object closer, squinting, then turned to fix an elderly man in the audience with a piercing gaze. "Einar Sorenson, I saw you bring this in. What the heck is it?"

"Aw, Lena," the man said, his eyes crinkling as he grinned. "You oughta know. It's a Swedish library book."

Lena grimaced and pulled a rolled-up television schedule from the center of a roll of toilet tissue to howls of laughter from the audience.

"Hey!" someone shouted. "The guy who sold me one of those said it was a Norwegian encyclopedia."

After the second wave of laughter died away, Lena, with an air of affronted dignity, sniffed. "Now, I think we should move along to the serious bidding."

"That's the trouble with Swedes," Dan offered from a safe distance. "No sense of humor."

"Heck, no sense, period," Einar Sorenson added.

Einar's wife, a dainty white-haired lady, reached up and swatted him on the back of the head. "Just remember, Norsky, you've gotta go home with a Swede tonight."

The elderly man eyed the crowd and, catching Andrea's eye, winked broadly. "Oh, I don't know. I might get a better offer."

Dan laughed. "I think your luck's about to run out, Einar."

Einar glanced at his wife, who was now looking at him with one eyebrow raised, and subsided with a furious blush.

Dan leaned toward Andrea. "I think old Einar had a couple nips during the picnic."

She nodded. "I don't think he was the only one, either." She'd noticed more than one picnicker discreetly sipping from a small flask or bottle, apparently not content with the Rorvik ladies' offerings of soft drinks and strong coffee.

Lena moved on to the next item up for bid, a handmade birdhouse on a stand. "Okay, let's start at one dollar."

A hand went up in the audience.

"One dollar. Do I hear two?" She nodded to the next bidder. "Two. Who'll make it three?"

The bids rose as Lena went on, her professional auctioneer's call surprising Andrea. White Thunder's housekeeper was a woman of many talents.

Caught up in the action, Andrea raised her hand as the bidding went to eight dollars and was almost relieved when someone raised the offer to nine.

At twelve dollars, Lena announced, "Going, going, gone. Sold to Doc Coggins."

Grinning, Doc stepped forward and picked up his prize, handing the money to a woman seated next to Lena.

"What are you going to do with that, Doc?" Lena asked.

"I'm going to set it up near the window that Ole sleeps beside. He likes watching birds. He's a bird dog, after all."

Lena snorted. "That animal has about as much bird dog in him as I do, but I hope he enjoys it."

She moved on to the next item, a hand-painted ceramic bowl. "All right, let's start the bidding at two dollars."

The auction went on through a number of items, ranging from homemade preserves to heirlooms to practical jokes. At one point, she held up a rolled tube of paper.

"Another Norwegian encyclopedia?" she asked, unrolling the paper.

"Nope. That's my contribution." Bert Petersen rose in the audience.

Andrea wondered how she'd missed the banker, then realized it was probably because she hadn't recognized him out of uniform. Instead of his usual gray suit, Bert wore khaki shorts and a T-shirt that advertised a UFO-themed restaurant in Bismarck. A grinning alien on his chest raised a glass in salute as a spaceship hovered in the background.

Lena opened the paper and squinted at it, reading aloud. "In the event that the bearer is abducted or experimented upon by aliens or extraterrestrial beings, this policy will pay the bearer the sum of one thousand dollars." She raised an eyebrow at Bert.

"It's an insurance policy against alien abduction." He glanced at Andrea. "You can't be too careful in times like these."

Lena rolled her eyes. "Fine, Bert. Thank you. Let's start the bidding at fifty cents."

When the last bid was made, Lena clapped her hands.

"Okay, that's all for this year. It looks like we did real well. If you haven't paid Tillie—" she gestured to the woman next to her "—give her your money now. She'll add up the contributions and let us know the grand total by the end of the evening." She glanced out at the audience and nodded at a man bearing a huge accordion case. "Now Barney and his band are going to get set up for some dancing. Plenty of food's left, too, so don't let it go to waste."

The crowd applauded as she stepped down and walked to Andrea's side.

"Where did you learn auctioneering, Lena?" Andrea asked.

The older woman shrugged. "Well, after you've been to a few hundred auctions, you just kinda pick it up. I do it for a couple different fund-raisers every year."

"It sounds fun."

Lena grinned. "I'll teach you if you like. Maybe you can do it next year."

Behind them, Barney and his group launched into a polka.

"Maybe so." Andrea smiled back at her but couldn't help thinking that next year things would be very different around here. She'd come to care about Dan and Lena, she realized. They were part of the appeal of White Thunder. Was there any way they'd stay on?

The Vidtel prize included the services of the ranch staff for two months, until she was settled in and they made other arrangements. She and Mike had an arrangement. As her partner, he would, of course, stay. As would Lena. But what about Dan? Somehow, she couldn't imagine the ranch without all of them.

Mike sat on a long bench watching the dancers, his mind wandering pleasantly when the music stopped, snapping him out of his thoughts. He glanced toward the musicians and noticed that the members of Rusting Hulkk were speaking intently with them. He'd wondered where they'd gotten to after their assault on the food table.

The older men rose and relinquished their instruments to the boys. Todd took Dan's accordion, Jock, the guitar and Stench, oddly enough, the fiddle. They played experimentally for a few moments, getting the feel of the instruments, then launched into a lively and unexpected reel. The startled dancers began again, while the spectators clapped in time with the music.

Mike grinned. So they were folk musicians, too. He looked at Andrea and she smiled at him. She mouthed a question at him, something he couldn't quite make out.

"If you're not going to tell me the story, how about dancing with me?" she called, moving through the crowd toward him.

Dance? A moment's panic struck him. He hadn't danced since... Maybe a round of storytelling would be easier.

Within moments she was right in front of him, her eyes bright.

"They're very good, aren't they?" she said. "I'm ashamed to say, I'm a little surprised."

He nodded, trying to cover his nervousness. "Me, too. I thought they just played that heavy-metal stuff."

"So, do you want to?" she asked.

"Dance? I'm a pretty bad dancer." He gave a self-deprecating laugh. Maybe she'd ask someone else, he thought, then realized that wasn't what he wanted. He longed to feel her in his arms, even if he made a complete fool of himself in the process.

"I'm not exactly Ginger Rogers myself, but I just can't let that music end without dancing to it." She held out her hand.

He took a deep breath and reached for her. Together they stepped onto the makeshift dance floor.

Andrea's hand was soft and warm in his. He pulled her close, placing his other hand in the curve of her lower back, feeling the tension in her taut muscles. She was slender, but her hips curved softly below his hand and he could feel her firm, rounded breasts against his chest. He tried to keep from looking down. It was all he could do to avoid an embarrassingly physical reaction to her as it was.

He gazed into her eyes, and she returned his look boldly as they moved together across the floor, their bodies rhythmically synchronized to the flowing beat of the music. Her lips parted slightly, as though she were about to speak, then she smiled and surrendered herself to the dance.

"I know virtually nothing about you," he said, looking down at her. But even as he spoke, he recalled the phone call he'd overheard her first night at the ranch—her apology for embarrassing her mother, her promise to call someone else, obviously a man. Was there someone else back home? Someone who was waiting for her?

It's none of your business, he thought. *You shouldn't have been listening, anyway.*

"What's there to know?" she said lightly. "I'm a veterinarian from Seattle. I'm an air force brat. There's not much else."

Fine, he thought. If she had nothing to tell him, that was the end of it.

So why did it bother him so much that she wanted to keep her past to herself?

CHAPTER SIXTEEN

THE FESTIVITIES at the lake had lasted well into the night and were, in fact, still going on. Rusting Hulkk, the unexpected life of the party, elected to stay and continue playing as long as the evening lasted. Friends of Dan's had offered to put them up in town for the night. Most of the older crowd, though, Mike and Andrea included, started for home shortly after ten.

She stifled a yawn, exhausted after dancing for hours. Mostly with Mike.

She glanced at him out of the corner of her eye. He sat beside her, close but not touching, his head against the seat back, his eyes closed.

He'd changed today, she realized. He'd come to life in a way. Had she played some part in that?

They drove across the darkened prairie, Dan and Lena quiet, probably exhausted, in the front seat. Andrea gazed out the window absently. The moon and stars shone brightly, with little competition from man-made light. She could make out considerable detail in the grassland around them, spotting fence posts and windmills, oil derricks and even the occasional cow.

Dan slowed for a turn, and Andrea was surprised to discover she now recognized the roads around White Thunder. The fields they passed were hers. She watched carefully, hoping to catch a glimpse of her bison out there somewhere. Did bison sleep standing up? She'd never make them out if they were lying down. They'd look just like dark mounds or shadows out there.

In the distance, a flash of light caught her eye. Lightning? She watched for it again.

There!

Not lightning, but a glowing object she lost momentarily when it disappeared behind a hill.

It was moving. Slowly. Dipping and bobbing as though at the mercy of the breeze, or perhaps just skimming low over the terrain in an effort to evade detection.

"Mike," she whispered. She reached beside her and shook his arm, afraid to take her eyes off the object lest she lose it again. "Look."

He leaned across her to gaze out the window as she pointed. "What is it?"

"I don't know. Clarissa and Connie again?" Even as she said it, she knew she was wrong. This light was different. Its shape was definite, rounded. And it moved *above* the ground. It was flying.

"Dan, stop the car." Mike's voice was low and urgent.

"What's up?" the older man asked as he pulled the station wagon onto the shoulder.

"Where are we?" Lena muttered sleepily, and sat up straight.

"Just outside the ranch." Mike pointed toward the light. "Do you see it?"

"Well, I'll be." Dan looked back at Andrea. "Is that the light you saw your first night here?"

"I'm not sure. I think so. It seems to move the same way."

Mike climbed out of the vehicle and walked to the fence. Andrea got out, as well, but waited by the car.

He called to her. "See if Dan has his binoculars."

She relayed the question.

Dan shook his head. "They're back at the house. I had to clean the lenses."

"He doesn't have them," she told Mike. "Should we go out there and have a look?" She didn't relish the thought of another late-night crawl through the underbrush, but they had to find out what was going on.

Dan disagreed. He cranked down his window. "Mike, wait till morning. You don't know what might be out there."

Mike stepped back to the car. He studied Dan in the eerie, greenish glow of the dashboard lights. "You don't really think it's aliens, do you?" A note of humor softened the concern in his voice.

"I don't know what it is, but I don't want you taking the chance." Dan laid his hand on Mike's arm. "Mark the spot and you can come back and investigate tomorrow. You're not likely to find anything in the dark, anyway."

Mike looked at Andrea. She shrugged. Dan was probably right. Chances were they'd find nothing out there tonight. "Can we find this spot again in the morning?"

Mike raised one eyebrow. "We?"

"*We*," she said emphatically. "This is my problem, too." Besides, she wasn't about to let him investigate on his own. It might be dangerous. "I'm the senior partner. Rank has its privileges, as you should know."

He rolled his eyes but appeared resigned. "Lena, reach into the glove compartment. I think there's a bandanna in there."

Lena did so and handed him the red cotton kerchief.

"I'll tie this to the fence post. *We* can start at this spot in the morning and work our way out." He cocked his head to one side, a crooked grin on his face. "If that meets with your approval, boss?"

He's enjoying this, she realized. Did he miss the excitement of his old life so much, then? "Sounds like a plan.

Partner," she emphasized as a final reminder that he was
not in this alone, whatever his wishes to the contrary.

Mike walked to the fence and tied the bandanna around
a strand of barbed wire, then returned to the car. "We'll
head out in the morning, before the boys get back. That
ought to keep the fuss to a minimum."

"I don't know," Andrea said. "They'd probably enjoy
the opportunity. Especially Stench."

"No doubt. But if there's something dangerous going on
out there, the fewer people we risk, the better." Mike met
her gaze, his eyes onyx in the darkness. "I'd rather not risk
you, in fact."

"And I won't let you go alone," she replied softly. "So
I'll see you in the morning. And," she said for the benefit
of the others, "I'll trust Dan to make sure you don't leave
without me."

Dan glanced at her in the rearview mirror. "You have
my word. I don't want him out there alone any more than
you do."

They drove the rest of the way to the house in thoughtful
silence, watching the light until it was no longer visible.

ANDREA LAY IN BED, willing herself to relax, but the more
she concentrated, the more knotted her muscles became and
the faster her mind raced. She'd been exhausted only a
short time ago, but the "UFO" sighting had driven all
thought of sleep from her mind.

She rose and went to the window. The lights were still
on in Mike's trailer, where he was taking advantage of the
band's absence to tidy up the place. Or so he'd said.

She hoped he'd been honest with her. She wouldn't put
it past him to go off on his own in search of the light in
some misguided attempt to protect her.

The thought nagged at her. He was more than capable,
she knew, but what if something happened to him out

there? It would be hours before anyone discovered him missing and started a search. If he got hurt...

She shook off the thought. What could possibly hurt him out there? Space aliens with death rays? The idea was too ridiculous.

Of course there were more mundane concerns. He could drive into a gully or fall and break something.

She was silly to worry and yet she couldn't stop. First one, then another disastrous scene played out in her mind until finally she spun away from the window.

Honestly! Did he know what he was putting her through?

Shivering, she climbed back into bed and sat there with the covers pulled up close around her chin. She looked at her watch. It was 1:00 a.m.

If he wasn't inside in fifteen minutes, she was going out there. She propped herself against the headboard and listened for the sound of his footsteps while the seconds ticked past.

If he took the truck, she'd have a problem. She could chase him in Lena's car, but only if he stayed on the road. The station wagon wasn't built for rough terrain.

She glanced at her watch again. Five after.

It felt like an hour had passed.

She settled back against the pillows. Ten more minutes, then she'd throw her jeans back on, go out there and find out just what Mr. Winterhawk was doing.

A NOISE BROUGHT ANDREA sharply awake. She looked around the room groggily, then sat up and looked at her watch, struggling to bring the lighted dial into focus.

Two o'clock!

Damn! She'd fallen asleep!

She leapt out of bed and darted to the window.

The lights were still on in Mike's trailer, and the truck

was parked in its usual spot. As she watched, something moved down near the corral. A person. No, two.

Not Mike, then. And she couldn't blame this on the band's propensity for late hours, with them staying in town tonight.

She watched the figures move together through the shadows. Did they have something to do with the light? she wondered.

She had to tell someone. Dan?

No, his health was too fragile. It was no job for Lena, either, although she had little doubt the woman could handle most intruders.

No, she had to find Mike.

Andrea pulled on her jeans and shirt, then, slipping on her green boots, tiptoed out of the room and down the stairs to the front door, checking the sofa, just in case.

He wasn't there. He had to be out in the trailer.

A moment's trepidation shook her at the thought of going out to him.

Of being alone with him.

She hadn't been alone with Mike since the afternoon they'd gone to the homestead.

A lot had changed since then, for both of them.

But she had no choice. She had to find out what was going on here, and Mike was the only one who could help her.

She opened the door and stepped out into the cool darkness.

MIKE FLIPPED THROUGH the past couple of days' Minot newspapers and the latest *Rorvik Herald*, looking for any reports of unusual lights or objects in the sky, announcements of military tests or weather research, anything he might have overlooked.

He was grasping at straws, he knew, but he couldn't pass

up the opportunity to check, even though he'd carefully reviewed all the papers already.

The boys had left the trailer in remarkably good condition, only lightly strewn with clothing and candy wrappers. They apparently weren't one of those bands that made a habit of trashing their hotel rooms. Luckily for them.

He glanced at his watch. It was already past two. The time had really gotten away from him. He was going to regret this in the morning when Andrea was up to get an early start out to the "UFO" site.

Someone knocked at the trailer door. He looked up, startled. Who could be out here at this time of night? Had something happened?

He walked to the door and opened it. Andrea stood on the top step, her face pale in the yellowish light from the porch lamp.

Heart pounding, he opened the screen door and pulled her inside. "What's wrong? Are you all right?"

Her curls were tossed around her head as if she'd just come in from a windstorm, and he couldn't stop himself from reaching up to smooth them off her face.

She gasped, whether in reaction to his touch or in an effort to catch her breath, he couldn't tell. He guided her to a chair.

"What's going on?" he said gently, fighting a sudden urge to take her in his arms and comfort her.

She stared up at him, her eyes huge. "I saw someone outside. Two people."

"Where?" *Now what?*

"Near the corral. Heading toward the barn."

"I'll go take a look. Stay here." He went to the kitchen for a flashlight, then started for the door.

She reached for his arm. "No. Mike, I want to go with you. Whatever's going on here is my problem, too. I can't let you walk into it by yourself."

He looked into her worried eyes. His best judgment told him to argue, to make her stay here where she'd be safe. But then again, his judgment concerning Andrea had been a little cloudy of late. "Okay. But stay close."

She nodded and followed him out into the darkness.

Crossing the ranch grounds with Andrea at his side, Mike held the flashlight like a club, its light off to preserve their night vision. They hardly needed to worry, though, as bright as the moon was tonight. As they walked toward the corral, they cast their own shadows.

The night was cool and quiet, the sky brilliant with stars. The softest of breezes carried away the dust they kicked up as they walked. Mike neither saw nor heard any hint of movement beyond the snoring of Gypsy in her pen. He moved stealthily around the barn, Andrea close on his heels, and looked inside. Nothing. He then checked up the road a distance in case any strange vehicles might be parked on the property.

"I don't see anything out of the ordinary," he whispered. "How 'bout you?"

"No. Nothing." Relief mingled with frustration in her voice.

He turned to her. "Maybe you imagined it. Or dreamed it?"

She shook her head, frowning. "It was no dream. I was wide-awake and standing at the window."

He surveyed the deserted yard and corrals one last time, and they started back to the trailer. "Well, if someone was out here, they're gone now."

"I guess so," Andrea said. "We should check around tomorrow and make sure nothing's been disturbed."

Mike nodded, opening the trailer door. "Good idea." He hesitated, then asked, "As long as we're both up, do you want to come in for a minute? I could put some coffee on."

A note of warning sounded in her head, but Andrea ignored it. "Sure," she said. "I'd like that."

They stepped inside.

"Make yourself at home," he said. "I'll get the coffee going." He started down the narrow hallway toward the front of the trailer.

"Thanks," Andrea said. Taking a seat in a comfortable armchair, she looked around the room, recognizing much of Mike in it.

The furnishings were simple and uncluttered, but not the unrelieved earth tones she'd come to associate with bachelors' dwellings. The living room was done in deep rusts and reds with accents of blue and green, all in geometric, Native-looking patterns. The inviting sofa and a matching chair were detailed in rustic, heavy oak. A solid oak desk topped with a computer and printer, brass lamp and a stack of printed white sheets, facedown, completed the room.

A collection of several Indian shields hung on the opposite wall. Andrea recognized them from the Native art galleries she'd visited back home. She rose to examine them more closely.

Made of tanned hide stretched over a round frame, the shields were painted with symbols of animals, birds, stars, geometric patterns and surrealistic shapes whose nature she couldn't begin to guess. Feathers, beads or bits of carved bone dangled from some of them. All were gorgeously colored in tones ranging from rich red, orange and brown to dusty blue and green.

The central shield in the display was a cream-colored circle painted with a design of horns in malachite green. In the center was a figure of a blue-and-white bird with talons and a sharp, curved beak. Eagle feathers hung around the lower edge of the shield, decorated along their quills with red clay beads.

The stretched hide was yellowed and bore crackled lines

of age. It bore scars, as well. Battle scars, deeply incised as though it had warded off the blows of an enemy weapon.

The beautiful power of the object struck Andrea almost physically. This shield, she knew, had been used by a warrior, had perhaps saved his life. She could almost sense the owner's history, his life force emanating from the simple disk of hide and feathers.

Behind her, a floorboard creaked. Startled, she spun around.

Mike held a pair of stoneware mugs. "Sorry. I didn't mean to sneak up on you." He handed her a mug. "This won't be up to Lena's standards. All I had was instant."

She pretended to look aghast. "What? You'd give instant coffee to someone from Seattle? Sacrilege." She sipped the hot beverage and grinned. "It's good, though. Really."

"For instant. What can I say? You'll have to send the coffee police after me." He took a seat on the sofa and placed his cup on the table, studying her. "Are you sure you didn't dream whatever you saw out there?"

Andrea sighed. "I'm sure. In fact, I saw someone out there once before, but I thought it was someone from the band."

"What?" Mike frowned. "You saw someone walking around the property and you didn't tell me? When?"

"My first night here," she said with a shrug. "The band had gone out to your trailer. I just thought it was a couple of them wandering around. I thought they probably weren't used to calling it a night so early."

He nodded. "You're probably right, but you should have said something, anyway."

"If I'd known I'd see someone out there again tonight, believe me, I would have. Unfortunately, clairvoyance is not one of my gifts."

"Well, you aren't lacking because of it," he remarked cryptically.

Was that a compliment? Unsettled, she changed the subject, gesturing to the shields. "I was admiring your collection," she said. "The shields are wonderful. Have you been collecting them long?"

"No," he said, stepping closer to stand beside her. "Just since I've been out here."

He stood so near she could feel the night air's lingering chill on his skin. She longed to touch him, to transfer her own warmth to him, to take away the cold that seemed so much a part of him.

"I've managed to accumulate quite a few of them in a short time," he said with a gentle laugh. "I guess it's become a sort of obsession. Part of finding my roots."

She shook her head in disagreement. "I wouldn't call it an obsession. It's natural to want to learn about your heritage. Especially when you've only just become aware of it. Which reminds me, you never did complete your homework assignment."

He laughed. "The story of White Buffalo Woman."

"Yes," she said. "Would you tell it to me?"

"All right. I have to apologize in advance for my presentation, though. I'm not much of a public speaker." He took a sip of coffee, then cleared his throat. His eyes seemed to cloud, as though he was seeing something far away. "Many years ago, the Sioux had suffered a difficult winter. They fought and argued among themselves, children disobeyed their parents, and the elders who tried to keep the peace were ignored.

"The elders of the village hoped that when the buffalo returned, peace would come back to the village, but as spring began, the buffalo did not come back. The people's discontent grew, and finally two young scouts were sent out from the village to seek the herd.

"The scouts searched for days but could not find the buffalo. Then, one morning, they discovered a set of footprints. Human footprints. One of the scouts wanted to follow, but the other argued, wanting to return to the village. At last, though, the first scout convinced him that someone might be lost and in need of help, so they followed.''

Mike looked at Andrea. She had her eyes closed, as though concentrating on his words. He went on. "Ahead of them the scouts saw the most beautiful woman they had ever seen. She wore a dress of pure white buckskin, intricately beaded. The second scout was overcome with lust for the woman and determined to take her back to the village, even against her will. The other scout argued that they must respect her. He asked her gently if they could help her.

"The woman looked at the second scout and told him she knew what he was thinking. When he angrily reached for her, a cloud surrounded him. When it lifted, he had disappeared. Only his bow and arrows remained.

"The first scout was stunned. He realized the woman had great powers and he was frightened. She spoke gently to him, though, telling him not to be afraid. 'I bring a message for your people,' she told him. 'Tell them what you have seen and that they must stop fighting and work together. Tell them to build a great tepee in the center of the village, and when it is finished I will come to them.'

"The scout returned to the village and told them of the woman and her message. The chief realized that the scout had met a sacred woman and that they must do as she said. He asked the tribe if they agreed, and each member said yes. So together they began to build the tepee, each member of the tribe helping and bringing something to contribute. At last a great white tepee rose in the center of the village. And when it was finished, the woman returned, carrying a bundle in her arms.

"'I am White Buffalo Woman,' she told them, 'and I bring you a gift.' She entered the white tepee, where the chief and the elders waited, and knelt in the center to open her bundle. The gift she carried was a pipe. A buffalo was carved on one side, and twelve eagle feathers were attached to the stem, along with four ribbons in black, white, red and yellow. 'This pipe is your gift,' the woman said, 'because you have proved yourselves worthy. The buffalo stands for the earth, which nurtures us, the eagle feathers for the sky and the twelve moons of the year. The ribbons stand for the four corners of the earth and the four winds, and you must offer it to each corner in respect when you use the pipe. The black ribbon stands for the west wind, which brings us rain, the white for the cooling winds of the north, red for the east, which brings the sunrise, and yellow for the south and the summer sun, which makes the grasses grow. You have worked together in peace. Now use this gift in peace and you will prosper.'

"White Buffalo Woman gave the pipe to the chief, then rose and walked out of the village. As she reached the fields, she began to run and suddenly changed into a magnificent white buffalo. Then a herd of buffalo appeared, grazing in the fields. The herd had returned, and with them, the tribe's prosperity.

"The people of the village used the pipe whenever they were tempted to fight among themselves to remind them that only through peace could they prosper. Soon they began to offer the pipe to others in neighboring villages, explaining White Buffalo Woman's message of how they must respect nature and the earth, which had provided for them."

Andrea opened her eyes. "Mike, that was beautiful."

He looked at her then, and the distance between them seemed to disappear as she gazed into his eyes.

"There are a lot of things I've become aware of recently," he whispered. "A lot of things I thought I'd never know."

He made no move toward her, but the very space between them seemed to crackle and hum.

She took a deep breath, fighting the tide that roared in
her ears and threatened to consume her.

When he pulled her into his arms, her last vestige of will
fled. His mouth closed fiercely on hers, warm and moist
and incomparably sweet.

She melted against him as he slid his hands along her
back, twined them in her hair. Raising her arms around him,
she felt his strength, reveling in it and drawing it to her
like sustenance.

He lowered his head, and she caressed his dark hair as
his lips moved down her throat and into the warm hollow
at its base. His fingers brushed the top button of her blouse.

Someone knocked at the door.

Mike released her slowly with a soft groan of regret.

"Who could that be?" Andrea whispered. She looked
around quickly, overcome by a sudden desire to hide.

"Probably your phantom." Mike walked to the door.
"But who knows? Everybody seems to be out and about
tonight."

He opened the door. Dan and Lena stepped inside. They
started, almost in unison, when they saw Andrea.

"Oh, it must have been Andrea," Lena said as Dan
asked at the same time, "Andrea, what are you doing out
here?"

"What are both of *you* doing out here?" Mike asked
them.

"We were out walking, and on the way back to the house
we saw someone moving around near the barn."

Mike laughed. "That was probably us. Andrea saw
someone—two people, actually—walking around outside
and came to find me. We went to take a look."

"And the two people Andrea saw were probably Lena

and me." Dan shook his head. "I think we're all getting a little jumpy with all this UFO talk."

Andrea's embarrassment subsided in the wake of the rational explanations. Her hair felt tousled, her lips swollen with the pressure of Mike's kisses. She hoped Dan and Lena wouldn't notice, but Lena was eyeing her with a curious and pleased expression on her face.

"So what were you two doing out at this hour?" Andrea couldn't resist asking.

It was Lena's turn to blush. "We were just getting some fresh air."

Andrea refrained from pointing out that they'd spent most of the afternoon and evening in the fresh air. Not to mention the fact that it was nearly 3:00 a.m.

Dan met her gaze. Was the older man blushing, too? There seemed to be a definite tinge of pink under his tan.

"I think it's about time we all turned in," he said. "Andrea, you want to walk back to the house with us?"

She nodded, not at all sure she wanted to leave Mike but positive that doing so was for the best.

"Wait. It's chilly out," Mike said. He glanced around the room, then pulled a creamy wool afghan off the sofa. "My jacket's back at the house. Wrap this around you." He draped the afghan across her shoulders like a shawl, then reached for her hand and gave it a gentle squeeze. "Good night," he said.

"Thank you," she whispered, then walked in silence back to the house with Lena and Dan.

CHAPTER SEVENTEEN

MIKE WATCHED FROM the door of the trailer as Andrea walked away. Her dark hair moved against the creamy afghan around her shoulders, bringing to his mind the image of the beautiful buffalo woman in her white buckskin gown as she magically transformed herself into the white buffalo.

He could almost see it happening, as though in a vision.

A tremor ran through him. A vision?

No, he thought, this was ridiculous. Visions, and the vision quest, were a part of his Sioux heritage, certainly, but surely he wasn't the recipient of some kind of spiritual message. Especially a message telling him that Andrea belonged at White Thunder.

Not that he didn't want her. He more than wanted her, he was beginning to care for her despite all his intentions to the contrary. In fact, it was all he could do to keep from following her back to the house to tell her how he felt.

Trouble was, he didn't *know* how he felt. Despite his plans to get her off the ranch and all his promises to himself that he wouldn't get involved, he'd let himself get close to her. He wanted to trust Andrea, to believe she was different. It felt right, but what if he'd misjudged her? Could he live with the results again?

He tried to clear his mind, but memories, still so close to the surface, drifted into focus. He still remembered the look on his fiancée's face.

Michelle's golden tan had washed out of her face as she

stared at his injuries with horror, hearing the news that he might never walk again.

The doctors had told him she'd get over it. That she'd come to accept it. Give her time, they said.

He gave her time. It was a commodity he had in abundance, and for a while, it seemed she was coming around.

But his own feelings had begun to change. His injuries made him realize what was truly important and how much he had to learn. When he made the decision not to return to the army, Michelle became angry. As his interest in his heritage grew, her visits became less frequent.

Finally he told her about his plans to seek his father's people. Michelle had slipped his ring off her finger and set it beside his bed. He'd changed too much, she told him. His injuries had crippled his mind, as well as his body. He was no longer the man she loved, the man she'd planned to marry.

He'd thought they loved each other, but she'd abandoned him when he needed her most.

Mike had decided then and there that it was for the best. He didn't need anyone. He'd recover on his own, seek his past, and from that moment on, rely only on himself. And he had.

Perhaps Dan and Lena's interruption was for the best, as well.

ANDREA WALKED INTO the house with Dan and Lena, feeling like a teenager caught sneaking home late from a date. She wondered what they'd say to her.

But Dan just said, "Well, it's late, and you'll want to get up early to look for your 'UFO,' so we'd best turn in. Good night." With no further comment, he headed to his room.

Andrea looked expectantly at Lena, anticipating the third degree she knew the housekeeper was dying to give her.

But Lena just gave her a slow wink, then went to her own room.

Somehow that was worse than questions. If Lena had asked, Andrea could always deny her interest in Mike. But the older woman seemed to view her relationship with Mike as a foregone conclusion.

She crept up the stairs to her room, closing the door softly behind her, then sinking against the door, limp and shaken.

Mike's kisses still burned on her lips and throat. She trembled at the memory of his caress, a warm throbbing ache rising within her at the memory of his hands on her body.

She'd never felt this way with Jeffrey, she realized, and once again she was filled with guilt. In her ignorance, she'd led him to believe she was in love with him.

She hadn't known what love was.

Until now.

She was falling in love with Mike.

Andrea took a deep breath. Was it really possible to fall in love with someone in the space of two weeks?

What if Dan and Lena hadn't made their timely appearance? Would rationality have prevailed? Would she have stopped Mike before things went too far? He was her partner, after all. If she risked everything for a relationship with him and it turned out to be a mistake, what would she do then? Leave?

She couldn't go through that again. And, more important, she couldn't treat Mike that way. He knew little about her previous relationship. Why should he have to pay the price for her naiveté?

She pulled off her blouse and jeans, slipped on her nightgown, then climbed beneath the covers and turned out the lamp. She doubted she'd sleep much.

THE AIR SEEMED DIFFERENT, still and oppressively heavy, when Andrea woke the next morning.

It was probably her mood, she thought. She'd dozed fitfully most of the night, awakening almost hourly until shortly after dawn when, more tired than when she'd gone to bed, she decided to get up and shower. The combination of a new time zone and ranch hours had really messed up her body clock.

Maybe I should try melatonin, she thought.

The idea brought her up short. What was it about the sleep hormone that nagged at her memory? Something she'd read in a medical journal? Try as she might, she couldn't recall the article.

Well, it would probably come to her once she woke up.

Dressed and somewhat refreshed, she surprised Dan at his morning coffee.

"Well, you're up early," he commented, winking at her. "All ready to go hunt aliens?"

"Ready as I'll ever be, I guess." She poured herself a cup of coffee and took a seat next to him. "Dan, what do you think is out there?"

"Not aliens," he replied, laying down his paper. A broad grin split his lined face. "I don't know what it is, but I don't think it's little green men. Or even little whitish men with oversize heads."

She must have looked surprised, because his grin widened. "Sure, I've watched those UFO shows, too, ya know. So dang many of 'em on lately they're hard to miss.

"Thing is," he continued, "why would any space alien want to come out here and fly around making lights in the sky? I mean, it seems kinda pointless, doesn't it?"

Andrea shrugged. "I'd never really thought of it that way. People just assume if there are aliens out there, they want to study us or take specimens or something."

"Harrumph," Lena muttered from the doorway. "So

what do they think, that aliens shine their spaceship lights and make crop circles just to watch us act silly about it? 'Cause that's about as extensive as it's gotten out here.''

"You've had crop circles out here?" Andrea asked. Lena had said something about them before but hadn't mentioned that they'd been seen on the ranch.

Dan shook his head. "Not really. Not like those ones they show over in England and those places. Ours are small areas where the grass is flattened and dead, like something landed on it."

"Something like a spaceship?" Andrea asked with one eyebrow raised.

Dan shrugged. "Don't know. I've never seen a spaceship. When I do, then I'll worry about it."

Mike came in through the screen door. "'Morning, Dan, Lena. 'Morning, Andrea."

Andrea's pulse quickened as she recalled the kisses they'd shared. He wore faded jeans and a plain white T-shirt. He looked fantastic, and she picked up a section of Dan's paper to distract herself as the blood rose in her cheeks.

"Hi," she answered noncommittally over the farm reports.

He gave a brief, crooked smile, almost of sympathy, she thought, and turned away to pour his coffee. Well, this probably wasn't any easier for him than it was for her. Being alone with him again was going to be awkward, as well.

"Dan?" she asked. "Would you like to come with us today? You know the property better than anyone else does. If there's anything out of the ordinary, you'd be the best one to notice it."

Dan shook his head. "I'd like to help, but Lena's driving me into town for a doctor appointment. I'm sure Mike will be able to spot anything strange. He's probably more familiar with the terrain than I am these days."

Well, it was worth a try.

She glanced up to see Mike watching her. Had he guessed she was trying to line up a chaperon? From the way he lifted one eyebrow, she expected he had.

He probably thought that either she didn't trust him or, worse, that she couldn't trust herself. She glanced at her watch. Not even eight o'clock and the day was already starting to go to hell.

Mike gulped the last of his coffee, half relieved to discover Andrea was as nervous as he. He apparently wasn't the only one who'd had a sleepless night. Dark circles shadowed her eyes, which were a brighter green than usual.

Andrea Moore looked better exhausted than most women looked wide-awake, he thought. So much for the concept of beauty sleep. What would it be like to wake up next to her?

He pushed the thought from his mind. That was dangerous territory. Best not to even consider it. Too bad Dan hadn't taken her up on her invitation. His presence would certainly have defused the situation.

Or just postponed the inevitable.

"Are you about ready?" he asked.

She looked up at him again and nodded. "Anytime."

"Let's go."

In virtual silence, they drove out to the main road. The air was warm and heavy, the usual morning breeze absent. It weighed on him as oppressively as his thoughts, and he scanned the horizon for signs of the storm he knew it heralded.

The sky was clear and blue. Cloudless—at least for the moment.

"The air's stuffy today," Andrea commented. "Feels like it'll be a warm one."

"Yep." He glanced at her. "I think today you'll get a taste of what summer's like around here. Keep a lookout along here. We should be getting close to the spot."

She turned away and stared out the window, watching the fence line. "Look," she said, pointing out a flash of red ahead of them. "There it is."

"I see it." Mike pulled the truck over onto the shoulder and looked past Andrea out the window.

"How far out there do you think the light was?" she asked.

"Hard to say. I think our best bet is to just head in that direction and see what we find."

"Sounds reasonable to me. Any idea just what we're looking for?" Her tone was light, as if she were having as much trouble as he accepting what they were doing.

He shrugged and couldn't keep from grinning at the absurdity of their activity. Alien hunting. Who'd believe it? "Probably nothing as obvious as a sign reading This Way to the Aliens," he said. "Just keep an eye out for anything unusual and we'll stop to investigate."

A gate broke the fence line a few hundred yards from the spot where the red bandanna hung. Mike opened it while Andrea drove the truck through, then closed it again and took his place once more behind the wheel.

"Ready?" he asked.

"Let's go find some spacemen," she replied.

He drove slowly to allow them to scan the terrain for anything out of the ordinary. With the rolling hills out here, they'd have to double back in a sort of grid pattern to make sure they covered everything. And keep track of the ground they'd already examined to avoid checking the same spots over and over again. The search would be tedious and time-consuming.

"How far from the fence line should we go?" Andrea asked.

"Hard to say. We don't know the altitude of that thing last night. Flying near the ground, it would have to have been relatively close to the road. But at a higher altitude, well, we'd have been able to see it from a long way off. It could have been quite a distance away."

They continued on, bouncing over the rough pastureland. Mike noted that Andrea sat rigid in her seat, clutching the grab strap against the frequent bumps. He tried to concentrate on his observation of the area but couldn't resist darting occasional glances at her. Should he say something about last night or would it just make her more uncomfortable?

Andrea scanned the green countryside as they made slow passes, watching carefully for anything that stood out or seemed unusual, glad to have something to occupy her. Anything to distract her from the close proximity of the man beside her.

It took all her willpower not to stare at him, to search his face for some clue to his feelings. If only Dan had agreed to come along. At least she might be able to relax a little instead of jolting along with every bump, too tense to let her body absorb the impacts.

Around noon they bounced through a shallow gully and up onto a low rise. Several hundred feet ahead of them lay an odd-looking area of grass, regular in shape and shorter than the surrounding vegetation. Was that unusual? Andrea wondered. Or was it just a patch of some kind of plant she didn't recognize.

She pointed it out to Mike. "What's that spot out there? That weird-colored area."

He followed her gesture. "I don't know. It doesn't look normal. Let's take a closer look."

They pulled up to the area and climbed out of the truck. Ahead of them lay a broad, roughly circular area of flattened grasses, covering several yards.

"A crop circle," Andrea whispered. She crouched and extended trembling fingers to pluck a strand of straw-colored vegetation. Something had been here, she realized, struggling to accept the truth that lay before her. Whatever they saw last night had caused this.

And threatened White Thunder and everything it was beginning to mean to her.

She remembered Clarissa Hale's comments about the medicine wheel and Mike's heritage and caught herself watching him, wary.

Mike's expression was grim. "I guess so. Kind of a small one, though." He reached down to take her arm, raising her away from the grass, and turned her hand palm up, studying the strands she'd picked. "The grass doesn't look damaged. Just crushed, like something big and round sat on it."

Andrea looked down at her hand in his. "Like what? It's smaller than I'd have expected for a spaceship. Unless they're really little aliens." Her tone was light, but her heart was racing. Could this truly be evidence of flying saucers?

Mike didn't release her hand, and Andrea made no move to pull away from the only safe, secure thing she had to cling to. "Mike, do you think we *are* dealing with UFOs? Professor Hale said something about Indians, about the medicine wheel, that it was similar to crop circles." She stopped, realizing she was babbling.

"The medicine wheel? Crop circles?" He frowned and shook his head. "There's no connection that I'm aware of. The medicine wheel is, well, not to be trite, but it symbolizes the circle of life. The way all people and animals and plants, even what most people consider inanimate objects, are interconnected. It has nothing to do with aliens."

He let go of her and crouched to study a sandy area next to the grassy patch. "*This* has nothing to do with aliens, either. Look here." He touched the ground lightly, and Andrea leaned over to see what he'd found.

Imprinted in the dirt was a series of diamondlike patterns.

"Tire tracks?"

Mike nodded. "I doubt if space aliens use four-wheel drive."

Andrea shuddered, feeling strangely violated. Someone had come out here, onto her property, and caused this damage. Someone human. The thought bothered her more than the possibility of aliens.

Why would someone do this? And how long had it been going on?

"Whatever they've been doing out here might be what's causing the bisons' problems." The realization left her feeling sickened. "Mike, we need to find out who's been here and why."

"I agree." He looked out across the plains. "It's not going to be easy, though. We'd practically have to catch whoever it is in the act."

"Do you think it might be Professor Hale?" Andrea wiped a bead of perspiration from her forehead. If only the breeze would pick up. She glanced up at the sky. Heavy clouds had started rolling in. "Would the professor stoop to faking evidence?"

"I don't know. I wouldn't put it past that Chambers woman, though. Let's take a few samples for analysis, just in case, and I'll take them to Minot. I have a friend in the chemistry lab at the university."

"Good idea," Andrea said. Dan had already had tests run on the soil and water at the ranch, but he couldn't test every acre and probably hadn't tested any sites where there had been evidence of...whatever was happening.

She studied the sky once more. The clouds were oddly

colored, almost greenish, and dark with rain. Lightning flashed in the distance.

Funny, she thought, how still the air was. She'd have expected some wind, at least, with the change of weather. But the atmosphere was heavy, almost palpably so, and humid.

Mike was familiar with the weather here. She turned to him, about to ask whether they were in for a storm, and noticed he was already contemplating the growing billows of dark clouds, his brows drawn low in a worried frown. "What is it?" she asked.

"We'd better head back. I don't like the looks of this weather."

She agreed. As bad as the clouds looked, though, the feel of the air was worse, disturbing her at some instinctive level. She'd never felt anything like it before.

They climbed into the truck. Mike started the engine and began to turn back the way they'd come, but after a quick check of the sky appeared to think better of it.

"We'll go cross-country," he said. "It'll be a little faster."

They turned again, and Andrea looked back over her shoulder toward the road. The clouds were heavier in that direction. Thick and low, they seemed to dip almost onto the road, rolling toward their fleeing vehicle like an inexorable gray-green tide.

Mike accelerated, and the truck bounded over the terrain. Andrea clung to the strap with one hand, steadying herself against the dash with the other. He glanced at her.

"Sorry," he said. "We have to get out of here fast."

Andrea looked behind them again. The bruise-colored clouds seemed almost in pursuit, rolling in to overtake them. Ahead of them a short distance, she recognized the low buildings of the Amundson homestead. They were still a long way from home.

Mike glanced in the rearview mirror. "Damn."

"What's wrong?" Andrea asked, but Mike didn't answer as he swerved the vehicle sharply toward the decrepit cabin.

He stopped between the building and the nearby creekbed. "Let's go." His voice was low and urgent. "Into the root cellar till it blows over."

His insistence brooked no argument, and Andrea followed him from the truck. "Till what blows over?"

"That." He nodded past her, and she turned to stare at the swirling tentacle of black that angled from the roiling clouds toward the earth, along the path they'd come.

It was a tornado.

CHAPTER EIGHTEEN

THE STORM RUSHED TOWARD them, a deadly finger of destruction. Here and there it touched the earth, sucking clouds of dust and debris into the maelstrom. Andrea stared at the approaching cyclone with morbid fascination, unable to tear her gaze from it.

"Oh, God, Mike. What about Dan and Lena? What about Gypsy?"

"It's not heading their way. They should be fine." Mike grabbed her hand and pulled her with him into the cabin. "Come on! We don't have much time." He wrenched open a trap door in the floor, then hustled her down a narrow ladder into the darkness.

Following her down, he slammed the door closed behind him, shutting off the only source of light. Andrea blinked futilely in the musty blackness.

"Mike?" she murmured. She knew he was behind her; she could hear him moving on the steps. But she needed his reassurance in her sudden blindness.

"I'm right here." His voice was calm but almost lost in the roar of the approaching storm.

His fingers closed on her shoulder in the darkness, steadying and strengthening her.

"Relax," he said, close to her ear. "We'll be fine."

She felt him move beside her and heard the jingle of keys. A tiny light came on, a bright spot smaller than a candle flame that, nonetheless, provided enough illumination for her to see some details of their shelter.

"That's a little better." Mike winked at her by the light of his key-chain flashlight.

It was a lot better, Andrea thought. Her ears no longer bore the brunt of her senses, and the noise of the storm seemed to diminish, if only because she could distract herself by looking around.

The cellar was small, roughly half the size of the cabin above it. Its walls and floor were dirt, shored up in places with old timbers. Piles of debris formed dark, amorphous blobs in the corners, and she could hear an occasional skitter as if tiny animals had been flushed from their homes by the intruders.

Mike began to investigate several boxes stacked near the steps, holding the light over his head to provide the widest area of illumination.

"We stashed some supplies down here a while back," he explained. "Just in case of an emergency like this. I think there's a battery-powered lantern in here somewhere."

Above them, the storm's fury increased, approaching them like a runaway freight train. She stepped nearer to Mike and feigned interest in his investigation of the supply boxes. If he wasn't worried, she thought, she wouldn't be, either.

Mike set aside jugs of bottled water, a first-aid kit and boxes of batteries, then pulled out a small plastic lamp, complete with a molded shade. He switched it on.

Pale light flooded the little space, banishing much of Andrea's fear along with the shadows.

The tornado roared overhead, its frenzy deafening. Andrea pressed her hands to her ears but couldn't shut out the raging wind. The cabin shuddered above them, and she recalled the scene from *The Wizard of Oz* in which Dorothy's little house was lifted off its foundation and hurled into the air. Could a storm really do that? Or would it just smash the cabin to splinters above their heads?

Mike glanced up at the trap door. Andrea followed his gaze. The aged wooden planks of the door flexed upward under the pressure of the wind.

"We'd be better off away from the door." Mike slid the boxes across the floor to the far side of the cellar and gestured for Andrea to follow.

A loud crash sounded above them. Dust rained down from the ceiling and Andrea screamed involuntarily. Mike pulled her into his arms and pressed her to the ground alongside the boxes, shielding her with his body.

Andrea clung to him, oblivious to everything but the safety of his arms. Her face pressed against his throat, she breathed in the masculine scent of him. She didn't care what happened to them as long as he held her.

Gently he lifted her off the dirt floor, and they settled onto the makeshift bench, still holding each other.

"Are you okay?" he asked, almost shouting to make himself heard over the storm. His breath was warm against her ear.

Andrea nodded. "Are you?" She looked up, expecting to see daylight through the cabin floor, but it was still intact. The impact of the storm had only shaken dirt and fragments of rotten wood down on them. She was amazed that the whole structure hadn't collapsed.

"I'm fine."

"How long will it last?" Andrea shouted at him despite the fact that his face was only inches from hers. His eyes were black in the lantern light.

"Not long." He stroked her hair out of her eyes. "Don't worry. We'll be all right."

"Are you sure it won't hit the ranch?" She wondered about Dan and Lena. And the boys. Were they back yet? What if they had gotten caught in the storm?

He shrugged. "I'm sure. The storm's moving in the opposite direction from the ranch." He squeezed her shoulder reassuringly. "They'll be fine. They've been through this often enough. The house has a good storm cellar."

"Just how many tornadoes have they been through?" she asked, trying to keep the tremor out of her voice.

Mike's arms tightened around her. "Actual tornadoes? Not many. Lots of tornado watches and warnings, though."

"What's the difference?" She was determined to keep him talking, as absurd as it was for them to sit here shouting at each other while a killer storm raged over them.

"Watches are announced when the conditions are right to produce a tornado," he explained. "That happens practically every time a thunderstorm moves through. A warning is when a funnel cloud has actually been spotted. Those are rarer, but not unusual. What's rare is for the tornado to actually touch down somewhere it can do damage.

"So what's the deal with mobile home parks?" she asked. "Every time there's a tornado, there seems to be a demolished trailer park involved."

"Oh, I have a theory about that." He took her hand in his. His tone was light, almost teasing, as though he sensed her need to keep talking.

Andrea raised an eyebrow. "This better not have anything to do with UFOs."

He shook his head emphatically. "No, not at all. Actually, my theory is that trailer parks, with their high concentration of metal and the electrical current from their power supplies, set up a magnetic field that attracts tornadoes."

"An electromagnetic field? You're kidding, right? You sound like Doc and the power lines."

"No, really," he said. "How else would you explain it?"

"Well, I can't, but I think the coincidence theory is a

little more likely—apart from the fact that trailers are less stable than houses.''

Mike rolled his eyes. ''They laughed at Einstein, too, at first. One of these days I'm going to apply for a grant to test my hypothesis.''

''I won't hold my breath.''

''It's always the scientific establishment that's the last to believe,'' he said in mock despair. He tilted his head. ''Listen.''

''What? I don't hear anything.''

''Exactly.''

She realized what he meant. Silence, almost eerier than the storm itself, had descended on the cabin. ''It's over,'' she murmured, then glanced at him for affirmation. ''Isn't it?''

''It is.'' He nodded and stood up, pulling her to her feet, then let go of her and walked to the stairs.

She stood below while he climbed up and opened the door. Daylight streamed into the cellar, followed by the thundering sound of rain on the wooden roof.

Mike climbed out and looked around. The cabin was still intact, or at least it was in no worse condition than it had been. He turned back to help Andrea out of the storm cellar, almost regretting that the storm had ended. The brief time he'd spent holding and reassuring her had, unbelievably, been the most peaceful he'd ever known.

She walked past him to the window. ''Mike,'' she said, worry in her voice. ''You'd better come look at this.''

He stepped up beside her and looked out the window. Rain poured down in silvery sheets that caused sky and land to meld into a single mass of gray beyond the cabin porch. He could just make out the pale blur of the truck, parked a few feet from the cabin.

She looked at him. ''Should we run for it?''

''No. The visibility's too bad to drive. We'd probably

end up in a flooded gully somewhere. We'll have to wait it out. It shouldn't be too long."

Glancing at his watch, he hoped he was right. It was late afternoon and ominously dark. The storm showed no sign of abating. "Are you hungry?" he asked to change the subject.

She nodded. "Starving. It's been a while since breakfast."

He glanced back out at the downpour, annoyed with himself. He should have gone with his first instinct and left early before she got up. If he had, they wouldn't be in this mess. He wouldn't be risking Andrea's life. "I have some emergency supplies in the truck. Part of my blizzard kit. There's some food. Well, granola bars, at least."

Andrea shook her head, concern in her eyes. "You don't need to go out in that. It should let up soon. I can wait."

"No, it's no problem. I'm pretty hungry, too," he lied. He'd do his best to make her comfortable. It was the least he could do. "Wait here. I'll just be a few minutes."

He stepped off the porch. The rain hit him like an intense cold shower, immediately drenching him to the skin. Thick mud sucked at his boots, making progress nearly impossible. The wind drove stinging drops of water into his face, forcing him to make his way forward almost blind.

At last his fingertips brushed the smooth side of the truck. He felt his way back to the tailgate and swung it open, then climbed into the bed to reach the utility box behind the cab. He opened it and pulled out a plastic storage box of emergency supplies, which he dropped over the right side of the truck to the ground.

Nearby, rushing water gurgled loudly, audible even above the pounding rain. Mike glanced down at the creekbed to the left of the truck.

The torrential downpour had flooded the little creek.

Swiftly flowing water stroked the sides of the left rear tire, rapidly carrying away the bank on which it rested.

Mike jumped out of the truck bed, made his way forward to the cab and climbed in. He had to move the vehicle before it slid off the embankment. If he could drive up alongside the cabin, the truck would be out of danger. If not...

He started the engine and accelerated forward. The mud refused to release its hold on the tires. Mike rocked the truck backward, infinitesimally—too much and he'd land in the creek—then he shifted into drive again and tried to roll forward.

The rear corner of the truck dropped with a sharp jolt.

Damn! The bank had given way.

Mike switched to four-wheel drive, but it was no good. The vehicle slipped downward again, then the rear swung in a quarter turn as the stream's current caught it. His back tires were in the water and the front ones couldn't grip the muddy slope.

Something pounded on the window. He leaned toward the passenger side, now slightly elevated, and looked out. It was Andrea, her face pale with fear.

"Get back!" he shouted. "It's too dangerous." What was she thinking? If the unstable truck rolled with her so close, she might be hit as the front end came off the ground.

She ignored him and swung open the passenger door. "Mike, get out!" she screamed. "The water's rising too fast." She reached frantically for his hand.

The truck twisted again, dropping further into the water. Mike glanced toward the rear and saw water creeping up the bed toward him. With the pouring rain, the creek had become a raging river.

Adrenaline surged through him. She was right. He was out of time. He clambered toward the passenger door.

Andrea had backed off and stood a few feet away, her

arms outstretched toward him, her hair drenched and her rain-soaked clothes plastered to her body. Mike slid over the edge of the doorway and dropped awkwardly to the ground, slipping in the mud. A shaft of pain shot through his ankle.

He had no recollection of crying out, but he must have, because suddenly Andrea was beside him, drawing his weight against her.

"What's wrong?" she shouted over the rain. "What did you hurt?"

"My ankle. It's nothing." He tried to push away from her and stand on his own, but another stab of pain made him clutch her shoulder to keep from falling.

"You *are* hurt," she said. "Come on, let's get inside."

"Bring the supplies." Mike gestured toward the plastic box he'd set aside.

She shook her head. "I'll come back for them. We have to get you inside first so I can have a look at that ankle."

Mike allowed her to support him as far as the porch, then insisted she save the supplies before the water swept them away. They might be trapped here awhile if the creek stayed high. The box contained blankets and other supplies in addition to the food. They'd need those once it got dark, especially soaked as they were.

Andrea looked rebellious but left him and went back into the rain to drag the box to the cabin. Once it was safely on the porch, she helped Mike inside.

"You don't have to do anything," he said, settling carefully onto the floor as his drenched clothing dripped a puddle beneath him. *Damn, it hurt to move.* "I'm fine."

She raised one eyebrow. "Oh, really? Can you walk on that foot? Can you even move it?"

He flexed his ankle experimentally. Pain lanced up his leg, and he couldn't suppress a grimace of pain.

Her expression said "I told you so." "Take off your boot," she ordered.

He shook his head. "I just twisted it. It'll be fine."

"Right." She stepped out onto the porch and dragged the heavy box of supplies inside. "Do you have any extra clothes or blankets in here?" Without waiting for an answer, she opened the case and began to tick off the contents. "Blankets, a sleeping bag, a snowmobile suit, first-aid kit, food." She looked at Mike intently. "We should get these soaked clothes off. It's not too cold out, but it doesn't take much of a chill to bring on hypothermia."

"Go ahead," Mike said.

Andrea scowled at him, then grabbed a blanket and pulled it over herself like a makeshift tent. After a moment, a sopping T-shirt flew out from under it, followed seconds later by a pair of soggy green boots and her drenched jeans. She poked her head free from the blanket and wrapped it togalike around herself, then wrung the water out of the cotton shirt and draped it over the windowsill to dry.

Mike stared at her. She was incredibly beautiful, even wrapped in an army surplus blanket with her hair hanging in damp strands over her shoulders.

Her bare shoulder and throat were smooth and pale. She was close enough that he could see the goose bumps on her arms. He longed to wrap his own arms around her and share his warmth.

Mike felt the blood rush from his head to other parts of his body and looked away quickly at the pouring rain. Maybe another trip outside would be a good idea, he thought. The cabin wasn't equipped with showers, cold or otherwise.

Andrea looked down at him. "Your turn."

He met her gaze and silently stripped off his sodden shirt, then took the blanket she offered and wrapped it around his shoulders. Its warmth felt good. He hadn't realized how chilled he was. He peeled off his boots, wincing at the pain in his ankle as he did so.

Andrea dropped to her knees beside him and reached for his foot. "Just let me take a look at it."

He shrugged and allowed her to extend his leg in front of her. She ran her hands expertly from knee to ankle, raising goose bumps that had nothing to do with the temperature. He fought to keep from his expression neutral, to keep from grimacing in pain.

She released his ankle and lowered his foot gently to the floor, then rocked back on her heels and studied him. "Well, I don't think it's broken, but you should probably get it X-rayed when we get back just to be on the safe side. I suspect it's only a bad sprain."

"Well, that's not so bad."

"No. You'll be dancing again in no time." She looked away, nervously, then glanced at him again. "How long do you think we'll be stuck here?"

"Probably overnight unless someone comes looking for us. The storm looks like it won't let up for a while. If it's still daylight, we can walk back to the house, but we don't dare try it at night, with the flooding."

"Not to mention your ankle," Andrea pointed out. "I doubt you'd get far with that."

"So I guess we're not so far removed from Dan's pioneer ancestors, after all."

Andrea nodded. They were trapped here in a primitive cabin, at the mercy of the elements. She remembered Mike telling her how Dan's great-uncle had died here in a storm. An involuntary shudder went through her and she caught her breath.

"Cold?" Mike asked. He reached out to her, offering her the warmth of his blanket, of his arms.

With a sigh, she went to him.

CHAPTER NINETEEN

MIKE WRAPPED HER in his arms. "Somehow these past weeks have seemed so unreal to me, like awakening after a long sleep to a reality I never knew existed. I feel like you've become part of White Thunder in that time. Like you've become part of me."

She didn't resist as he pulled her closer. "I feel the same, as though I belong somewhere for the first time in my life. I tried so hard not to admit it to myself, though. I couldn't face a new complication in my life."

Lightning flashed, momentarily brightening the dim cabin. A long, rolling peal of thunder followed.

He searched her eyes for any sign of hesitation or regret. "Can you face it now?"

"I have to. I can't hide from the truth anymore." She lowered her head and pressed her lips gently to his.

Her mouth was hot and soft on his, and the last vestige of his resistance fled. This woman held the key to his future. She offered him a chance to live again.

It was time to take that chance.

Andrea caught her breath as Mike pulled her across him to cradle her against his bare chest. For a brief moment some still-rational part of her brain told her to stop, to think about what she was doing. Then his mouth came down on hers, driving away all reason. She clutched at him, gripping his shoulders, stroking the muscular column of his neck, holding him against her.

Mike caressed her face and throat with his free hand,

then very slowly, as though offering her the chance to demur, he peeled back the layers of the blanket that covered her.

She looked up into his face as he bared her to his gaze. He closed his eyes, then opened them again, as though unable to believe what he'd seen.

"God, you're so beautiful," he whispered. His mouth claimed hers again. He stroked her shoulders and arms, easing the thin straps of her bra down out of his way, then reaching behind her to unfasten the garment.

She slid it off, freeing herself to his touch.

He inhaled rapidly, then reached to cup her gently, his thumb stroking, teasing, caressing her nipple.

Andrea gasped and arched her back, pressing into his hand as exquisite pleasure shot through her. He bent to kiss and suckle first one breast, then the other. Her pulse pounded, her body taking up the beat, throbbing and insistent. Hunger rose from deep within her, an aching desire that begged for fulfillment. She'd never felt anything like it.

Mike rolled her gently onto the discarded blanket. His jeans were still wet from the rain and cold against her bare skin, but she could feel his heat and hardness through the fabric as she moved across him.

He rose onto his knees over her and Andrea reached out, emboldened by her desire, to grasp the buckle of his belt. He worked the leather strap free as she let her hand stray to his zipper. He gasped and closed his eyes as she pressed her palm against his hard length.

He slipped off the damp jeans and stretched out beside her on the blanket. "Are you sure this is what you want?" he asked, suddenly uncertain. He was risking everything. If this was a mistake, he had to know now.

"I've never been so sure of anything before," she replied, and drew him into her arms.

AFTERWARD, THEY LAY entwined together, spent and sated, as the rain slowed to a gentle shower, then faded away in the darkness.

"Thank you," he said.

She rose on one elbow and blinked at him. "For what?" She traced the bow of his upper lip with the tip of her finger.

He caught her hand and kissed it. "For giving me my life back. I'd forgotten what it was like to trust someone. I almost missed the truth that was right in front of me."

She cradled her head on his shoulder, wrapping the blanket around them. "If you want to talk about it, I'll listen."

Mike stroked her bare arm, hesitating but realizing he wanted to tell her. He owed it to her.

"I was in the army when it happened," he began slowly. "We were sent out of the country on what was called a training exercise. It turned out to be something else."

He recalled the instructions his unit received as the plane approached the drop zone. They were to attack a guerrilla stronghold in retaliation for a raid that had killed several American soldiers. The mission was top secret. Its details were still classified and he could give her no more than a vague hint of what they had done in the jungle that day. The less she knew the better.

"We parachuted into the area and everything went as planned. Then, as we were returning to our rendezvous point, one of my men was hit by a sniper. I went back to help him."

"Was he badly hurt?"

"No," Mike said. "It was a deep flesh wound, but not too bad. I helped him back along the path the rest of the squad had taken. I was only a few minutes behind them when it happened."

Andrea waited, silent, her expression grave.

"The path had been mined." The jungle soil had been

soft and covered with leaves. It was so easy for someone to bury several antipersonnel mines and wait for the enemy to come along. He hadn't even considered the possibility of mines. Probably wouldn't have even if he hadn't been busy with his injured comrade.

"The mine exploded as I stepped on it. I was lucky, in a lot of ways. It wasn't a Bouncing Betty, for one thing." He saw the question form on Andrea's face and explained. "That's a type of mine that springs into the air when someone steps on it. Then it explodes. Not too many people survive those. The one that got me was triggered to explode when stepped on. I felt the trigger click, and it registered enough that I was able to shove the other guy out of the way before it went off. That movement knocked me off balance slightly and probably saved me. Most of my injuries were from shrapnel and concussion."

"Oh, Mike." Pain and horror mingled in Andrea's expression. "What happened to the other man?"

"He was hit by shrapnel but wasn't too badly injured. I'd taken most of the explosion, shielding him. My legs got the worst of it."

"When I got home..." Memories of his homecoming washed over him like icy rain. Andrea pressed against him to warm him with her own body, and he held her tightly.

"I was engaged to be married. My injuries were severe and I was in the hospital a long time. At first they didn't think I'd walk again. But I did. And I came to realize that the way of life I'd chosen was wrong for me. I needed to face my past so I could find my future. My fiancée couldn't accept the changes, though. She left me."

Clasped in his arms, Andrea gasped as though in sudden pain. He looked down at her. Her eyes were bright with unshed tears. He kissed her forehead and she trembled in his arms.

"I came out here after I was discharged. I met Dan and

went to work on the ranch. He was, well…'Like a father to me' sounds so clichéd, but he truly was. My own father had held back so much, I think, because of his own past. Dan welcomed me into the family. I belonged somewhere, for the first time in my life.''

Andrea snuggled closer to Mike, seeking his warmth as a wave of guilt swept over her. She'd been right. He had been hurt. Rejected and abandoned by a woman who left him exactly the way she left Jeffrey.

But it wasn't really the same, her mind struggled to rationalize. She hadn't abandoned an injured man. She could never have done such a thing.

But she had abandoned Jeffrey. *What would Mike think if he knew?*

It didn't matter. She owed him the truth, regardless of the consequences. He'd been honest with her. Did he deserve any less?

"Sleepy?'' Mike whispered.

"What?'' She turned to him.

He ran his fingertips over the curves where her breasts pressed against him. "You got so quiet. I wondered if you were sleepy.''

"Not at all,'' she said softly. She'd tell him about Jeffrey, but not now, she thought as she surrendered herself once more to his touch.

ANDREA AWOKE and stretched, her back aching from a night spent on the cabin floor. She opened her eyes. Pale gray light filled the room. *Up before dawn again.* Much more of this, she told herself, and she'd be a morning person in no time.

Warmth, nearly weightless, surrounded her. Mike's sleeping bag from the truck, she realized. He must have opened it up to cover them with during the night.

She felt the blankets next to her. Empty. Where had he gone?

"'Morning, sleepyhead."

Andrea sat up, clutching the covers around her against the early morning chill. Already dressed, Mike lounged on the windowsill watching her thoughtfully.

"Dan should be along soon," he said. He walked over to their makeshift bed, limping noticeably on his sprained ankle, and bent to kiss her cheek. "The clothes are still a little damp, but wearing wet denim is probably better than having him walk in on us without it." He grinned at her and wriggled his eyebrows in mock lasciviousness before handing over her jeans and T-shirt.

Andrea laughed, but her insides had twisted into knots. She hadn't expected Dan to come looking for them. What would he think? Would he guess what had happened to them last night?

"Thanks," she said, hoping her apprehension wasn't visible on her face as she pulled the clothing under the blanket. After last night, she shouldn't be shy about dressing in front of him, but she was.

As if he sensed her discomfort, Mike stepped carefully back to the window and looked toward the horizon. "It'll be a beautiful sunrise," he said. He turned to her and held out his hand. "Come watch it with me."

Unable to resist, Andrea pulled her T-shirt over her head and climbed out of the covers to pull on her damp jeans. She joined Mike at the window, where he warmed her with his embrace.

The prairie stretched endlessly away from them toward the horizon, where the gray predawn sky began to take on a faint yellow glow. Behind wispy trails of cloud that mottled it with shades of rose and mauve, the sky slowly brightened to pale peach, then soft lemon.

Andrea watched as the streaks of clouds, fading reminders of last night's tempest, lightened to buttermilk. Below them, the vast expanse of grassland glowed like spun gold.

"Oh, God, Mike," she whispered. "It's incredible."

He nodded. "This is my favorite time of day." He pressed a kiss into her unkempt hair.

"Out east they grow sunflowers," he continued. "Huge fields of them. Every morning they face the sunrise, thousands upon thousands of them, huge blossoms all lined up in one direction like an army in yellow parade uniforms standing at attention. Then, as the sun moves across the sky, they follow it until at the end of the day they all face the sunset." He gazed into her eyes, his face bright as she'd never seen it before. "I want to show it to you. There's so much that's beautiful about this land. I want to share it all with you."

Tears welled in Andrea's eyes. Blast it, she wasn't usually so weepy. What was happening to her lately? She raised her arms around his neck and pulled him down to her lips.

She knew what was happening. She'd fallen in love with him despite her best intentions. Despite the fact that she had recently left a fiancé at the altar.

Oh, God, she had to tell him. He needed to know, deserved to know the truth.

She disentangled herself from Mike and forced herself to meet his eyes. "Mike," she began.

Honk!

Andrea pulled away from him, guilty relief warring with frustration as a second blast of a truck horn shattered the stillness. She shielded her eyes against the rising sun and gazed out across the plain. A vehicle rumbled toward them.

"I think we're about to be rescued," Mike said, regret and humor mingling in his voice.

"I think you're right," Andrea replied. She didn't recognize the truck. "Well, I guess it was bound to happen sooner or later. Who is it?" *And why now?*

"Someone from town, I think. Maybe they brought the band back."

Andrea rolled her eyes. "You don't suppose the band's with them now, do you?" She could just imagine Stench's reaction to the news that she and Mike had spent the night together.

The truck came to a stop alongside the swollen creek where the truck sat in water that still reached above the rear bumper. Dan, Rusting Hulkk, and another man climbed out of the vehicle.

Dan hurried up to them, concern clouding his face. "Are you two all right? We were afraid that twister might have gotten you."

"We're fine." Mike clapped him on the shoulder. "We got through the tornado okay, down in the storm cellar. The creek flooded, though, and stranded us." He gestured to the truck. "We'll need a tow out of there."

"No problem," Dan said. "Steve's truck has a winch. We'll have you out in no time."

Steve, whom Andrea recognized as the owner of the Minot feed store, nodded. "It'll just take a few minutes."

Stench, Todd and Jock stepped up onto the porch, all three wearing meaningful grins.

Jock looked inside the old cabin. "Wow. You guys spent the night here, huh? Talk about rustic."

"Oh, I don't know," Stench remarked. "A little paint, some curtains, it wouldn't be so bad. Kinda drafty, though." He raised his eyebrows significantly. "Was it cold?"

Mike shook his head. "Nope," he said, refusing to be baited. "I had survival gear in the truck, so we stayed warm enough. Not that this is cold. We were equipped for blizzard conditions."

"So what was that you were doing on the front porch as we drove up," Todd asked, "if you weren't sharing bodily warmth?"

Damn, Andrea thought. She'd hoped they hadn't been seen. Oh, well, they'd all have found out eventually. She met Todd's teasing gaze. "Administering first aid. I'm a doctor, after all, and Mike's got a badly sprained ankle."

She glanced at Dan, who was watching the proceedings with twinkling eyes. He grinned broadly, and she felt her cheeks grow warm.

She gathered the supplies while the men worked to free the truck from the creek. Steve was right. It took only a few minutes to winch the vehicle back up to the bank of the swollen stream.

The boys helped her load the survival equipment. They started to climb in back for the trip to the ranch house, but Dan waved them over to him. Andrea couldn't hear what he said to them, but they ended up climbing into Steve's truck.

Mike rolled his eyes. "He probably thinks we'd rather be alone."

Embarrassed, Andrea took her seat in the vehicle. "That's okay. This will be easier. We'd never hear the end of it if they rode back with us. By the way, are you all right to drive with that ankle?"

Mike nodded. "It's sore, but I can move it without any problem as long as I don't stand on it."

"Good," Andrea said, settling back in the seat. "The station wagon I can handle, but this I don't know about."

The thought of the other vehicle brought its owner to mind. Facing Lena was going to be tough, too, she realized, but she suspected the housekeeper would approve of the direction her relationship with Mike had taken.

As the two trucks crossed the rolling prairie to the house, then to the main roads, Andrea was surprised to note that little standing water remained from yesterday's downpour. The earth had quickly absorbed most of it.

The breeze had returned today, and to her relief, the air no longer felt ominously heavy and still. Bright sunshine promised a warm day, and Andrea settled against the seat, drowsy and comfortable with the sun's heat on her face.

As they drove into the yard, she noticed an unfamiliar car parked beside the house. It bore a rental agency sticker on the rear bumper. Was it someone from Vidtel? She doubted it. Limousines seemed to be more their style.

Mike parked the truck, and Andrea climbed out as Lena stepped onto the front porch, her expression oddly strained. A woman, petite and smartly dressed, walked out of the house to stand beside her.

Andrea's heart skipped a beat.

It was her mother.

CHAPTER TWENTY

"ANDREA. SWEETHEART."

Mother covered the distance between them with a few dainty steps, looking model-chic in tan slacks and a nubby cream sweater. She clasped Andrea to her in a tight embrace, kissing the air beside her cheek, then gazed up at her. "Darling, it's all right now. I know you're sorry, and Jeffrey and I both forgive you. He's willing to overlook your behavior and take you back. Everything's going to be fine."

Wait a minute, Andrea thought. *I know you're sorry?*

Rigid in her mother's iron clasp, she looked into the petite woman's china blue eyes, bright under impeccably styled, dyed chestnut hair, and fought to stem a wave of anger. In a way it was comforting to know some things hadn't changed.

She threw a glance at Mike, who stood nearby watching with undisguised interest, as did Dan and the band members. Lena stepped up beside him and laid a cautioning hand on his arm.

Andrea extricated herself from her mother's grasp. "When did you get here, Mother?" she asked, trying to remain calm, to find a way out of this nightmare. "How did you find me?"

"I found out from Jeffrey's receptionist that Vidtel was running the coverage of your first day here," Mother said. "She saw it on television. I contacted the network and demanded that they tell me how to get here. Of course everyone knew where you were but your own family until you condescended to call. We were left to think you'd been abducted by some cult." She pouted daintily. "I got here about an hour ago."

Of course, Andrea thought. Vidtel was the last network Mother would willingly watch. But she hadn't even considered that she might be seen on television by any of her friends or co-workers.

Her mother stepped back and patted her perfect coiffure in a gesture of exasperation. "I immediately made plans to come out, then I called and called, but the woman who answered the phone kept telling me I had the wrong number and there was no one here named Andrea." She shot a withering glance at Lena.

Andrea glanced at Lena, too, and the other woman feigned interest in an imaginary speck of lint on her sleeve. Now that she thought about it, the phone *had* seemed to be ringing an awful lot, but she had attributed it to calls from Dan's friends asking about White Thunder's change of ownership.

She didn't know whether to be touched or irritated at the housekeeper's assistance, but at least Lena's tactics had stalled her mother while Andrea made her decision about the ranch.

"Anyway," her mother continued, "I've found you. Now, get your things together so we can get out of this godforsaken place." She looked around with an expression of distaste as she gripped Andrea's arm and tried to guide her toward the house. "I've been a nervous wreck, thanks to you. I took to my bed for a week after you disappeared. Dr. Jamison had to refill my tranquillizer prescription. It was all I could do to maintain my self-control." She shook her head. "And poor Jeffrey. He was stunned, the poor boy. Heartbroken. Oh, Andrea, how could you do this to us?"

Andrea winced, resisting both the tug on her arm and the

guilt her mother was determined to force on her. She'd hoped they could settle this and get her mother on her way with no mention of the wedding. If Mike found out…

She glanced at him. *Too late.*

He stepped closer. "Andrea." His voice was dangerously low. "What's going on here?"

Mother stopped pulling but maintained her hold, looking Mike up and down disapprovingly. "Who are you?"

"I'm Mike Winterhawk, the foreman here at White Thunder," Mike said. "Who are you?"

Mrs. Moore drew herself up in the way she always did when preparing to berate an impertinent salesclerk. Andrea caught her breath.

"I'm Andrea's mother, Helen Moore. I'm here on behalf of her fiancé, Dr. Jeffrey Miles."

She made a point of emphasizing Jeffrey's title. Andrea rolled her eyes.

Mother continued. "Andrea left the evening of her wedding, abandoning her fiancé at the altar, as well as her own mother and several hundred wedding guests. For this." She gestured at the house and barn, then turned to direct her comments at Andrea. "Jeffrey was very angry and hurt, but I've convinced him to forgive you and take you back. I know you were just confused, and I've tried to make that clear to him. He's a proud man, but I believe he'll excuse your miserable behavior so you can get on with your lives."

Mike retreated a step as if he'd been struck. "Pleased to meet you, Mrs. Moore," he said quietly. "If you'll excuse me, I have some errands to run in town." He turned away sharply, brushing aside Lena's fluttering hand, then stalked to the truck as fast as his injured ankle would allow and climbed in. The tires spewed dirt and pebbles as he took off down the drive.

Andrea closed her eyes and drew in a deep breath, fighting the sick, trembling sensation roiling inside her. When she opened them again, the vehicle was out of sight.

Oh, God. What had she done?

Tears sprang to her eyes, and she squeezed her lids against them, refusing to cry in front of her mother. A knot that felt about the size of Gypsy's head constricted her throat.

Fortunately her mother, caught up as usual in her own concerns, seemed oblivious to her distress. "Let's go, Andrea." She resumed her pull on Andrea's arm. "I have tickets for the eleven o'clock flight out of Minot and it's a long drive."

Andrea shook herself free and stood her ground. Did the woman have no sense at all? Of course not, she decided, answering her own question. Mother had always been so busy planning her life that she could never see what it was she truly wanted. She was very much like Jeffrey in that respect. It was probably why the two of them got on so well.

Mother turned to her, a familiar and infinitely irritating mingling of patient condescension and exasperation settling over her fine features. "Now what is it, sweetheart? Is it the ranch? I know you won it, but surely you don't want to keep it and *stay* here." She grimaced delicately. "You can sell it and have a tidy little nest egg for you and Jeffrey to start out. I'll contact a real estate agent as soon as we get back to Seattle."

"I'm not going with you, Mother. This is my home now." The words came out so easily, Andrea thought for a moment someone else was speaking. Even as she said them, the realization astonished her. She felt none of her usual guilt, none of the desire to appease her mother regardless of what she wanted herself. If the woman couldn't understand that she'd made her decision, that was her problem, not Andrea's.

Had she changed so much in such a short time? she wondered.

Her mother frowned, puzzled. "What do you mean, dear? Of course you're coming with me."

Andrea shook her head and noticed that the onlookers had started to discreetly disperse, leaving them alone in the middle of the yard. "No. I'm not," she said as clearly and concisely as she could, hoping her words would penetrate her mother's denial. "I'm staying here. *You're* leaving."

"Staying here?" Mrs. Moore blinked several times. "But, darling, you're engaged to be married. Jeffrey is willing to forgive and forget. You don't know how much effort it took me to convince him you were sorry you'd humiliated us. And after all, he certainly doesn't intend to leave his practice, and you can't conduct a marriage with both of you separated by half a continent."

Andrea sighed. How had she never realized before how truly blind her mother was to all but her own agenda? She placed her hands on her mother's delicate shoulders and faced her squarely. "Mother, I'm not going to marry Jeffrey. If I'd intended to marry him, I'd have stayed in Seattle and done it. I came out here because I couldn't marry him. Because I discovered that I wasn't in love with him." She let her arms drop to her sides, no longer seeing a need to fight. She'd made her decision. That was all that mattered.

Mrs. Moore chewed her lower lip thoughtfully. "I'm going to give you the benefit of the doubt, Andrea," she said in that cajoling yet self-assured tone she reserved for those moments when Andrea's rare stubbornness reared its ugly head. "I'll drive back to Minot for the night and give you a chance to think things through." She went to her car and opened the door, then turned back to Andrea. "I'll be back tomorrow and you can let me know your decision." She climbed into the car and drove away, leaving Andrea standing alone in the dusty driveway.

MIKE GLANCED AT the speedometer and noticed that it was pushing eighty. He was speeding and he didn't give a damn. He had to get away, and dropping off the soil samples was the perfect excuse. Of course, he had no idea what he'd do after that.

He'd known something was up when he'd overheard Andrea's phone call that first night. But he'd never have guessed she'd left her fiancé, literally, at the altar. The same way Michelle left him.

And she hadn't told him. Apparently she didn't think her engagement was important enough to tell him about. Even after he'd been open with her about his own past.

There was no way around it. It had happened again, despite all his intentions to the contrary. He'd fallen in love only to have that love betrayed.

And he *was* in love with her.

Damn! He slammed his fist against the steering wheel. How had it happened? What had he done to deserve this?

And more important, what was he going to do about it now?

Well, the problem might solve itself. Andrea might decide to return to Seattle with her fiancé.

The thought gnawed a cold, hollow ache in his guts. He didn't want her to leave. But could he trust her to commit to him and to White Thunder when she'd kept this from him? The ranch was in for some tough times. Would she stick it out when things got difficult, and if not, would she keep her promise to sell to him?

What if she ran like she had from her wedding? What if she sold White Thunder for the first offer she received? He'd lose everything.

He had to go back. To find out where things stood.

But not today. Today he'd drop off the samples from the "crop circle," find a comfortable hotel and have a night of peace and quiet before he returned. He had a feeling he'd need it.

TWO HOURS LATER, he lay rigid atop the covers of a hotel bed, ignoring a sports program on cable.

Why had Andrea left the guy?

Maybe she had a good reason. He knew deep down that it wasn't for the same kind of reason Michelle had dumped him. As briefly as he'd known Andrea, he knew her well enough to realize she wouldn't be so cruel. She'd stand by a man who'd been through what he had. She'd help him recover. To regain his life. To find his vision. At least, she would if she loved him.

He had to give her a chance to explain. He owed her that. He owed himself, as well. The loss of Andrea would be a wound he could never overcome.

ANDREA WALKED BACK into the house after her mother drove off. Its occupants scattered before her as though she was carrying the plague, leaving her alone in the kitchen. She sank onto one of the dinette chairs and rested her head in her hands.

Mike hated her. She knew it. The expression on his face when Mother told him about the wedding would be etched in her memory the rest of her life. All the pain and longing and betrayal he must have felt when his fiancée left him had come flooding back.

Now she was in love, for the first time in her life, and she was about to lose everything because of the way she'd left Jeffrey. It was a terrible irony, she thought, that she'd finally grown strong enough to put her own needs first and by doing so had probably destroyed her only chance for love.

She felt a hand on her shoulder and looked up reluctantly. Lena stood beside her. The lanky redhead pulled up a chair and sat down.

"He'll be back." She patted Andrea's arm. "He loves you, you know."

Andrea shook her head, the hated tears filling her eyes. "Oh, Lena, if he did, he doesn't anymore. I've ruined it."

"Bull pucky," Lena snorted. "You did what you had to do. That young man you were going to marry sounds like a real horse's hind end. You're lucky you got out when you did."

"I know. I had to do it. But now Mike thinks I'm just as terrible as the girl who left him when he was hurt." She gave a shuddering sigh.

Lena shook her head. "Mike's like all men. Sometimes it takes a little while for sense to penetrate their thick skulls. It will, though, and he'll realize that what matters is that he's in love with you. Eventually he'll figure out why you had to leave the way you did."

"Do you think so?" Hope flickered. Mike had to come back sometime, after all. When he did, she'd tell him the truth and why she kept it from him.

"You betcha." Lena grinned at her. "Now, why don't you give Doc a call and see if there's anything he needs help with this afternoon. It'll do you good to get away for a few hours. No sense having you moping around here all day."

"You're right," Andrea said. An afternoon at the clinic, in Doc's buoyant company, would definitely help distract her from her troubles. She picked up the phone.

MIKE SAT IN THE DIMLY LIT hotel bar nursing his light beer. He wasn't normally much of a drinker. Tonight, though, he thought, that might just change. If ever he'd felt like drowning his sorrows, it was now.

He glanced around the nearly empty lounge and wondered why all bars looked the same. Dark, smoky and earth-colored with an abundance of wood and black Naugahyde. Had someone conducted a study years ago and determined that people drank more in gloomy surroundings? Or was the uniformity intended to keep the more inebriated customers in a familiar milieu to minimize their disorientation?

Mike took another swallow of his beer. Whatever the intent, the decor did make it easy to sit here and concentrate on drinking. There wasn't much else to do.

"Bartender. Bourbon and water," a woman said behind him. "Double."

Mike turned to face the auburn-haired woman who slid onto the bar stool next to him. It was Andrea's mother.

Great, he thought. *Of all the gin joints in all the towns in all the world...* Leave it to him to pick the same hotel where Andrea's mother was staying.

She glanced at him, her smooth brow wrinkling slightly. "Aren't you the foreman from my daughter's ranch?"

Mike nodded. "Mike Winterhawk."

Something akin to relief relaxed her features, as though she was glad to see a familiar face, no matter how awkward the situation. "That's right. Mike."

The bartender placed a glass in front of her, and she gratefully took a swallow of pale golden liquid, then turned back to him. "Mike, do you have children?"

"Um, no, ma'am." Mike surreptitiously glanced around for some means of escape. The last thing he wanted was to sit here with Andrea's mother, discussing her parenting problems. He feigned interest in his beer.

"You're lucky. Because no matter what you do to help them along, eventually they'll break your heart." She took another sip of her drink. "I've tried and tried to make her happy, to help her make the right choices, and now, when I've finally managed to convince Jeffrey that she still wants him, what does she do? I'll tell you what. She refuses to come home."

Mike looked up in sudden interest. "She did?"

"Yes." Mrs. Moore's tone was indignant. "Can you believe that? After all we've suffered. And when I come all the way out here to tell her she's forgiven, she tells me to go home. I might as well catch my flight home tomorrow. This time I don't think I'll be able to change her mind."

Mike felt as though a half-ton weight had just been lifted from his chest.

"I don't know why she insists on staying," Mrs. Moore continued. "There's nothing out here. I pointed that out to her. And poor Jeffrey, he'd tried so hard to plan everything out for her, to guarantee she'd be taken care of. Do you think she was grateful? Not at all."

She took a swallow of her drink. "I tried to convince Jeffrey to come with me. I was so sure that was what she wanted. For him to prove his love by chasing after her."

"And he wouldn't come?" Mike asked.

"No. He refused to stoop to begging." Mrs. Moore shook her head. "He had everything planned out to the last detail. They were going to have a wonderful life together. He would have taken care of everything. He'd have given her the security I never had. Why would she leave?"

Mike finished his beer, wondering whether he could make his escape. The bartender asked if he wanted another drink. He shook his head and pulled out his wallet to pay.

"And what is it with this career thing?" Mrs. Moore added. "Jeffrey planned for her to stop working when the babies came. After all, a child's place is with its mother, don't you agree? But she didn't seem to like that idea at all." She shook her head in obvious exasperation. "I mean, here he was, offering to take care of her for the rest of their lives. Everything was arranged. Then what does she do? She runs."

Mike collected his change and paused, staring at her.

Suddenly he saw his situation and Andrea's as clearly as if a bright light had been shed on them.

Michelle had run because everything she'd counted on, the stability she'd come to expect, had disappeared with his injury and the changes it had wrought. She'd lost control of her future.

And Andrea had run because her fiancé had taken control of her life and intended to enforce his brand of stability on her, just as her mother had tried to do all her life. She must have felt the cage door starting to close behind her as her wedding approached. And just like any caged animal, though she would have been protected and cared for, she took advantage of the chance to make a final break for freedom. The news that she'd won White Thunder was the key that opened her prison.

He couldn't blame Andrea for her decision, just as, suddenly, he could no longer blame Michelle for hers. Both had done what was necessary to protect themselves, though it had meant hurting someone else in the process.

He had to get back to White Thunder. He looked at his watch. Nearly nine. It would be almost eleven before he reached the ranch, but he had to get back. He'd call the lab for the test results tomorrow.

"I just remembered I have an appointment," he said to Mrs. Moore, who watched him curiously as he hurried out of the bar.

CHAPTER TWENTY-ONE

HOT BREATH GUSTED against Andrea's cheek and something tickled her nose. Groggily she raised a hand to brush the offending object away from her face. Her hand touched a large, hairy shape, and she opened her eyes just as a pink tongue descended on her face.

She thrust herself upright in Doc's wing chair, and Ole, standing on his hind legs, front paws on the arm of the chair, gave her a "woof" of greeting.

"Okay, okay, kibble breath." She grabbed the dog's muzzle playfully, directing it away from her face. "I'm up. Back off."

She looked at her watch. Almost 10:00 p.m. She'd dozed for nearly two hours.

Doc appeared in the doorway carrying two steaming mugs. "I see Ole's given you your wake-up call." He handed her a cup. "This'll get you back on your feet."

"I don't care about my feet. As long as it gets the taste of dog breath out of my mouth."

Doc laughed. "Well, if nothing else it'll kill the germs. I've yet to meet any bacteria that can survive my coffee."

Andrea took a swallow of the strong brew. "I'd bet a few higher organisms wouldn't survive it, either." She stretched and took another sip, letting its warmth soak into her. Doc and Lena must have learned their coffee-making skills at the same place, she thought, probably some secret Defense Department chemical lab.

"I looked in on our patient and gave him his last meds

for the night," Doc said. "He's doing fine. We'll keep him on a restricted diet for a few days, and if there are no further complications, we may be able to send him home Monday."

"Great, I'd hoped we would," she said, relieved. The Doberman pinscher had come in late in the afternoon with severe pain, abdominal distention and shock. A series of X rays had revealed twisting of the stomach known as gastric torsion, and emergency surgery was necessary.

After the long surgery, Andrea stayed with the dog so Doc could have supper and nap for a few hours. She knew if she went back to White Thunder too soon, she'd spend the whole evening worrying about Mike. Better to stay at the clinic and occupy herself with her patients.

She spent the early evening listening to the radio and reading between checks on the Doberman and other patients. Near 8:00 p.m., she'd settled down to read a textbook on farm animal nutrition. The last thing she remembered was a comparison of protein levels in feed grains. She'd fallen asleep with the book in her lap.

"Why don't you head home and get some sleep?" Doc said. "You're probably exhausted."

Andrea nodded. "I guess I'm more tired than I thought. It's been a trying day."

Doc studied her, but she didn't elaborate. He probably knew everything, anyway.

"Is your mother still at the ranch?" he asked, confirming her suspicions.

"No, she left just before I came over. Mother threatened, I mean, promised, she'd be back tomorrow, though. So, what do you have lined up for tomorrow?"

"Why? Do you plan to stay the night and avoid her?" A grin lit Doc's face.

"Don't tempt me." She shook her head. "No, I'll have to face her eventually. I might as well get it over with."

"Well, I have a few morning appointments here, then a couple farm calls to make. Nothing major unless we get another emergency, but come on by if you want to." His brown eyes twinkled. "You've been good for business. I've had more unusual cases in the past couple weeks than I've had in months."

Andrea considered her alternatives. If Mike didn't return by morning, she'd spend the whole day watching for him. Or arguing with her mother. She made her decision. "I'll be in around ten unless something comes up."

"Great. I'll see you then."

A few minutes later she maneuvered the station wagon out of the clinic driveway, stifling a yawn and hoping, after numerous trips to town, that she'd be able to find her way back to the ranch. She rolled her window halfway down, counting on the cool evening air to keep her alert so she could watch for familiar landmarks.

It felt like a year rather than a day had passed since she and Mike had been stranded at the old homestead. Only a day since they'd lain together in the cool darkness of the cabin listening to the beat of raindrops on the roof. Since she'd felt his hands on her body and realized that it was what she'd wanted since the first moment she saw him.

The tears she'd fought so hard spilled over at last, tracing warm trails down her cheeks.

If Mike wasn't at White Thunder by the time she got there... She'd throw herself at his feet the minute he got home and beg his forgiveness for not telling him about Jeffrey.

Tears drying, she glanced down to check the odometer. She was close to the ranch now. Time to start watching for the turnoff.

There it was, right on schedule. She signaled from force of habit and slowed to make the turn.

Ahead of her, some distance off the road, a light flashed.

No, she thought, *not again.*

She slowed the station wagon to a crawl and rolled her window down the rest of the way to allow herself an unobstructed view of the object.

It disappeared for a moment. Then it was back, bobbing and dipping as though carried along by the evening breeze. This time it was closer, no more than a few hundred yards from the road. She turned off her headlights and pulled to the shoulder, where she sat watching the object's passage across the night sky.

That thing, whatever it was, was the root of all the ranch's problems, she was sure. She had to get to the bottom of this.

She climbed out of the car and closed the door quietly. A gust of wind fingered her hair, making goose bumps rise along her arms and back.

What if it is a UFO? Pale, bug-eyed creatures danced in her imagination.

She shook herself sharply. The worst thing she was likely to find would be Clarissa Hale and her party of alien-hunting flakes. And as strange as the little professor was, Andrea was fairly certain she wasn't dangerous. Even in association with Connie Chambers.

If it was Clarissa, though, she'd take more definitive action this time. There was no excuse for trespassing after the warning she'd given the woman, science or no.

She started down the shallow slope of the ditch between the road and the fence, actually wishing for once that she were wearing her hated snakeskin boots. They'd provide better support on the uneven terrain than her sneakers did, but they were back at the house drying out after their drenching in the storm. She'd have to be extra careful. The last thing she needed was a twisted ankle out here in the middle of nowhere.

At the barbed-wire fence, she hesitated. *Over or under?*

The idea of getting hung up astride the fence was too painful to even consider. She raised the second strand from the bottom and crouched to ease under it. The barbs grabbed a few flyaway strands of her hair, tugging them painfully, and she paused to free herself, leaving a few hairs caught in the fence wire.

Then she was inside. Ahead of her, the glowing object moved slowly away. She followed.

She hadn't underestimated the ruggedness of the terrain. It was slow going. She kept her eyes on the ground, picking her way over hillocks and around gullies and stumbling more than once on rock chunks jutting up from the soil.

Overhead the moon edged out from behind a cloud, illuminating the ground in front of her. Taking advantage of the light, she moved quickly, topping a low rise. She crouched down, as she'd learned from Mike, to keep from being seen. Just in case.

Ahead of her something moved, casting shadows against the ridge beyond. Andrea ducked back behind the crest of the hill, dropping onto her stomach in the tall grass. Her pulse raced, and struggling to breathe both deeply and silently at the same time, she listened.

A muttered curse came to her over the nighttime sounds of the prairie. It was quickly shushed.

"Yeah, right," a harsh female voice replied acidly. "Like there's anyone to hear us out here."

Andrea collapsed against the hillside with an odd sensation of mixed relief and anger. That was Connie Chambers, no doubt about it. And Clarissa Hale was probably with her. Despite the warning she'd given them after the last time.

And this time there could be no question of their wandering onto the ranch accidentally. The federal grasslands were all the way on the other side of the ranch.

This was really too much. This time she'd make it clear

to them in no uncertain terms that she'd had enough. Maybe a night in the Rorvik jail—if Rorvik had a jail—would make an impression.

Clenching her teeth, she climbed to the top of the hill and looked down at them, hands on her hips.

She'd been right. Connie and Clarissa, the latter clad in a safari outfit complete with bush helmet, had their backs to her and didn't notice her arrival. Only one of Clarissa's technicians was present, standing beside them aiming some sort of device toward the plains. Where was Tweedledee?

After a moment, Andrea cleared her throat loudly.

The technician dropped his instrument as all three of the trespassers whirled to face her.

"Good Lord," Professor Hale stage-whispered. "Get down from there. Do you want to give away our position?"

Before she could answer, something struck her from behind, carrying her over the crest of the hillock. She landed in a heap at the professor's feet. The bulky body of her attacker came to rest on top of her, then scrambled off, mumbling apologies.

Stunned and breathless, she lay still a moment before sitting up. Technician number two, Tweedledee, crouched beside her, his expression sheepish.

Clarissa Hale hurried over to her to help Andrea to her feet and shook her head at her assistant, clucking disapprovingly. "That wasn't necessary, Rudy."

Rudy looked worried. "I'm sorry. You told her to get down. I got carried away." He studied Andrea, squinting at her in the moonlight. "Are you all right, Dr. Moore?"

"I'm fine." Andrea rose and shook herself free of the professor's ministrations. "Despite the fact that you've added assault and battery to trespassing. I suppose there's no need to tell you you're on my property again. What part of *no* don't you understand?"

Connie Chambers, who had watched the proceedings

with uncharacteristic silence, spoke up. "We know we're on White Thunder, Andrea, but I think you'll admit that this time it's with good reason." She pointed away from them toward the darkened plains. "We were following that."

In the distance a glowing object bobbed and danced just above the horizon. And this time Andrea could see that it was no car headlight.

CHAPTER TWENTY-TWO

"You see?" Professor Hale's voice was filled with awe. "They're here. The visitors are among us."

Andrea shot a glance at Connie, who rolled her eyes.

"Well, it's not us," Connie said. "So it's gotta be something. Frankly, after tromping around out here for the better part of a week, I'm counting on little green men."

"Well, I doubt it's aliens, green or otherwise." Andrea headed for the professor's Jeep, parked a few yards away. "Are the keys in that thing?"

"Yes, but…" Professor Hale started toward her. "What are you going to do?"

"I'm going to settle this once and for all." Andrea climbed into the vehicle and twisted back to look at the protesting woman. "You wait here. If I'm not back in a reasonable amount of time, get to my car—it's parked out on the road—and go for help." She felt more than a little stupid suggesting she might need rescuing, but whatever was out there, alien or not, was an unknown. She had to be prepared for anything.

"You can't just leave us here in the middle of nowhere," Connie yelled, ignoring the professor's shushes and lunging for the Jeep.

Andrea started the engine. *Now you know how it feels,* she thought, recalling how Connie had abandoned Rusting Hulkk. "I'll be back soon." *I hope.*

She took off into the darkness, fighting to control the vehicle over the rough terrain. Headlights would have made it easier, but she didn't dare turn them on, not knowing what might be waiting for her out there on the prairie.

With only the bright moonlight for illumination, she scanned the ground ahead of her. Would she even have time to react, she wondered, if a gully suddenly appeared before her?

Ahead of the Jeep, a dark shape rose out of the shadows, and her breath caught in her throat. Reflexively, she slowed the vehicle. Her heart hammered against her ribs.

Then she realized what she was looking at. The cabin. She had reached the Amundson homestead.

And she wasn't the only one.

Dim light glowed from around the side of the cabin, a tiny glimmer in the darkness. Hoping she hadn't already been heard, Andrea parked the Jeep a short distance from the cabin and climbed out.

She stepped through the brush, straining to hear any telltale noises over the pounding of her heart in her ears. She'd never expected that as a rancher she'd spend so much time creeping around in the grass.

A soft click sounded around the corner. Andrea jumped, stifling a squeak of alarm as she pressed herself into the shadows along the side of the building. She waited, her heartbeat so deafening she was sure that whoever, or whatever, lay around the corner could hear it, too.

How long she remained there, motionless against the rough timbers, she couldn't tell. She heard an occasional soft rustling from around the side of the cabin, but nothing further happened. No space aliens waving ray guns appeared demanding she take them to her leader.

After a further moment's hesitation, she crept forward again and peered cautiously around the corner.

A stocky form crouched at the back of the house, partially obscured behind a round, gently glowing object roughly three feet in diameter.

The figure rose, lifting the lighted sphere with it. For a moment, it—he—held the globe aloft, then released it. The object, a sort of balloon tethered to a small container, hovered for a few moments until the breeze caught it and carried it upward.

The man who had launched it laughed softly as the balloon climbed, its pale glow illuminating an expression of childlike delight on his face.

It was Bert Petersen.

Andrea resisted her first impulse to race out and confront him.

He might be dangerous.

Hell, he was probably nuts.

Why else would he be on her ranch in the middle of the night launching hot air balloons, or whatever they were?

But she couldn't believe he'd harm her. She glanced back the way she'd come. Would Clarissa and Connie follow her out here, in case she did need rescuing? Should she wait in case they showed up? She suspected neither the professor nor Connie was likely to have followed her across the prairie on foot.

She was on her own.

At last she made up her mind. Bert was a little strange—well, maybe a *lot* strange—but she knew instinctively he wouldn't intentionally harm her. Besides, she had to find out what the hell he was doing out here.

She took a deep breath and stepped out of the shadows, clearing her throat loudly to avoid startling him.

"Um, good evening, Bert."

He started nonetheless, dropping the new balloon he was assembling. He squinted into the darkness at her. "Dr. Moore—Andrea? What are you doing out here in the middle of the night?" His tone was one of genuine, innocent surprise.

Andrea stifled a sudden and unexpected urge to laugh. "I was going to ask you the same thing."

"Oh, well, yes," he stammered. "I suppose you were." He looked about him in apparent confusion.

"Are you all right?"

He nodded quickly. "Oh, yes. I'm fine. Oh, there it is." He crouched to pick up the balloon.

"What *are* you doing out here, Bert?" She stepped closer.

Bert fluffed out the balloon portion of the object.

Up close, Andrea could see it was a large bag of some kind of very thin material. "What's that?"

"This?" He held up the balloon and grinned. "Well, you might call this my sideline. In fact, you could even say I'm moonlighting." He chuckled at his joke, a pleased look on his plump face, then waved her closer. "This is my UFO. It's really very clever if I say so myself."

He held the "UFO" out to her. Not sure what else to do, she took it gingerly in both hands, examining it in the beam of the small flashlight he shone at her.

The balloon was a thin plastic bag from which dangled strings that had been punched through the plastic at regular intervals. The ends of each string were fastened to the four points of a small crisscrossed structure made of wooden ice cream sticks. A can of jellied alcohol fuel, the kind used for chafing dishes and camp stoves, rested on the wood support.

"I launch them like this." Bert pulled out a match and ignited the fuel, which burned with a low bluish flame. He carefully lifted the strings to open the bag over the flame. Heated air filled the lightweight bag, inflating it into a glowing orb. Bert released the apparatus and it soared into the night sky, a miniature hot-air balloon. "Voilà. UFO."

Andrea watched the rising sphere in amazed silence, then turned to face him. "But why? And why here? Bert, do you realize I have a whole pack of UFO hunters swarming across my ranch looking for these things?'' Well, Connie and Clarissa hardly constituted a pack, but they certainly caused as much trouble as ten people.

"Oh, I know." Bert beamed at her. "Isn't it wonderful?''

Andrea shook her head. "I don't understand. What is this all about?''

"Publicity." Bert laughed. "Do you know how much business the news of UFO sightings will bring to Rorvik? This is better than my giant bison idea. It's better than bringing Wal-Mart to town. Why, when I learned Clarissa Hale and her people were investigating out here, I knew this was my chance. She's been out here off and on for years, setting up her equipment and taking her readings. Did you know she's erected a series of heavy-duty radio and microwave transmitters and receivers on the edge of your ranch, just inside the federal grassland? Mounted them on the transmission towers out there. She had a grant.''

Andrea shook her head.

"The area around White Thunder has always had a history of strange sightings," Bert continued. "That's what brought her here in the first place. And that's what gave me this idea. Sometimes I even make 'crop circles.' Oh, I've led her a merry chase." He snickered.

"So you're responsible for all the weird stuff that's been happening out here?'' Andrea found herself unable to get angry. In fact, she rather liked the idea that Bert was perpetrating an elaborate hoax on Clarissa Hale and the overbearing Connie Chambers.

Bert nodded, his grin widening, and Andrea felt a smile tug at the corners of her mouth.

Now what? She couldn't let this continue, but she didn't know what to do. She didn't want to have Bert prosecuted for trespassing. He'd done no actual harm, and she actually rather admired his audacity.

Of course there was the vague possibility that his UFOs had spooked the bison, contributing to their problems. Stress certainly had an impact on fertility. But she had to admit it wasn't too likely. He was conducting his activities irregularly and on a fairly limited basis. Chances were the animals hadn't even noticed him.

She glanced back up at the rising balloon, noticing that the wind had picked up considerably. And changed direction. The little balloon floated just beyond the cabin's yard. It danced in the breeze for a moment, then moved toward them, dropping slightly in the downdraft. She caught her breath.

"Bert, look. It's moving toward the cabin!"

They watched helplessly as the balloon carrying its flaming fuel dropped toward the wooden roof of the cabin, where it landed with a soft clunk.

Andrea ran to the side of the building and stretched on tiptoe, feeling with her fingertips in the hope of catching hold of the balloon. All she felt was rough, splintered shingles, now ominously dry despite yesterday's rain. Above her head something flared brightly. The scent of burning wood reached her nostrils.

She spun toward Bert, who stood behind her, his face crinkled with worry. "The roof's on fire!"

Bert turned and looked frantically around the grassy yard. "Quick," he said. "Bring your Jeep alongside the cabin and I'll climb up on it."

Andrea dashed to the vehicle and started it, pulling it up to the side of the building. Before she had even turned off the engine, Bert clambered onto the fender, then balanced precariously on the hood.

"I don't think that's such a good idea." She stood up in the open Jeep and reached for him, but she was too late.

With surprising agility, he hoisted his plump body onto the smoking roof.

"Bert, be careful!" Andrea shouted. "That roof is partially collapsed already." She climbed onto the seat of the Jeep, straining to see what was happening. He should have let her go, she thought. She was younger and lighter. He was risking his life climbing up there.

"Don't worry," he called, his voice breathless. "Just a foot or two more and I've got it."

Above Andrea's head, ancient timbers creaked. "You'd better get down, Bert," she shouted. "The roof is too weak."

"No, it's fine. This is my fault. I have to take care of it before it's too late."

She heard a pounding noise from the roof, as though he were trying to beat out the flames with his bare hands.

"There. I think that's got it," he called down to her. "I think—"

Whatever Bert had been about to say was swallowed by the crash of splintering wood. His short cry of surprise was abruptly cut off as he fell through the roof.

CHAPTER TWENTY-THREE

MIKE SAW THE CAR on the shoulder as he approached the ranch. It looked like—it was. The station wagon.

What was Lena's vehicle doing out here along the road?

He pulled to the curb behind the car and got out to investigate, wincing as he put weight on his ankle. Damn, if this kept up, he'd probably have to get it X-rayed after all.

The vehicle was empty, except for a white jacket and a black leather bag. Andrea's medical gear! She must have driven the car into town to assist Doc.

But where was she now? Had the car broken down?

He got in and started it with his own key. Everything seemed normal. The gas tank was nearly full. He turned off the engine and climbed out, looking around for any sign of the vehicle's occupant.

A glow in the distance caught his eye.

No, he thought, *she wouldn't.* But he knew otherwise.

This is Andrea you're dealing with, remember? If she saw the lights again as she was driving home, she'd probably stopped to investigate. Maybe she thought Professor Hale was back.

But what if it was someone whose intentions were far different than those of the dotty professor?

Fear gripped him. Damn it, he thought, if she got hurt because of his stupid pride, he'd never forgive himself. He didn't want to imagine life without her. He couldn't even think of the possibility.

He went back to the truck for his flashlight and looked

around for anything else that might serve as a weapon. Reaching under the seat, he gripped cold metal. A tire iron? He pulled the object out and looked at it.

The emasculator.

It would have to do. He swung the steel implement in one hand, testing its balance. *Not bad,* he thought. He tossed it onto the seat beside him, then unfastened the fence wires, drove the vehicle through and headed across the field toward the gradually intensifying glow in the distance.

Before he'd gone too far, a wavering light appeared ahead of him. Not the light they'd followed before—this was more like someone signaling. He drove toward it and wasn't too surprised when Professor Hale and Connie Chambers appeared out of the darkness, Connie waving a huge flashlight.

He pulled alongside them and rolled down the window. Whatever was burning was still ahead of him, but Andrea might be here. He had to make sure she was safe.

"Thank God you've come!" Clarissa Hale cried. "You must help us."

"She took our Jeep. We've been stranded out here for ages," Connie added.

Mike waved a hand to silence them. "Where's Andrea? Isn't she with you?"

Connie shook her head. "No. That's what I'm trying to say. She took our Jeep and went that way." She pointed toward the distant glow.

"She went after the UFO," the professor wailed. "We couldn't stop her." She opened the door of Mike's truck and climbed in. Connie squeezed in beside her, and the two technicians clambered into the back.

Professor Hale wrung her hands. "We must go to her. She may be in terrible danger."

Mike sighed. No use fighting it, he thought. There was no time. The professor could be right.

As soon as they were all secured in the vehicle, he started again toward the glowing light, praying silently for Andrea's safety.

ANDREA LEAPT OFF the Jeep and landed hard on the packed earth. Staggering slightly, she caught her breath, then picked up the flashlight and started for the front of the cabin.

Burning splinters tossed up by the collapsing roof had settled onto the tall grass in the yard. Despite the soaking rain the area had received yesterday, the vegetation caught fire quickly and burned with a heavy smoke.

She ran up onto the porch, forgetting that the wood there was every bit as brittle as that of the roof. As the boards flexed threateningly beneath her, she slowed down and picked her way carefully into the building.

The interior of the cabin was dark. A thin veil of smoke stung her eyes, making visibility even worse. The fire was still smoldering at the very least. She had to get Bert out of here before it flared again in the dry, dusty interior.

"Bert!" she called.

A groan answered her. She followed the sound blindly, praying that no more of the roof would come down on top of her.

Bert lay semiconscious on the floor near the section of collapsed roof. Apparently his weight on the already weakened structure had caused the new collapse.

She dropped to his side and examined him for injuries. His pulse was rapid but strong, his breathing normal. She checked for fractures and found nothing obvious, but that didn't rule out the possibility.

And it didn't eliminate the possibility of neck or back injuries, either.

Something popped in the broken debris nearby. Andrea aimed the flashlight beam at the wreckage and watched as a wisp of smoke curled out of the wood fragments. Then a small finger of flame tickled the fallen beams. Her heart began to race once more.

They had to get them out of there before the whole cabin went up.

She leaned over the injured man and tapped his shoulder firmly, careful not to jar him. "Bert. Bert, can you hear me?"

Bert groaned again and opened his eyes. "What happened?"

"The roof collapsed under you. Are you hurt? We have to get out of here."

"I think I'm all right," he said weakly. "Just a little stunned." He started to sit up, then winced and fell back onto the floor. "Head hurts."

"Can you move your arms and legs?" Andrea ran her hands over them again, watching him carefully for any signs of pain.

He moved them slowly. "I think they're okay." He turned his head slightly. "Neck's okay, too. My head just hurts. But I think I'm bleeding somewhere." He held up a bloodstained hand.

Andrea checked for lacerations and found a broad but shallow gash behind his right ear. "It's not too deep, but it'll probably need a couple of stitches. It looks a lot worse than it is." She tried to sound upbeat and encouraging, despite her rising panic. "Can you stand if I help you?"

She glanced from Bert to the growing flames. The smoke was getting thicker, burning her throat. She didn't like the idea of moving him without something to stabilize his head and back, but she suspected that shortly his injuries would be the least of their concerns. Once the fire began to spread, the entire cabin would be engulfed in moments.

She rose and bent to help Bert. Behind her the fire

snapped and popped menacingly. He leaned heavily on her and they made their way slowly to the cabin door.

As HE CROSSED THE DARK prairie, Mike could see the spreading flames. They were coming from the Amundson homestead.

Behind him, Connie shrilled, "This wouldn't have happened if you hadn't insisted on dragging me out on this wild-goose chase, you loony."

Clarissa Hale shushed her. "I am a scientist, not a loony. And this is no time for placing blame. Dr. Moore may be in danger. We don't know what she's dealing with."

"Well, you'd better hope it's aliens, or I'm outta this dump." Connie sank back against the seat, muttering to herself as Clarissa began to lecture her once more about the unpredictability of scientific investigations.

Mike accelerated toward the flames, ignoring them both.

He pulled to a stop alongside the cabin, well back from the bank of the creek where, an eternity ago it seemed, he and Andrea had been stranded. He leapt from the vehicle and instantly regretted the act as pain shot through his ankle. He forced it from his mind.

"Andrea!" *Please God, Creator,* he prayed. *Let her be all right.*

Dense smoke from the burning wood and grass billowed around the cabin and yard. Mike could barely make out any details of the area. He yanked a handkerchief from his pocket and, clutching it to his nose and mouth, stepped into the thick cloud, concentrating his attention on the ground to make his way through the smoke.

At his feet, he noticed long scuffs in the dirt, as though someone had staggered along here. He crouched to study them more closely and saw something else in the dust. Blood. The drops shone like black pebbles in the dancing firelight.

"Andrea!" he shouted again.

"Mike?"

The voice came from his left, toward the still-swollen creek. He made his way toward it.

At the edge of the creek, something began to take shape through the haze of smoke.

Andrea.

She was crouched on the bank beside an injured man he soon recognized as Bert Petersen, her face and clothing smudged with soot and dirt.

No woman had ever looked more beautiful.

"Mike!" She rose and threw herself into his arms.

BACK AT WHITE THUNDER, Andrea held an ice pack against the minor burn on her arm. The paramedic who looked her over when the ambulance came for Bert had strongly recommended she be transported to the hospital, as well, just in case, but she had refused. She'd been away from Mike long enough.

Dan had grown concerned when she didn't return from the clinic. He'd called Doc to confirm that she had indeed left, then he called the police. They had discovered the flames and contacted the fire department, which arrived shortly after Mike reached her.

The entire ranch was in an uproar. Rusting Hulkk was, to a man, miffed at having missed all the excitement. They pumped her for endless details of her ordeal.

Clarissa Hale, her staff gathered around her in the living room like chicks around a mother hen, brooded silently over Bert's hoax while Connie stormed around the room, muttering under her breath about being had. Andrea was almost relieved once Bert was hauled off to the hospital. She wouldn't have given a buffalo nickel for his health if he'd stayed within Connie's reach.

Lena bustled about the kitchen, brewing her most powerful coffee and filling a plate with cookies for her unexpected guests. Mike was glad she had something to occupy her. He didn't want her turned loose on Connie and Prof. Hale. The three of them together would be more than anyone could take.

"How are you?" he asked Andrea tentatively, still embarrassed at his earlier behavior. She'd forgiven him if her reaction to his arrival at the cabin had been any indication. Under the circumstances, though, he wouldn't have blamed her for greeting anyone who'd shown up with such enthusiasm.

"I'm okay," she said softly. "Only a minor burn and some new bruises to show for the evening."

He smiled but was determined to keep the conversation businesslike. "That was some scheme Bert had going. Do you think he might have caused the bison's problems?"

Andrea shook her head. "It's possible but not likely. In fact, Bert mentioned something else while we were at the cabin, and it's been nagging at me ever since." She looked up at him. "He said the professor set up some powerful transmitters on the towers on the federal grassland. Remember the towers we saw when we were repairing the fences? Those have to be the ones."

Mike nodded. "You're probably right. How long do you think they've been out there?"

"Bert said she's been investigating out here a couple years. How long has the herd been having trouble?"

"A couple years. Do you think there's a connection?"

"Well, it's kind of farfetched," she said, "but it's been in the back of my mind since Doc mentioned power lines. I remember reading some medical studies about the effects of electromagnetic fields on humans and animals."

"Reproductive effects?"

She nodded.

Dan stepped closer to listen, his expression curious.

"The herd likes to graze out in that area," he said. "They spend a lot of time there. What do the transmitters have to do with them?"

"They generate a strong electromagnetic field," Andrea explained. "It's a type of radiation, and there's been some controversy in recent years about whether it might cause cellular mutations that result in cancer and other medical problems. It hasn't been proven definitively, but there's speculation that the radiation reduces melatonin levels in animals. Melatonin's a hormone that regulates the circadian rhythm, the body's biological clock. I recall thinking about it a few days ago, but I didn't make the connection."

"Which could affect the reproductive season of the female bison," Dan concluded for her. "So you think Professor Hale's equipment might have caused the problems?"

"I don't know. I don't even know how we could find out. But it is one possibility."

"One more possibility than we had before," Mike said. "Maybe the best way to test the hypothesis is to get that equipment away from the ranch and see what happens."

"It's worth a try," Andrea said. "We haven't found anything else that could be the cause."

Mike reached down and gave her shoulder a reassuring squeeze. "Believe me, if either Bert's or the professor's activities are to blame, we shouldn't have anything more to worry about after this."

The doorbell rang and Andrea heard Lena at the front door talking to an equally insistent woman. The housekeeper came into the kitchen, followed by Andrea's mother.

Andrea glanced quickly at Mike. He nodded a terse greeting at Mrs. Moore, then excused himself and went outside. Lena threw her a look of exasperation and shooed Dan and the band out of the room. If Andrea had hoped for safety in numbers, she was out of luck.

Mother pulled out a chair and sat beside her.

"What are you doing here this time of night, Mother?" She didn't look very well, Andrea thought. Her eyes were shadowed and narrowed strangely, as though sensitive to the light.

Mrs. Moore came right to the point. "I'm sorry to come out so late, but I've decided to go back tomorrow and I just wanted to give you one last chance to change your mind." She smoothed her still-perfect coiffure and glanced around the kitchen. "I was afraid you'd all have gone to bed. I thought farm people went to bed with the cows and got up with the chickens."

Andrea stifled a sudden urge to leap to the defense of White Thunder's residents. She smiled at her reaction. Not too long ago, she'd felt the same about country folk. Funny how everything could change so quickly. She said nothing, waiting for her mother to continue.

Her mother patted her hand. "Everything can still be like it was, dear. It's not too late to make everything all right."

"Thanks, Mother, but I really don't want everything like it was. That's why I came out here in the first place." She patted her mother's hand comfortingly—she'd always wanted to be the one to do that for a change.

"For the first time in my life I'm doing what I need to do to take care of myself. I spent my whole life living the way you expected me to. I wore the clothes you selected for me, went to the schools you chose. Mother, I wore flats because you thought I was too tall."

Her mother stared at her in silence, her expression contrite.

"When I found myself engaged to the man you'd selected for me, with the promise of a life ahead of me just like the one I'd had with you, I decided I'd had enough." She stood and pulled her purse off a hook by the kitchen door, rummaging through it. When she found the diamond ring—her engagement ring from Jeffrey—she dropped it into her mother's open palm.

"I forgot to give that back. Take it to him, would you? I'm staying here. I love this place and its people." One in particular, she thought, but continued, "White Thunder is my home now."

For once she felt no urge to add the words "I'm sorry." For the first time in her life, she wasn't sorry. "I love you, Mother, but you have your own life to live and I have mine. You'll just have to learn to accept that."

To her surprise, Mother nodded, understanding dawning on her face. "You know I only wanted what was best for you. I wanted you to have the stability I never had," she said softly. "Because you're my child and I love you."

"I know, Mother. But sometimes what's best for me isn't what's best for you."

"I guess I can see that. It just never really occurred to me before. Well," Mrs. Moore said, rising, "I guess there's no reason for me to stay." She pressed a cool kiss onto Andrea's cheek. "Give me a call when you're settled. I'd like to visit again." Her words were an unspoken question.

"I'd like that," Andrea said, hugging her mother.

Mother dabbed at the corner of her eye with a manicured fingertip.

"It's too late for you to drive back tonight, Mother," Andrea said softly. "Why don't you stay till morning? You can sleep in my room. I'll have Lena get you settled in."

She suspected she wouldn't sleep at all tonight anyway, the way her mind was whirling. She poked her head into the living room. "Lena, would you take mother up to my room? She's going to stay till morning."

The living room was full of people, Andrea noticed as her mother followed Lena up the stairs. The professor and her entourage, along with Connie, were still here, and neither Dan nor the band seemed willing to call it a night. The boys in particular seemed to be waiting for something to happen; maybe they expected a fight to break out between Connie and Clarissa. She wouldn't have been surprised, herself.

The only person missing, Andrea noticed, was Mike. He hadn't come back into the house. He'd seemed glad to see her at the cabin, but maybe she'd misinterpreted his concern. Maybe he was still angry with her.

She bit back a sob of frustration. She'd made her decision and burned her bridges. But Mike had been a very large part of that decision.

Lena walked back into the kitchen, her face bright with unabashed curiosity, her footsteps louder than usual. Andrea glanced down at the housekeeper's feet.

Lena was wearing her green boots.

Andrea looked up at her, and the housekeeper blushed to the roots of her russet hair. "I've been wanting to try them on ever since you got here."

Andrea grinned. "They look good on you," she said sincerely. Lena was one of the few people she knew who could carry off green snakeskin.

Lena patted her shoulder. "Your mother's all settled, and I've laid out fresh towels for you in my bathroom. Go get cleaned up while I go out and talk to Mike."

Andrea glanced toward the group congregated in the living room.

"Don't worry about that bunch," Lena said. "I'll take care of them."

Andrea nodded her gratitude and headed for the bathroom, suddenly realizing how sore and exhausted she was. A few minutes later, she had washed the soot from her hair and face and returned to the kitchen to look for Lena, noting that the crowd in the living room had disappeared. The housekeeper had probably sent Clarissa and company packing. The boys and Dan were nowhere to be seen, either. And as for Lena, she'd said she was going to talk to Mike.

Talk to Mike about what?

She cringed at the thought that Lena was going to intercede with Mike on her behalf. Surely she wouldn't get involved.

Then again, this was Lena.

CHAPTER TWENTY-FOUR

OUTSIDE, MIKE PACED restlessly beside Gypsy's empty corral. Dan had moved the bison into the barn during the storm, and since she was nearing her calving time, had decided to keep her there.

Lena watched him in silence and shook her head with an air of resignation. Or disgust.

He halted, glaring at her. "What's that supposed to mean?"

She looked up at him, her blue eyes wide and innocent. "What?"

"That head-shaking business." He managed to keep from snapping at her, but only just.

She did it again. "Nothing at all. It's just that I can't understand why you men have such trouble seeing what's right in front of your eyes."

Mike drew his lips together angrily and said nothing.

"She's getting cleaned up," Lena said. "So go in there and tell her you love her, you stubborn jackass."

"I can't. Not till I'm sure."

"Sure of her or sure of yourself? She loves you, you young fool. Don't wait around or you'll blow it." She looked wistful for a moment. "Like Dan and I nearly did."

"Dan and you?" Mike's mouth dropped open in surprise.

Lena nodded. "It took us a long time to realize we cared about each other." She fixed him with a penetrating gaze.

"Even longer to get up the courage to do something about it."

Mike grinned. He should have known there was something between his two friends. How could he have been so blind?

He knew Lena spoke the truth about Andrea, too. He knew now why she'd left her fiancé and that it had nothing to do with her feelings for him. Still, he had to be sure—to hear it from her. Otherwise he could never be sure he wouldn't wake up someday to find her gone.

The screen door slammed and Mike looked up.

Andrea stood on the porch, smoothing her damp hair away from her face. She started in his direction.

"Andrea! Come quick!" Todd raced toward them from the barn and slid to a halt in the dust, gasping. "Dan sent me to get you. Gypsy's in labor!"

Andrea started to follow Todd, then turned back to Mike. "Is my medical bag still in Lena's car?"

Caught off guard, he could only nod. He mentally shook himself. Gypsy—in labor. The first calf born on the ranch in years. "Go with Todd." He waved her toward the barn. "I'll bring it."

Todd took off at a run, with Andrea following, while Lena brought up the rear, her orange mane flying. Ignoring the pain in his ankle, Mike darted around the side of the house to where the station wagon had been parked after the fire. Flinging open the door, he grabbed the black leather bag from the passenger seat.

He tucked it under his arm like a football and raced toward the barn, all thoughts but Gypsy banished from his mind. At the barn door, he slowed to a walk. Everything was quiet. *Too quiet,* he thought, conscious of the cliché. Shouldn't they all be bustling around like mad or boiling water or something?

Oh, no!

They'd been too late. Andrea hadn't been able to save the calf.

Andrea glanced up and saw him. "Mike. Come in."

He edged into the silent crowd, including Connie and Professor Hale, gathered around the stall. They parted to make way for him, and the first thing he saw was Andrea's dark head as she knelt beside the bison. Gypsy lay on her side in the straw, panting, her flanks shuddering periodically with her labor. Mike held the bag out to Andrea.

She waved him down to a spot next to her in the straw. "Thanks, but I won't be needing that," she said softly, her eyes brimming.

His heart sank. It was over. Everything he'd hoped for, all his dreams for White Thunder.

Then she smiled at him. Radiantly. "No. Mike." She shook her head. "Everything's fine. Perfect. It should be any minute."

He dropped to his knees beside her. Gypsy snuffled and turned her head to nuzzle his hand.

"Sorry I don't have any marshmallows, girl." He felt tears spring to his own eyes. "As soon as you're done I'll get you some. I promise."

A heavy contraction rippled the bison's side, and she bellowed in protest. Andrea stroked her and leaned forward to check her again, then looked at Mike and grinned. "She's on her way."

Gypsy shuddered through another contraction, and for just a second the tip of a hoof protruded from the birth canal. As the contraction subsided, the tiny foot disappeared again.

Mike gave a snort of frustration, and Andrea patted his arm comfortingly. "It's all right. It just takes time."

"And bison are fast at calving," Dan said.

"These expectant fathers," Lena murmured with a softness he'd never believed her capable of. "Good thing it's not a baby. Imagine what he'd be like after a few hours of labor.''

Another contraction exposed both hooves, and this time they stayed visible. A blunt, pale nose followed.

Mike gripped Andrea's hand. She moved closer and he pulled her into his arms.

Gypsy heaved a sigh and pushed through another contraction. Suddenly the calf's entire head was visible.

Then, all at once, the whole tiny calf slipped out onto the straw.

Andrea flew into action, pulling the little animal free of its birth sack, siphoning fluid from its nostrils and rubbing it briskly with straw to stimulate breathing before Gypsy, having caught her breath after her labor, turned to investigate the new arrival.

Andrea moved aside to reveal a small, damp, woolly creature that looked for all the world like an overgrown lamb. She grabbed Mike's hand and pulled him forward to help. He grinned, running his hands over the small, wet, warm body.

An overgrown lamb?

He looked at the calf again. Something wasn't right. This calf wasn't the ruddy cinnamon brown of the few bison calves he'd seen.

The calf was white!

Mike's breath caught in his throat. It wasn't possible!

Gypsy had borne a white bison calf!

"She looks like a healthy little girl," Andrea said, reaching out to him.

He took her hand and sank back down beside her in the straw, awestruck. News of this birth would send reverberations throughout the lands of the Sioux and across the entire country. He'd gone in search of his heritage and it had come to him.

The white buffalo calf was the confirmation of something

he'd finally come to believe. That with time White Thunder would heal as he had healed.

Andrea hugged him. "Oh, Mike, isn't she beautiful? This has to be a good sign for the ranch." She looked into his eyes. "For our ranch."

He kissed her cheek. "She's perfect. I'd never dreamed..." He paused and took her hands in his. "Andrea, darling, would you be willing to consider a change in our partnership agreement to something more permanent? I can't guarantee it'll be easy. White Thunder still has a long way to go. These first couple years might be rough."

"Not as long as I have you," she said, her green eyes bright. "Equal partners this time?"

"Equal partners," Mike said, and pulled her into his arms.

EPILOGUE

SURVEYING HER REFLECTION in the wavy glass of the dresser mirror, Andrea put the finishing touches on her hair.

Her gown was simple, sleeveless, silk, uncluttered by the rows of lace and beading that had adorned her mother's gown.

Her mother's reflection smiled at her in the mirror, and she dabbed at a tear. "You look lovely, dear. Your father would be so proud of you."

Andrea turned and hugged her. "Thanks, Mother. It means a lot to hear you say that."

Someone knocked at the door. Startled, they both turned toward it.

"Who is it?" Andrea asked.

"Me." Mike's voice came from the other side of the door.

"Mike, what are you doing here?" Mrs. Moore asked. She opened the door a crack and peered out at him. "You aren't supposed to see the bride before the wedding. It's bad luck."

He stepped past her into the room, grinning wickedly. "It's worse luck for the bride to run off on her wedding day, Helen. Given her history, I thought I'd better be here to make sure it doesn't happen again." He looked at Andrea, admiration and desire in his eyes. "Wow. Now I'm really not going to let you out of my sight. You're beautiful."

"Mike," Andrea said with exasperation, but she couldn't help smiling at his teasing. "Are you ready to go?"

"Yep. We don't want to keep Dan and Lena waiting. They're counting on a double wedding, and that's hard to do with just one couple."

She took his arm and they started downstairs.

Doc greeted them at the bottom, and Mike transferred Andrea to him.

"Thank you for offering to give me away, Doc," she said. "It means a lot to me."

"My pleasure. Anyway, I promised Mike I'd be here to make sure you showed up." Doc's grin echoed Mike's. "He told me you haven't had the best attendance record where weddings are concerned."

Andrea rolled her eyes. Was there nothing this man didn't know?

"You'd better find Dan and get outside, Mike," Doc said. "The minister and the guests will be wondering what's up."

Mike nodded and pulled Andrea into his arms for a brief but passionate kiss. He released her and started for the backyard.

Doc sighed. "Aah, youth."

"Doc, you're not that old." Andrea took his arm. "We just need to find the right woman for you."

The veterinarian grimaced. "Don't even think it."

Outside, the remaining members of Rusting Hulkk played classical music on borrowed instruments. Andrea and Doc hurried to the back porch where Lena waited, resplendent in lavender lace.

Lena took Doc's free arm and leaned toward Andrea. "Glad you made it, hon. Dan hid the car keys, though, just in case." She laughed heartily, gave Andrea a crushing hug, then called to the band, "Okay, boys. Let's get this party under way."

Rusting Hulkk struck up the wedding march.

IT WAS DARK by the time Mike and Andrea headed back to White Thunder from the reception in Rorvik. The party was still going when they'd left, with Rusting Hulkk—on loan from their extended gig at the Viking—providing the entertainment. Dan and Lena had left early, as well, to drive to Minot and the flight to their Hawaiian honeymoon, courtesy of Andrea's cashed-in Vidtel ticket. When they returned, they'd be taking over Mike's trailer. Lena was ready, she'd said, to start taking care of a smaller place.

Andrea leaned against Mike's shoulder and watched the nighttime prairie as they drove, at peace for the first time in ages. Maybe the first time ever.

Out of habit, she found herself scanning the dark horizon.

A dimly glowing triangular light moved slowly across her field of vision.

She gripped Mike's arm and pointed to the object. "Oh, no," she groaned. "What's that?"

His initial burst of laughter died in his throat. "Looks like our friend Bert is up to his tricks again. He's not on White Thunder, though. Too far south."

"Well, he's probably not hurting anything, then." She settled back down and tucked Mike's arm around her. "Let him have his fun. As long as he doesn't burn anything down."

Mike nodded and drew her closer, stroking her arm in a way that sent shivers through her.

BERT PETERSEN STOOD outside the Sons of Norway Hall in Rorvik, catching his breath after a full evening of dancing. A moving light out on the prairie caught his eye, and he grinned. Maybe the truth was out there, after all.

HARLEQUIN SUPERROMANCE®

GUARANTEED
PAGE-TURNER!

Every now and then comes a book guaranteed
to enthrall the reader from start to finish.
Harlequin Superromance—the series known for its
innovation and variety—is proud to add these
books to their already outstanding lineup.

IT HAPPENED IN TEXAS
by Darlene Graham

Marie Manning wakes up to discover that there's a body on her
property. And Marie's world goes from safe to scary. It doesn't
help that Sheriff Jim Whittington thinks she knows more than
she's telling. And it certainly doesn't help that Marie's heart
beats a little faster every time the officer comes around....

Be sure to watch for it in November 1998
wherever Harlequin books are sold.

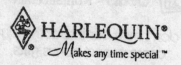

HARLEQUIN®

Makes any time special ™

Looking For More Romance?

Visit Romance.net

Look us up on-line at: http://www.romance.net

Check in daily for these and other exciting features:

Hot off the press

View all current titles, and purchase them on-line.

What do the stars have in store for you?

Horoscope

Hot deals

Exclusive offers available only at Romance.net

Plus, don't miss our interactive quizzes, contests and bonus gifts.

PWEB

What do you want for Christmas?

A DADDY FOR CHRISTMAS

'Tis the season for wishes and dreams that come true. This November, follow three handsome but lonely Scrooges as they learn to believe in the magic of the season when they meet the *right* family, in *A Daddy for Christmas*.

MERRY CHRISTMAS, BABY
by Pamela Browning

THE NUTCRACKER PRINCE
by Rebecca Winters

THE BABY AND THE BODYGUARD
by Jule McBride

Available November 1998
wherever Harlequin and Silhouette books are sold.

HARLEQUIN®
Makes any time special™

Silhouette®

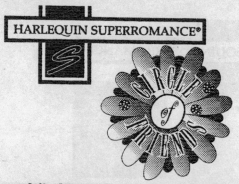

HARLEQUIN SUPERROMANCE®

Love **THAT MAN**

He's the guy every woman dreams of.
A hero in every sense of the word—strong, brave,
kind and of course, drop-dead gorgeous.
You'll never forget the men you meet—or the
women they love—in Harlequin Superromance®'s
newest series, **LOVE THAT MAN!**

BECAUSE IT'S CHRISTMAS
by Kathryn Shay, December 1998

LOVE, LIES & ALIBIS
by Linda Markowiak, January 1999

Be sure to look for upcoming **LOVE THAT MAN!** titles
wherever Harlequin Superromance® books are sold.

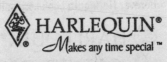

HARLEQUIN®
Makes any time special ™

COMING NEXT MONTH

#814 O LITTLE TOWN OF GLORY • Judith Bowen
Men of Glory
Honor Templeman is a Calgary lawyer, who makes the
shocking discovery that her husband, Parker, had another
wife, another family...in a small ranching town called Glory.
Now that he's dead, she wants to meet Parker's children—but
their uncle and guardian, Joe Gallant, is fiercely protective of
them. Inevitably, when Honor fills in because Joe's desperate
for a nanny, she grows to love these kids. *And* their uncle....
He's a man for all seasons, from the heat of a prairie summer
to the joys of a Glory Christmas.

#815 BECAUSE IT'S CHRISTMAS • Kathryn Shay
Love That Man
To most people in the small town of Bayview Heights,
Seth Taylor's a hero. But Seth can't forgive himself for a
mistake in his past. And neither can Lacey Cartwright—the
woman he loves. If Lacey takes his side, she'll lose what's
left of her family. It's a risk she can't take—and a choice Seth
can't allow her to make.

#816 LET IT SNOW • Sherry Lewis
Marti Johansson has brought her troubled teenage son to
spend a quiet Christmas on his grandfather's Colorado ranch.
Unfortunately, the holiday is anything but peaceful. Her father
is feuding with his neighbor, Rick Dennehy. Her son wants
her to forgive his father, who has his own reasons for wanting
Marti back. And then there's Rick....

#817 THE HEART OF CHRISTMAS • Tara Taylor Quinn
Abby Hayden is at loose ends until Nick McIntyre persuades
her to spend the Christmas season helping out in a home for
pregnant teenagers. This place is where Abby learns about
trust and happiness and letting go.... And this Christmas is
when she falls in love with her very own Saint Nick! By the
author of *Father: Unknown.*